# Smoky Mountain Judge

## Foggy Mountain Intrigue

### Book Six

## Ashley A Quinn

TCA Publishing LLC

*This book is dedicated to my grandparents. Thank you for being not just my babysitter growing up, but for being a friend as an adult. I miss you.*

# ONE

"Pax!" Kennedy Davidson stood at the end of the hallway near the kitchen, yelling toward the stairs for her son. She let out a long breath as she looked up, praying for patience. "Come on. We're going to be late. It's your first day. Your sister is already in the car."

Heavy footsteps thudded on the stairs, and a moment later, her tall, lanky fifteen-year-old rounded the banister, backpack slung over one shoulder. A lock of his wavy, light brown hair fell over his forehead. He tossed his head, getting it out of his eyes.

"You ready?" Kennedy raised an eyebrow as he walked toward her.

"I guess." He marched past her into the kitchen, snagging the breakfast sandwich she made for him off the counter as he headed toward the door.

Kennedy rolled her eyes. One day soon, they were going to have a "Come to Jesus" type talk about his attitude, but not today. Not when they were already running behind on the first day of school—at a new school.

Snagging her purse and lunch sack from the counter, she

followed him out the door into the garage, where they piled into the car, joining his twin, Paige.

"You're worse than a girl." Paige pinned her brother with a dry look.

"Shut up."

"Hey." Kennedy glanced in the mirror. "Can we please not fight? Today's supposed to be exciting. It's a new start for all of us." She didn't want to start her new job as a magistrate for the federal district court stressed out because her kids were at each other's throats. One morning without an argument was all she was asking for.

Paxton rolled his eyes and looked out the window. Paige gave her mother a naughty smile, but stayed silent.

Thanking her lucky stars they'd listened, Kennedy opened the garage door and started the engine. Sunshine streamed inside. It was a nice change from the dreariness of the last several days. Spring had arrived and brought rain with it.

"Everyone have everything?" She glanced in the back.

"Yes," Paige said.

Paxton nodded, now focused on his food.

"Good." Kennedy pulled out of the garage.

The ride to the kids' school was short. When she'd looked for houses in Asheville, she'd restricted the area so she wouldn't have to get on the highway to take the kids to school. It was bad enough she'd have to use it to get to work. Driving was not her favorite pastime.

Turning off the main road, she joined the line of cars in the drop-off zone. When they were within a few car lengths of the doors, she glanced back. "Do you guys remember where you're going?"

Pax rolled his eyes and reached for the door handle.

"We'll be good, Mom." Paige opened her door. "See you this evening."

"Okay. Have a good day."

Paige waved, but Pax just got out, shutting his door without a backward glance.

Blowing out a breath, Kennedy shook her head. She knew this move would be hard. Especially with only a few weeks left of the school year. Her appointment to the court was terrible timing, but it was an opportunity she couldn't say no to. Especially when it brought her closer to her oldest brother and his family. And away from her useless ex-husband and her overbearing mother.

Back on the main road, Kennedy headed for the interstate loop to take her downtown. At least the federal building wasn't far off the interstate. She was not sorry to get away from the congestion in Richmond. Hoping her drive would be easy, she turned on her radio, searching for a traffic report as she merged onto the highway. Song after song greeted her until an announcer's voice droned over the speakers.

"An accident on two-forty just north of Tunnel Road has slowed things down for eastbound traffic."

Kennedy frowned. She wasn't sure where that was. But she was traveling westbound, so hopefully, things were clear for her. Listening to the rest of the report, the announcer said nothing else of note, so she changed the station to one with music. She hummed along as she drove, soon exiting the morning rush and weaving her way through the surface streets to the federal building. Parking in the staff lot, she grabbed her things and headed inside, glad she'd come in late last week to get her security badge and orient herself to her surroundings. Today would go much more smoothly with all the admin stuff out of the way.

After passing through security, she took the elevator to the office suite she shared with her new boss. Excitement fluttered in her veins as she paused outside the door. She'd been a judge at the local level for several years. A lawyer for several more before that. But this was a different playing field. One day, she wanted to be the one on the other side of the door, waiting for her new magistrate to arrive.

"You got this. Rock your new role," she muttered to herself. Extending a hand, she grasped the knob and turned it, stepping inside.

Chaos greeted her. Two law clerks scurried from desk to desk, while behind the central reception area sat an older woman with a deep frown between her eyebrows and a phone receiver tucked into her shoulder. Kennedy learned last week that Suzie MacKinnon ran a tight ship. If there was this much chaos, something was wrong.

Suzie glanced up as Kennedy walked in, her expression morphing to one of relief. Murmuring into the phone, she hung it up. "Oh, thank God you're here."

"What? Why? What's wrong?"

"Judge Jedynak was in an accident on his way to work. We're trying to figure out which cases we can reschedule or pass off to another district judge and which ones you can handle."

The announcer's report echoed through Kennedy's mind, and she wondered if that had been him. In any case, she hoped the judge's accident wasn't serious. "Okay. Let me put my things in my office, and I'll help you." Her feet were already moving toward her office door. She found the key on her keyring and unlocked it. Inside, she dumped her stuff on her desk, then turned around and pushed up her sleeves. So much for an easy first day.

# Two

An edginess skated along Finley Porter's spine as he walked out of the courtroom. That hearing didn't go the way he expected. Gustavo Herrera's attorney was like a piranha, devouring every statement, every *thing* in his path. Finn wanted to see the drug lord put away for a long, long time. He thought they'd built a solid case, but much of it hinged on Piper Riordan's testimony, and the defense counsel was out for blood. The man had latched onto her background, and was attempting to make her sound forgetful and lazy, which called her suitability as a witness into question. Thankfully, she wasn't there to hear him berate her character. At least Judge Stechschulte dismissed the motion to suppress her testimony. It didn't bode well for the trial, though. Finn was glad Piper had thick skin. She would need it when Herrera's attorney cross-examined her.

"Porter!"

Finn paused, glancing back. Another federal prosecutor, Joe Caster, walked toward him.

"I wondered if I'd see you here today." Joe stopped several feet away and held out a hand.

"Yeah." Finn shook it. "Wilkins asked me to be here. To give my impression of his main witness." He'd stayed up late, prepping for today, but even with that, Herrera's attorney still surprised him.

"He told me about that after I overheard him on the phone with Ms. Riordan. She was ticked there was even a question about whether she'd be allowed to testify." Joe shook his head, one corner of his mouth kicking up.

An answering smile lifted one side of Finn's lips. "Yeah, she's a firecracker. It's why she's still alive." Piper's unwillingness to give in and let Herrera win saved her life. "You didn't stop me, though, to talk about Wilkins' case. What's up?"

Joe sobered. "I figured talking to you now would save me an email. I need everything you've got on Javy Gonzales."

Finn frowned. "Javy Gonzales? Why?" He'd been chasing the mid-level drug boss for over a year as part of the task force trying to take down the Vargas-Ruiz cartel. But he didn't think they were close to arresting him yet. They didn't have enough evidence on any of the charges they were pursuing.

"I just came from his bail hearing with Judge Davidson. It was denied. Now I need to review all the evidence and build my case."

"Bail hearing? When was he arrested? And for what? By whom?" Finn reached into his pocket for his phone to check his email, then remembered it was in his office since he couldn't have it in court. Clenching his teeth, he pierced Caster with a stare.

"Wait, you didn't know? The DEA brought him in yesterday on federal drug trafficking charges. They caught him in a sting they did."

Finn's frown deepened. Why hadn't Sharpe told him about this? They'd been working to bring Gonzales in on not just drugs, but on illegal firearms sales too. Gonzales' little operation was funneling weapons to other cartel sects and terrorist groups around the country.

"I'll have to get back to you on that. I need to talk to Nick and find out what happened. And who's Judge Davidson?" That was not a name he was familiar with.

"She's the new magistrate. Seemed competent. But she ruled in my favor. Ask me again when she shoots me down."

Finn chuckled. "True. But, hey, thanks for the heads-up. I'll talk to Nick and get back to you."

"Sounds good." With a wave, Caster walked off.

Smile fading, Finn's frown returned. He bit the corner of his mouth, glancing back at the direction Caster came from. Why didn't Sharpe let him know about Gonzales' arrest?

His feet carried him down the corridor. He doubted Nick was on this side of the complex; Caster would have mentioned it. But maybe he could catch a glimpse of Gonzales and get a sense of his mood. The man was a cocky bastard, but if Sharpe's team had him dead-to-rights, he might feel a little deflated. That could give Finn the in he needed to get some information out of the man. He wanted him to roll on Herrera, but that was likely wishful thinking. It would take more than a few trafficking charges to get Gonzales to turn on his boss. No, he'd need to prove weapons charges too. Unless Nick had something extra-juicy on the guy.

Finn's shoes scuffed softly on the marble floors, the sound echoing off the walls as he moved down the corridor. It was probably a video hearing. They'd been doing a lot of those lately. Saved on staffing. Mouth flattening, Finn picked up the pace. On the off-chance it wasn't, he wanted to catch a glimpse of him.

At a quick clip, he soon reached the area where the magistrates held court. A quick scan of the hallway revealed no one of note, but defendants went out another door.

Which he didn't have access to.

Biting back a groan, Finn pressed the heels of his hands to his eyes. He needed sleep. All his late nights were catching up with him.

"You okay, Agent Porter?"

Finn lowered his hands and looked at the court officer standing outside one of the rooms, recognizing him. "Hey, Shawn." He gave the younger man a polite smile. "Yeah, I'm fine. Just tired."

"I hear that. Do you know how little newborns sleep? I thought I did. Then I had one." He shook his head. "I don't remember what it's like to sleep all night."

Chuckling, Finn walked closer. "You got new pictures?" He'd seen some right after Shawn's son was born, but none since. Finn liked kids, so he didn't mind when his colleagues showed off new pictures.

"Not on me." Shawn shook his head. "My phone's in my locker." His expression changed, and he gave Finn a small frown. "What are you doing over this way, anyway? I heard Herrera had a hearing today, but it's not over here."

"I actually just came from it. I ran into Joe Caster on my way out. He said the DEA arrested someone I've had my eye on. I wanted to see if I could catch a glimpse of him. Gauge his mood. He's got information I want."

"Ah. I think you're out of luck on that front. All the hearings are video conferences today."

The doors behind him opened, and several people filed out. Finn glanced inside, his eyes pausing on the woman behind the bench. "That the new judge?"

Shawn nodded. "Poor woman got thrown into the fire."

Finn frowned, turning away from the dark-haired, bespectacled woman in black robes. "What do you mean?"

"It's her first day of actual hearings, and Judge Jedynak was in a bad car accident on the way into work this morning. She's had to take on extra work."

"What? Oh, man. Is he okay?" Finn wasn't going to ask how Shawn knew all this. He'd learned the court officers knew everything.

"Not sure. All I've heard was it was bad. He's alive, but I don't know the extent of his injuries."

"Damn. Well, I hope he's all right." He liked Elijah Jedynak. The man was fair in his rulings and knew the law backwards and forwards. It kept Finn on his toes and made him be a better agent; he didn't want his cases to get tossed because he didn't follow the correct procedures.

"Me too."

Finn took one more look at the woman at the head of the courtroom before the door swung shut behind the last person. She didn't look frazzled. She looked in control.

And sexy in those dark-framed glasses.

*Whoa.* Finn shifted on his feet. Where did that thought come from? Gritting his teeth, he took a step away and glanced at Shawn. "Hey, thanks for the info on Jedynak. I'll see you later." He backed up, then pointed a finger at the man. "Print out some new pictures and carry them around. I want to see how Aidan's changed."

Shawn smiled. "Will do. Go get some sleep."

Oh, if only he could. He still had a full day ahead of him. "I'll try."

Grinning, a knowing look entered Shawn's eyes. "Cuppa makes a strong Americano." He winked, referencing the coffee shop around the corner.

Finn returned his smile. "Oh, I know." Backing away, he lifted a hand in farewell, then turned, heading back the way he came. He'd definitely hit up the coffee shop at some point today. They kept a coffeepot in the office, but even with as strong as they made it, it didn't match what he could get at Cuppa. Nor did it taste as good.

But first, he wanted answers. Nick had some explaining to do.

Bypassing the ATF offices, he wandered up a floor to the DEA's offices. Finn stepped off the elevator and went down the hall, his stride purposeful. He supposed he probably should have called ahead first to see if Sharpe was even there, but his impulse control was in short supply thanks to his lack of sleep.

Finn stopped outside Nick's door and rapped his knuckles on it. A low voice on the other side told him to enter. He twisted the doorknob and stepped into the opening.

Nick's expression turned apologetic when he saw Finn, and he held up a hand. "I know. I'm sorry. Things happened quick yesterday. I didn't realize who we had until we had him. Once we had everyone processed, I went home and crashed. I was going to catch you later this morning. How'd you find out, anyway?"

"Joe Caster." Finn strolled in, shutting the door, and sat down. "We met in the hallway. He asked me for what I had on the guy. He's been denied bail, by the way."

Nick's head bobbed. "Good. That should give us enough time to gather more evidence on the other charges we want to throw at him. I'm glad Jedynak saw things our way. I was afraid he'd discount Gonzales' ties to Herrera."

"Jedynak wasn't the one who denied bail. He was in a car wreck this morning. It was the new magistrate."

"Oh?" Nick's dark brows furrowed over his brown eyes. "He okay?"

Finn lifted one shoulder. "Don't know. It was nasty from what I heard. Hopefully, we'll hear more soon."

"Yeah, hopefully. Damn. That throws a wrench into things. They'll have to postpone a bunch of stuff if he's going to be out for a while. The magistrates can only do so much. At least they have a full team now, though. Did you meet the new guy?"

Dark glasses perched on a straight nose flashed through Finn's mind. "It's a woman. And no. I only caught a glimpse of her. Caster seemed to like her. Said she appeared more than competent."

"I wouldn't expect less from someone Jedynak hired."

"Me, either. Tell me more about your case against Gonzales." Finn didn't want to focus on the pretty magistrate. He was sure he'd learn more about her as the days went on. Right now, though, he wanted to talk about why he was sitting in Nick's office. "What happened?"

Nick blew out a short breath and sat back. "The city arrested a low-level dealer a couple months ago. The man wanted out of the life, having only gotten in it to pay off some of his kid's medical bills, but then he couldn't get out. The city prosecutor's office called me, wanting to know if I wanted to interview him. That was a no-brainer, so I sat down with the guy, and he sang like a canary. Suddenly, I had intel up to my eyeballs about stash houses, the distribution network, even some of the major players." He held up a finger. "He never mentioned Javy Gonzales. I'd have called you if he did." He lowered his hand. "Anyway, we set up a sting on one of the houses the informant mentioned. Undercovers went in, made some buys, and just as we were getting ready to move in, this fancy car rolls up and out pops Gonzales."

"Lucky." Finn shook his head. He wished some of his targets dropped into his lap like that.

"Yeah. Tell me about it. So, I'm in the surveillance van, screaming at everyone to hold their positions. Let him get into the house and see why he's there. He walks in, and the guy one of our operatives was talking to goes over and opens a wall safe and takes out a wad of cash and a bag of cocaine. Gonzales takes the cash and looks at it, then asks where the rest is."

"Why was he picking up cash from a stash house? Someone at his level has people to do that for him."

Nick shrugged. "Not sure, but from the conversation that followed that statement, I think he believes someone's been stealing from the organization."

"And with the power vacuum created by Herrera's arrest, he's probably trying to assert some extra authority."

"Exactly." Nick nodded once, and a smile tipped up one side of his mouth. "Except he picked the wrong day and the wrong house to do it."

Finn let out a snort. "That's for sure."

"So, am I forgiven for screwing up our original plan?"

With an overly dramatic sigh, Finn nodded. "I suppose." He chuckled. "Do you think he'll roll to save himself?"

Nick shrugged. "Maybe. We tried questioning him early this morning, shortly after booking him, but his lawyer wouldn't let him talk. He looked pretty dejected, though. With the evidence we have on him, he knows he'll lose at trial. I expect him to cut some sort of deal in the coming weeks."

Excitement created a buzz through Finn's body, waking him up some. They might not get Herrera out of the deal, but they could dismantle a significant portion of the Vargas-Ruiz cartel in the area with Gonzales' arrest. "Awesome. I'll get ahold of his attorney and make a formal request to do an interview." He stood. "Keep me posted on your end of things."

"I will. Hey, what did you learn at Herrera's discovery hearing? I wanted to go, but with the bust last night, time got away from me."

Finn's mouth flattened, some of his elation waning. "His lawyer's pushing hard to discredit Piper. The trial's going to be a rough one."

Nick's expression matched his. "I was afraid of that. Without her testimony, we don't have much. Just the break-in and armed assault at Dr. Tate's. That won't get him much time."

"True, but we have some options. Especially with Gonzales in custody. We might not need her." Finn had a feeling Javier Gonzales could be the key to bringing down the organization. The man was in the thick of it and knew all the key players, Herrera included. "I'm going to head back to my office. Gather up what I've got on their gun-running operation and give Gonzales' lawyer a call." He rounded his chair, turning toward the door. "I'll talk to you later."

"Sounds good."

Lifting a hand in farewell, Finn left Nick's office, his pace brisk as he made his way to the stairs, unable to stand still and wait for the elevator. He didn't need that coffee now.

# Three

Finn's energy rush only lasted a couple of hours before he found himself falling asleep at his desk. If he had any hope of making it the rest of the day, he needed a pick-me-up. Leaving the building, he lifted his face to the bright sunshine as he walked toward Cuppa. The warmth felt good after being inside the air-conditioned building. He was looking forward to this weekend. Unless one of his cases went topsy-turvy, he planned to take his friend, Ben, up on his invitation to spend it with him and some other friends at a cabin on the river. After the last few months, he needed to recharge for a couple of days.

The fresh scent of coffee hit him as he pulled open Cuppa's front door. He bit back a groan as he saw the line, then glanced at his watch. It was lunchtime. He hadn't even thought about that when he left his office.

That fact kept his feet moving forward. He needed something to help him reengage his agent brain. Since sleep was out, caffeine would have to do. It also afforded him the opportunity to people-watch. A person could learn a lot just by studying a crowd.

His eyes roved over those closest to him, recognizing several who worked in the federal complex. He didn't know them by name, but he saw them at least once a week. There, most people scurried from one place to another, always in a hurry. But here, their features were more relaxed as they sat and sipped their coffee and ate their pastries. Some even sat with friends, chatting and laughing.

The line shuffled forward, and Finn moved closer to the front, only two people ahead of him now. A woman at the end of the counter where patrons picked up their coffee caught his attention. About five-nine, her cream-colored suit and caramel leather heels showed off her trim figure. Finn's eyes strayed to the length of smooth, muscled leg peeking out below her skirt, then back up, over her firm rear to her straight shoulders. Her posture oozed confidence.

She turned, and a jolt of recognition hit him. It was the new magistrate. She was even prettier close up. And younger than he thought she'd be.

The line moved again, and Finn stepped forward, keeping his gaze on her as she walked deeper into the coffee shop and found an empty table near the window. She sat down and lifted her phone, sliding her thumb over the screen. A slight frown marred the space between her eyebrows as she read whatever she pulled up. Her dark-framed glasses slid down her nose, and she pushed them up with one finger, then took a sip of her coffee. When she glanced up, Finn looked away, not wanting to get caught staring.

He turned his attention out the window, his mind not registering anything beyond. What was wrong with him? Why did she enthrall him so? He saw tall, athletic, pretty women all the time. What was different about Judge Davidson?

Finn let his gaze stray to her again. She still stared at her phone, but her frown had intensified. Fine wrinkles now marred her forehead. He couldn't help but wonder what she read that caused her to frown so fiercely.

"Sir?"

Spinning to face forward, Finn looked at the barista.

She gave him an expectant look. "What can I get for you?"

He stepped up to the counter. "I'll take an Americano. Extra shot of espresso."

The young woman rang him up, and he handed her enough cash to cover the drink. He waved off the change, pointing to the tip jar, then walked down to the end of the counter to wait on his coffee. Again, his attention strayed to Judge Davidson. She now had the phone to her ear, her expression just as fierce.

"Here you go."

Offering the barista a smile of thanks, Finn took his coffee and headed for the table adjacent to the judge. Movement beyond the window snagged his attention as he neared. His gaze sharpened, and he perused the crowd outside. Something out there had subconsciously registered as not right. He looked from person to person, studying their body language, stopping on a man across the street. Dressed in a dark suit, he faced the coffee shop. Sunglasses covered his eyes, but he stared toward the café. Directly at the dark-haired woman frowning into her phone.

Finn changed direction, heading for the door. Passing behind the wall, he lost sight of the man as he exited the building. Outside, he dashed across the street, turning right and wandering down the sidewalk to where he'd seen him. Reaching the spot, Finn turned a full circle, but the stranger had disappeared into the crowd.

"Dammit." Something about that guy didn't sit right with him. He'd been watching the coffee shop. Blatantly.

Looking across the street, Finn saw the judge. She'd hung up and now stared at the table, the frown on her face evident from here. Apprehension tightened his muscles. He had no doubt that man had been watching her. There was nothing else in his line of vision. But why?

He faded back into the people milling on the sidewalk, taking up a spot in the shadows to keep an eye on Cuppa. Finn couldn't in good conscience go back to the office without making sure the judge made it back without mishap as well. She'd never know he was there.

# Four

She was going to kill him. Ground him for life and take away his phone until he graduated. After the morning she had, all she'd wanted was a short break to get some fresh air and a coffee, so she'd walked down the block to the coffee shop Suzie recommended. She had barely sat down when she got an email from the high school guidance counselor. Paxton had been in his new school one day—one freaking day—and was already in trouble.

Kennedy reread the message, biting back a groan. At least it wasn't bad enough for the school to call her office. They knew her ability to take phone calls was dependent on her caseload for the day, so instead, they'd agreed to email her with any issues, unless it was important enough to warrant a phone call. Apparently, squirting ketchup and mustard all over another student only necessitated an email.

Glancing up, she took another sip of her coffee, debating whether to call the school. She probably should, if for no other reason than to find out what the kid was wearing, so she could reimburse his parents for the cost of whatever clothing Pax ruined.

With a huff, she turned back to her cell and clicked the phone number at the bottom of the email, then brought the device to her ear. It rang several times before a woman picked up.

"This is Mrs. Pickerington."

"Hi. This is Kennedy Davidson, Paxton Cobb's mom. I got your email."

"Oh, yes. Hello. Thank you for calling me back so quickly."

"I was on my lunch break, so I have a few minutes free. Can you tell me what happened? Why did he squirt ketchup and mustard on the kid?" Kennedy put an elbow on the table and propped her head against her fingers.

"He won't say. Whenever we ask, he just shrugs and stares straight ahead. I have to say, Ms. Davidson, this is not the best way to start out at a new school."

Kennedy straightened, her frown intensifying at the woman's tone. It told her that she'd already deemed Pax a troublemaker, and it wouldn't matter what he did in the future to change that perception; he'd always be a trouble-maker. "I'm aware, Mrs. Pickerington. This move has been an adjustment for all of us. Is he there? I'd like to speak to him."

"We don't normally allow students to use the phone."

"If you want to find out why he did it, put him on the line." Kennedy used her judge voice; it brooked no argument.

A moment of silence passed, then Mrs. Pickerington let out a small sigh. "Just a moment."

There was a crackle on the line as the woman set the phone down. In the background, she heard the murmur of voices, then her son's voice sounded in her ear.

"Hello?"

"Paxton Andrew, it is the first day."

"So?"

Kennedy blew out a long breath and reined in her temper.

Getting upset with him would just make him clam up more. "Just tell me why, please?"

More silence passed. Kennedy wished she could see his face.

"He called Paige metal-mouth." His voice was low. "And four-eyes."

A new sort of anger curled in Kennedy's gut. As well as a surge of pride for her son's willingness to defend his sister.

"Am I in a lot of trouble?"

The tone of his voice brought back memories of the young boy he used to be, and how he would look up at her with those huge light green eyes swimming with tears whenever he did something he knew he shouldn't.

"Mildly. We'll talk about it when you get home. I'm glad you came to her defense, but covering the boy in condiments was not the way to do it. Put Mrs. Pickerington back on."

More crackling sounded as he handed the phone over. Kennedy didn't let her get out more than a hello before she interrupted.

"Did you hear what he told me?"

"Yes."

"Good. I will reimburse the dry-cleaning costs to clean the young man's clothes, but Paxton will not be apologizing. Not for defending his sister. What will be done about the boy who bullied my daughter?"

"Oh, um, well, I'll need to talk with him again. That's not what he told us."

Kennedy rolled her eyes. "I'm sure. What did he say?"

"He said he told Paige and Paxton that the table was full, so they'd need to find a different place to sit. Paxton responded by squirting his condiment packets on the boy's shirt."

"And you believed that?" That was over the top, even for the most troubled teen.

"Well, your son wouldn't say different, so..." Her voice trailed off, defensive.

"Obviously, there's much more to the story. I would say, at the very least, this boy should apologize to Paige for what he said. And perhaps you should rearrange their schedules so they don't all have lunch together."

"I already planned to."

"Good. Please have his parents turn in a receipt for the dry-cleaning to you, and I'll write a check. Is there anything else I should be aware of?"

"Just that Paxton will need to serve an hour-long detention. Either today or tomorrow after school."

Kennedy ground her teeth. She understood why—his response to the boy's comments was unacceptable—but it still stuck in her craw that his good intentions were being punished. "Fine. Today will work." She'd call Betty Ruth and tell her she'd need to make two trips to pick up the kids. Kennedy was happier now than ever that the woman agreed to move with them. She couldn't imagine springing her kids on some poor, unsuspecting person. They'd grown up with Betty Ruth. She knew how to handle them.

"I'll make a note of it. Thank you for your cooperation, Ms. Davidson. I hope this will be the last incident."

"So do I. Have a good day."

"You too."

"Thanks. Bye." Kennedy hung up and let the phone fall to the table. She scrubbed her hands over her face and let out the groan she'd been holding back. That kid would be the death of her.

Standing, she gathered her things and left the coffee shop, more keyed up than when she left the office. Any peace she'd found on the walk over was gone now.

She stepped out into the sunshine, barely noticing its warmth. Lifting her phone, she found Betty Ruth's name in her contacts. The line rang twice before her housekeeper-slash-nanny picked up.

"Hi, Ken. How's your first day been so far?"

"Insane. My boss was in a car wreck, so we had to scramble to cover his cases this morning. I took a break, only to get an email from the kids' school. Pax squirted ketchup and mustard on some boy because he called Paige names. Now he has detention."

"Oh, no. I'm glad he defended her, but really?"

"Yeah." The older woman's soft voice soothed some of Kennedy's anger. Betty Ruth could always make things better. Even if she wasn't trying. Her kind, sweet personality was like a balm to frazzled nerves.

Betty Ruth made a tsking sound. "Is your boss okay?"

"He will be." They'd received word on his injuries a couple hours ago. "He's got some broken bones and will need surgery and some therapy, but with time, he'll be fine." The next few weeks would be ridiculously busy, though, in his absence.

"Well, that's good. What time do I need to pick up Paxton?"

"An hour later than Paige."

"Okay. I think I'll switch up what I was making for dinner too. Enchiladas are quicker."

"That sounds good. Thank you, Betty Ruth."

"You're welcome, sweetie. We'll see you this evening."

They said their goodbyes. Kennedy quickened her pace. Betty Ruth hadn't smoothed away all of her agitation. She wished she had time for a run. At least she'd be too busy this afternoon to think about her problems.

# FIVE

The door to Kennedy's study creaked open. She glanced up from her laptop to see Pax poke his head in the door.

"Hey, honey. Come in." When she got home a couple hours ago, she hadn't mentioned the incident at school. Betty Ruth had worked her magic, and he was smiling. She knew he'd come to her eventually to talk. Despite his attitude of late, he was a good kid.

Pax entered the room, leaving the door open. He walked up to the desk, then hesitated.

Kennedy closed the lid on her computer and got up, rounding the desk. "Let's sit over here." She gestured to the couch along the wall.

He turned and crossed to the small leather sofa and sat down. Kennedy perched beside him. The boy twisted his fingers together, staring at his hands.

"I'm sorry, Mom." He peeked at her through the dark hair falling over his forehead.

Kennedy reached out and smoothed it back. "Hey. We all make mistakes. I'm not mad."

His head lifted. "You're not?"

"No. Not at your intentions, anyway. Your method? Well, there's a reason I didn't fight the detention you got. Why didn't you use words? Why go straight to slinging condiments?"

He sighed and scooted deeper onto the couch. "I don't know. He just made me so mad. We were a little late for lunch—we got lost—so there weren't many seats left. When we walked up and asked if we could sit at their table, Corey took one look at us and sneered. He said, 'Why would we want to share our table with a skater punk and his metal-mouth, four-eyed, flat-chested sister?'"

Kennedy's eyes widened. "You didn't mention that last part on the phone."

Pax glanced down again. "No. I was kind of afraid you'd come to the school if I did. No offense, but having my mom show up at school to defend me would just make things worse." He looked at her. "I'm sorry for how I reacted, but he can't talk to her like that." His silvery green eyes took on a flintiness that reminded her of her oldest brother. Ben got that same look when righteous anger reared its head.

She patted Pax's knee. "Thank you for apologizing. And for recognizing your mistake. I haven't said much about the attitude you've had of late, because I know this move was hard. But do you think you can try to curb it? To make the best of things? It might help you control your impulse to cover your classmates in sauces."

A smile quirked a corner of his mouth. "Yeah." He sobered. "I just miss my friends, you know?"

"I do. I miss mine too. And your grandparents." Despite her mom's willingness to butt in where Kennedy didn't want her, she missed the older woman. "But hey, at least we're closer to Uncle Ben. I think if you give this place a chance, you'll find that you like it here. There's a lot to do. And Aunt Gemma has already invited you over for riding lessons. That's something you've always loved." When the kids were younger, she and Pete would often take them horseback riding on vacation whenever they could. Both Paxton and Paige loved it.

He lifted a shoulder. "I guess."

"How about I give them a call and see if we can set something up for this weekend? We haven't seen them since we arrived."

That shoulder rose again. "You could."

Kennedy smiled. That was as close to a yes as she would get. "Okay, then. I'll get ahold of them."

He nodded, glancing away. Kennedy's smile faded as she took in the hesitant look on his face.

"Is there something else you wanted to talk about?"

His gaze darted to hers, then away again. "So, what's my punishment?"

Her brows dipped for a moment, then smoothed out. "Oh. For what happened at school?"

Pax nodded.

"Nothing."

His head shot up and his eyes connected with hers. "What?"

"You served your punishment at school. I am taking the cost to clean Corey's clothes from your allowance, but I'm not grounding you. Your intentions were good, Paxton. It's your execution that needed work. Can you promise me something?"

A wary look entered his eyes. "What?"

"That you'll think twice before acting out? That you'll try to do better? You're a good kid. I don't want to see you derail your future because you can't stay out of trouble."

He rolled his eyes. "A couple of detentions isn't going to mean I flunk out of school."

"No, but if you continue to make bad decisions, it could

mean you end up running with the wrong crowd. That could lead to even worse decisions. Those are the ones that could derail your future. I see it all the time."

Pax blinked, holding her gaze. Kennedy could see him considering her words.

"Okay. I'll do my best." His shoulders fell. "We really are stuck here, aren't we? No chance of going back to Richmond?"

Kennedy shook her head. "No. I'm sorry, honey. This is home now." She'd debated long and hard about taking this job. But her ex-husband's presence—or lack thereof—in their lives was causing more harm than good. He was supposed to spend every other weekend with the kids, but couldn't be bothered. Even when he deigned them important enough to schedule into his busy life, something always came up and he canceled. When they did go to his house, they spent most of their weekend roaming around his place by themselves while he went off to work or out with colleagues and friends. Or even on a date.

That had been the last straw; when he chose some woman he just met over his kids. She knew then she had to do something to keep them from feeling so worthless every other weekend. It hadn't taken much to get Pete to agree to let her move out-of-state with them. She'd never stop him from seeing them, but now it was up to Pax and Paige what interaction they had. They were no longer obligated to spend time with a man who didn't want them around.

She patted his knee again. "How about some dessert? We never had any." She stood.

Pax rose to stand beside her, making her feel short. Even at fifteen, he was over six feet tall. "What kind of dessert?"

"Ice cream? I think there's some in the freezer."

He headed for the door. "You better tell Paige before it's all gone."

Kennedy laughed, following him out. "You are not eating an entire carton of ice cream."

"Hey, I'm a growing teenager." He flexed. "I need fuel."

Laughing harder, she just shook her head.

# Six

Kennedy's heels echoed off the walls as she strode down the hallway from her courtroom to her office, done with her morning court sessions. Her stomach rumbled, reminding her how long ago she'd eaten breakfast. The sandwich and fruit she packed wouldn't be enough. Sure, it would tide her over for a little while, but by mid-afternoon, she'd be starving again. Hopefully, she'd get a short break, so she could raid the box of protein bars in her desk drawer. Though she wouldn't be opposed to the next few hours flying by. Once the day was over, she planned to order pizza, watch a movie with her kids, then take a long, hot bath and wash away the crazy week. Thankfully, it had calmed some after Monday. Paxton had stayed out of trouble, and her staff found a rhythm at work to cope with Elijah's absence. She was just tired.

The weekend would help recharge her batteries, though. She'd called her brother about getting together this weekend. He and Gemma already had plans with some friends. One of them owned a large cabin on the river, and they'd planned a short getaway. He'd invited her and the kids to join them.

At first, Kennedy protested. She didn't want to intrude. But Ben insisted, saying Brooke—the friend who owned the house—wouldn't mind. That she'd invite them herself if given half a chance. After a little more prodding, she'd finally accepted. Now, she was more than happy she had. She couldn't wait to dip her fishing pole into the water. But first, she had to get through her afternoon sessions.

The door to the judicial offices loomed, and she twisted the doorknob, letting herself inside. She stopped short at the sight of the woman standing in front of Suzie's desk. Dressed in a gray pantsuit with a light blue shirt, the woman had her dirty-blonde hair pulled into a tight bun. When she turned to look at who entered, Kennedy noticed the gun and badge strapped to her hip.

"Judge Davidson?"

Kennedy frowned and stepped further inside, closing the door. "Yes. You are?"

The woman walked forward and held out a hand. "Taylor Paulson, U.S. Marshals."

Taking it, Kennedy gave her a tentative smile in greeting. "What can I do for you?"

"Could we talk in your office?" The marshal dropped her hand and pointed toward the door with Kennedy's name on it.

"What's this about?"

Marshal Paulson gestured to the door again. "Please? Could we talk in private?"

The set to the woman's features told Kennedy she wouldn't say a word until they were behind closed doors. "All right." She walked to her door and opened it, motioning the woman inside, then shut the door.

"I know you're a busy woman, so I'll make this brief."

Kennedy set her briefcase on her desk, then turned to hang

up her robe on the coat rack in the corner. "I just want to know what this is about."

"We have reason to believe Judge Jedynak's accident wasn't an accident."

A frown formed on Kennedy's face, and her fingers paused in their task. After a moment, she resumed hanging up the black robe, then turned to face the marshal. "Not an accident?"

Marshal Paulson shook her head. "No. His transmission failed. He successfully steered the car to the shoulder, but someone plowed into him from behind, then fled the scene. Witness accounts state a truck with a push bar rammed into his car—deliberately—at a high rate of speed, then drove off."

Kennedy crossed her arms, then raised one hand to rub at her temple. She'd need to add a double-scoop of chocolate fudge ice cream to her relaxation routine tonight. "Do you have any leads? And why does this need to be a private conversation? This isn't anything Suzie can't know."

"Correct, but I'm not finished." Paulson's expression took on a note of concern.

An answering frown deepened the lines on Kennedy's forehead. "Oh?"

"Through investigating the judge's accident, we received information that there's a concerted effort to disrupt Gustavo Herrera's trial."

"Gustavo Herrera? He's not on our docket. Judge Stechschulte and her team are handling him." For which Kennedy was glad. If he'd been on Jedynak's docket, she would have needed to recuse herself because of her brother's involvement in the case.

"Right, but your team has Javier Gonzales. Word has it he's going to roll on Herrera to save himself."

"Why take out Jedynak, then? Why not Gonzales?"

"Because Jedynak's easier to get to. So are you."

Kennedy dropped her arms and straightened her spine. "Me?" Another thought hit her. "How did they know we had Gonzales? He hadn't been in a courtroom before Elijah's accident."

"Exactly." Paulson's gaze bored into hers.

Understanding dawned. "You think there's a mole in this office?"

"If not yours, then somewhere within the district court judicial offices, yes. Someone is feeding information to the cartel. I know it's not you, because you've been here a week."

Sinking into her chair, Kennedy propped her elbows on her desk, hands raised and folded. "So, what happens now?"

"You get a security detail, as do your fellow judges. I'm yours. During the day, anyway. Another agent will watch you at night."

"What?" Kennedy sat up and groaned. "Great."

A mirthless smile crossed Paulson's face. "It won't be that bad. I'll be as unobtrusive as possible. So will your overnight protection. We'll sit outside your house unless you need us. During the day, I'll sit in the back of your courtroom. Follow you to your car, then home—after I check your vehicle. That sort of thing."

Kennedy groaned again. "Does this mean I'm basically on house arrest?"

"We'd prefer if you limit your time outside, but we understand you have a life. We'll be around to help minimize the threat to you."

Leaning forward, Kennedy propped her head in her hands and stared at her desk. "What about my kids? Are they in danger?"

"So far, we don't think anyone's family is a target. The idea seems to be to disrupt the trial process. I would caution your children to be vigilant and not to go anywhere alone."

At least the latter wouldn't be hard. The twins couldn't

drive yet. "Okay." She sat up. "We have plans to spend the weekend up north with my brother's family and some of their friends. I'm not canceling. You're welcome to tag along, but I don't think it's necessary. I'll be surrounded by cops."

"You're talking about your eldest brother? Ben?"

Kennedy nodded, not surprised the marshal had done her homework.

The woman's head bobbed. "Okay. I'll pass the information along to my superior, but I can just about guarantee we'll still be your shadow." She offered another smile, this one with a touch of humor. "At least I'll have backup if I need it."

A short laugh left Kennedy's lips. "For sure." Her smile slowly died. "So, I guess this means my coffee break is out."

Marshal Paulson's face pulled. "Can you send someone to get it? Or have it delivered?"

"Probably, but it's not the same. I was looking forward to getting blasted with that coffeeshop smell, you know?" Reaching for her phone, she pressed the button to connect her to Suzie.

"Yes, Judge?" Suzie's perky voice came over the receiver.

"Could you send one of the interns to Cuppa to get me a latte? Medium salted-caramel, extra whip." She didn't care about the calories. Not today.

"Of course. Do you want anything else?"

"A chocolate croissant." Yep, totally didn't care. "Have them stop in so I can give them some cash before they head out."

"Yes, ma'am."

"Thanks, Suzie."

"You're welcome."

The phone clicked in Kennedy's ear as Suzie hung up. She glanced up at Marshal Paulson. "So, who can I tell what?"

"You can tell your staff there's been a threat against you,

which is why I'm here. They don't need the particulars. As for your family, you can tell them the truth. I know I wouldn't want to hide something like this from my children. Not at their age."

"You have kids?"

"Yes, ma'am. Two girls. Sixteen and eighteen."

"Oh, you've conquered driving. Lucky. I get to start that soon." Kennedy rolled her lips in and pressed them together. She hadn't rambled when she was anxious in a long time. It was tantamount to the level of stress this situation caused that she'd fallen back on a habit long dead.

The marshal offered her a soft smile, understanding in her eyes. "It'll get easier. Once you acclimate to the situation, it'll get much easier."

Kennedy nodded. "I'm sure you're right. I just feel a long way off from that right now." She pushed away from her desk, unable to stay put. "Do you mind if I take a walk around the building? I need to move."

"Of course. I'll follow, but I'll stay back so you have a little space."

"Thank you, Marshal."

"Call me Taylor, please."

Giving the woman a small smile, Kennedy nodded, then opened her bottom desk drawer and reached into her purse for her wallet. She'd leave some money with Suzie for the intern. Taking out a ten, she shut and locked the drawer, then rounded her desk, passing the marshal.

"Suzie."

The woman looked up. So did the intern standing at her desk.

"I'm going for a walk. Here." She held out the money to the young woman. "Frannie, right?"

The woman nodded, taking the cash. "Suzie was just

telling me your order. You look a little frazzled. You sure you only want a medium."

A smile broke through the angst clouding Kennedy's brain. "I'm sure. Any more that that, and I'll be bouncing off the walls until midnight. Thank you."

Frannie nodded. "Okay. One medium salted-caramel latte with extra whip and a chocolate croissant coming up." She turned and walked out the door.

Kennedy waved at Suzie and followed Frannie, turning the opposite direction. Marshal Paulson trailed behind.

True to her word, the marshal hung back, giving Kennedy the illusion she was alone. She wished she could go outside. Fresh air and sunshine always helped clear her head. But she didn't want to push her luck. She was still shocked enough that the idea of exposing herself freaked her out some.

Which was probably why she nearly collided with a man as she turned the corner. An apology on her lips as she side-stepped, it died in her throat as her gaze connected with a pair of steel-gray eyes set into a tanned, square-jawed face. He offered her a smile, crinkles fanning out from the corners of his eyes and dimples forming in his cheeks.

"Whoa, there."

Kennedy cleared her throat and found her voice. "I'm sorry. Excuse me."

"No problem, judge."

Nodding, she took a step around him, then stopped and looked up as his words registered. "Have we met?" She studied his face. He didn't look familiar. She'd remember a man like him. Handsome, but rugged. Tall. Nice smile. Shoulders for days.

Her eyes strayed to his muscular chest. Yeah, she'd remember him.

"No, I've just seen you around."

His voice brought her head up. A small smile toyed with his mouth, giving him a rakish air.

"They pay me to pay attention." He pointed to his hip.

Brow furrowing and cheeks reddening at the innuendo behind his gesture, she glanced down anyway, unable to help herself. What she saw pulled a soft laugh from her. On his belt was a gold shield with "ATF" inscribed on it as well as the words, "Special Agent." Smiling, she looked up. "Oh. Well, you have me at a disadvantage. You seem to know me, but I know nothing about you."

"Right. Sorry." He held out a hand. "Finley Porter. Finn."

"Kennedy Davidson." She shook his hand. Warmth permeated her palm and traveled up her arm. Even after she let go, it persisted, finding a place deep in her chest and settling there.

"It's nice to meet you. Formally." He gave a small bow. One side of his mouth lifted, that rakish look returning.

*Oh, this man is a charmer.* She'd do well to remember the power charming men had to hurt her heart. And her children's. Her ex-husband had charmed the pants off of her—quite literally. Though she'd like to think she wouldn't have stayed with him so long if she hadn't gotten pregnant. She was much more resistant to charm now.

Smile turning guarded, she nodded. "You too."

Something sparked in his eyes. An awareness that said he'd noticed the change in her demeanor. More than the charming smile ever would, that glint of intelligence drew her in. She had to slam on the mental brakes and throw up the barriers. A man complicating her life was the last thing she needed. No matter how handsome and intelligent he was.

Kennedy turned up the wattage on her smile. "Well, it was nice to meet you, Agent Porter. I'm sure I'll see you around."

"Undoubtedly."

Again, those eyes said he knew the thoughts running

through her head. She schooled her features and did her best to block him out. With a nod, she continued around him, applauding herself when she didn't look back.

She only wished it was as easy to keep his friendly smile and gorgeous eyes out of sight of her mind. Those were burned there now.

# SEVEN

"Paige, would you hurry up? Geez. How long does it take to pack a suitcase?"

Kennedy rolled her eyes as she zipped her tote bag closed, listening to Paxton yell down the hallway at his sister. Picking up her bag, as well as the small rolling suitcase she packed last night, she left her bedroom.

"Not all of us can fit everything we need into a single duffel, Pax." She flicked the strap of the backpack slung over his shoulder as she walked past. "That said—" She paused and glanced toward Paige's bedroom. "Paige! Let's go!"

"One second!" The girl's voice carried through the door to the hall.

Blowing out a short breath, Kennedy headed for the stairs. "Come on. She'll be down in a minute."

His heavy footsteps followed her down the stairs.

"Did you pack a bag with snacks, like I told you to?" She turned her head to look at him.

He nodded. "I left it in the pantry." Pax ducked into the small room and came back with a reusable grocery bag stuffed to the gills.

Kennedy couldn't stop the laugh that bubbled free. "We're only going to be gone overnight."

Paxton lifted one shoulder, a smile hovering over his mouth. "I wasn't sure what I'd want."

Shaking her head, she let him go. She wasn't going to quibble about a bag of snacks.

Running footsteps on the stairs heralded Paige's arrival a moment before she breezed through the door. "I'm ready."

"You're sure you have everything?" Kennedy glanced at her daughter and raised an eyebrow. The girl carried a backpack over her shoulder. "Where's your suitcase?"

"I didn't need it. It's only an overnight. I packed pajamas, my swimsuit, a couple changes of clothes, leggings, and a hoodie. Plus, my toiletries and flip-flops. I'm good."

Kennedy blinked, trying to reconcile herself as a teenager with the girl before her. She'd have needed a backpack just for her hair products and makeup. She still had a bigger bag than either of her kids. "If you're sure that's all you need, then let's load up."

"I just need to get my snacks."

"You have a snack bag too? How was there anything left for you to choose from? Your brother packed the entire pantry."

Paige reemerged with a grin, holding a sack similar to Paxton's. "I made him share."

Pax rolled his eyes. "Elbowed me in the gut and told me she'd crush my Oreos to crumbs if I didn't is more like it."

Kennedy stifled a laugh, spinning toward the garage door to hide her smile. "Let's go, you two." She reached for the door handle and led them to the car. Once they were situated, she started the car and pulled out of the garage, waving to Marshal Paulson as she turned onto the street. The marshal pulled in behind her. Her security team had decided to tag along, but would take more of a distance surveillance role. Kennedy had all the protection she needed with her brother and his colleagues in the same house.

"Are there going to be any other kids there our age?" Paige asked once they were on the highway headed out of town.

"I don't think so. I think all of your uncle's friends have young kids. Babies." Which Kennedy liked. She got her baby fix without all the work. Teenagers weren't easy, but they could at least care for themselves.

Pax groaned. "I hope they don't cry the whole time."

"I'm sure it'll be fine."

"Yeah, maybe." His tone told her he didn't believe that.

"We'll have fun, no matter what. The way Ben talked, there's lots to do there. The woman whose family owns the cabin keeps all kinds of water and yard toys on hand." She glanced in the rearview mirror in time to see him lift a shoulder. Holding back a sigh, she let the subject drop. She knew he'd have fun, even if he thought otherwise now. It's the way things always went.

Reaching for the radio, Kennedy turned it on, letting the music fill the silence so she wouldn't be tempted to convince him to be positive. He already knew. Singing along, the miles passed quickly, and soon, she turned off the state route and onto a county road. Following the GPS directions to the address Ben gave her, they passed into a dense thicket of trees, which grew denser when she turned onto the gravel drive.

"Anyone else feel like we're descending into a slasher film?" Paxton mumbled.

Kennedy smiled while Paige giggled. It did feel slightly ominous. The heavy forest felt a little claustrophobic.

They didn't stay in the trees too long, though. The forest gave way to a clearing, and the sight that greeted them took Kennedy's breath away.

"Holy crap!" Paige's exclamation filled the vehicle.

Holy crap, was right. The house was huge. Made of large

river rock and wood, the three-story house was more of a lodge. A porch, lined with rocking chairs, wrapped around three sides of the house. Kennedy followed the drive and drove around to the side, where several other vehicles were parked. Her mouth dropped open as she got her first glimpse of the rear. Massive windows spiked through all three stories. Covered porches on every level flanked them, offering relaxing views of the river and mountains.

"Geez. How much money do these people have?" Paxton tipped his head, looking up at the house as he gazed out the window.

"A lot," Paige answered. "Enough that I bet we all get our own rooms."

Kennedy wouldn't doubt that. She counted three sets of balcony doors on each side of the windows on the top two floors. There were probably an equal number of rooms on the front side.

She pulled in next to her brother's SUV and shut off the car. "Let's go find out."

The words barely left her mouth before the twins scrambled out their doors, chattering about the gigantic house and the view. Kennedy followed at a more sedate pace, leaving her bags in the car to fetch later. She glanced at Marshal Paulson's vehicle as the woman parked away from all the others. Her window rolled down, but she stayed in her car.

Gravel crunched under Kennedy's feet as she turned away and walked toward the structure. The back door opened, and she smiled when she saw Ben step out. He had his daughter, Meredith, tucked into one arm. The four-month-old clutched a plastic teether in her tiny fists; her bright blue eyes fixed on her daddy's face as she chewed.

"Hey, guys." He frowned slightly at the car parked at the edge of the grass, but said nothing.

"Uncle Ben!" Paige ran up the stairs to give him a hug.

He smiled and embraced her with one arm. "Hey, kiddo. How are you?"

"Good." Paige offered him a quick smile, then turned to Meredith. "Hi, sweetie." She glanced at Ben. "Can I hold her?"

"Sure." He shifted the girl and held her out.

Paige gathered her close. The teether popped free of Meredith's mouth, and she stared up at her cousin.

Kennedy smiled at the picture the two made as she ascended the stairs to greet her brother. "Hi, Ben."

"Hey, you." He held out his arms, and Kennedy slipped into his embrace and hugged him tight. She'd missed her brother's hugs.

"How was your drive?" He pulled back, smiling.

Kennedy chuckled. "Quick."

His grin flashed. "Did you find the place okay?"

She nodded. "GPS brought me right to it." She turned and glanced over the property. "This place is gorgeous."

"Right? This is our third or fourth time here, but it's still awe-inspiring every time." He tipped his head toward the door. "Come on. I'll give you a tour and show you to your rooms. Everyone is inside, getting ready to sit down for lunch."

Kennedy walked forward behind Paige. Ben clapped Paxton on the shoulder in greeting, then led them inside.

"Holy sh—crap." Pax sent Kennedy a sheepish look, changing his language mid-stream.

Again, she agreed. The interior of the house was no less grand than the exterior. The massive windows let in tons of light, illuminating the three-story great room. Huge timbers held up the roof, attached to equally large rafters. A staircase wound up the right side, leading to balconies on the second and third floors that ran three sides of the room. On the left, a stone fireplace sat cold in deference to the late-spring heat. Between them, a plush grouping of leather furniture sat clustered around an enormous cream-colored rug. To Kennedy's immediate left was a kitchen dreams were made of. Stainless-steel appliances, ensconced in rich pine cabinets only a shade darker than the log walls, gleamed like they'd never been used. Black granite counters with fine white marble veining topped them. Beneath her feet, the slate tile completed the river lodge look.

A chorus of hellos pulled Kennedy's attention away from her opulent surroundings. She smiled at the crowd of people milling around the kitchen island. "Hello."

"Everyone, this is my sister, Kennedy, and her kids, Paxton and Paige." Ben gestured to them, then glanced at Kennedy before introducing the others. "I'll just go around the room. You know my wife." He pointed to Gemma, who smiled and waved. "And her brother and his wife, and their son." Tristan and Laurel smiled. "Next to Laurel is Tristan's partner, Jake Maxwell. That's his wife, Mackenzie. Across from her is her friend, Piper Riordan and her fiancé, Cullen Tate. Then, on the end, is my K-9 deputy, Carter Townsend, and his girl-friend, Mara Roth."

A dog barked from beneath the table.

Ben smiled and tipped his head, looking at the animal. "Oh, and that's Maverick, Carter's partner." He paused and glanced around. "Where did Brooke go?"

Gemma rolled her eyes. "Johnathan called. She went upstairs to talk to him."

Ben's mouth flattened. Kennedy's brow wrinkled at the look on her brother's face. Something told her he didn't like this Johnathan.

"Let me guess, he's not coming?" Ben asked.

"Most likely." Gemma nodded.

"That throws off our numbers for any team things we do," Tristan said.

Kennedy's frown deepened. "How? Without him, don't we have an even number?"

"There's still one person coming," Ben said. "A friend of mine from work." He glanced at his watch. "He should be here soon. I got a text about half an hour ago that he was on his way. He actually doesn't live too far from you." He nodded at Kennedy, then shrugged and looked at Tristan. "We'll figure it out. One of us can always rotate if need be." He turned to Kennedy. "Come on. I'll show you to your rooms while we wait on him and Brooke."

With a nod, Kennedy motioned for her kids to follow. Paige handed Meredith to Gemma, then Ben led them upstairs to the third floor on the right side of the house.

"You guys get your pick of rooms. Finn's the only other one who will be up here. Gemma and I are on the other side with Tristan and Laurel. The other couples are on the floor below you. We decided to keep the babies on one side of the house so when they wake up at night, we don't disturb everyone else."

An image of stormy gray eyes and deep dimples flashed through Kennedy's head, but she quickly shoved it away. She highly doubted Ben's friend was the same Finn. Asheville was a big city, and her brother knew a lot of people in law enforcement.

"Sounds good." She turned to the twins. "Go pick."

They took off, opening doors. Paxton picked the room on the corner at the front of the house, while Paige picked the one across from him with French doors leading to the balcony. Kennedy had a feeling her daughter might end up asleep outside in one of the loungers tonight. The girl loved to sleep with the window open. Kennedy did too. She wandered into the middle bedroom on the back and went straight to the double doors, throwing them open.

"The view is incredible, isn't it?" Ben walked up beside her as she moved onto the balcony.

She glanced at him and nodded. "For as deep into the forest as we went, I wouldn't think there would be such a view here."

"I know. But it rises in elevation as you go through the trees. Brooke's ancestors knew what they were doing when they picked this land to settle on." He gestured to the landscape.

"I'll say. Thank you for inviting us. This will be a nice respite from our first full week since we moved. I know I should be home unpacking more, but—" She broke off and shrugged.

Ben waved a hand. "It'll all still be there when you get home. And I'm guessing you or Betty Ruth already put the essentials away."

Kennedy tossed him a sheepish smile. "You know me well."

He chuckled. "You probably had all that done within the first forty-eight hours."

She joined in his laughter. "Yep."

Ben touched her shoulder. "In any case, I'm glad you're here. Not just here, here." He pointed to the floor. "But here in North Carolina. It's nice having family close again."

"I'm glad to be here. I won't lie and say I don't miss Richmond, but it's nice having some breathing room. From more than just Pete. Mom was driving me crazy, constantly trying to 'help.'" She air-quoted. "But it was all comments about how I needed to find a man to lean on, disguised as advice."

"Yeah, well, you have to remember, she comes from an upbringing where women weren't the breadwinners. They raised the kids and kept their noses out of what was deemed a man's business."

Kennedy's eyebrows turned down, and she leveled a look at her brother.

He held up his hands. "I'm not defending her. Just telling you to look at things from her perspective."

Her face smoothed out, and she nodded. "I understand where she's coming from. It's still annoying. I don't need another man. The first one left me with a sour taste." When she and Pete first got married, she had high hopes. He treated her well and, after a bit of a rough start, seemed excited about becoming a father. But the harsh realities of parenting twins while in law school quickly showed her his true colors. His successes in his career showed her even more. The higher he climbed in the legal world, the more self-centered he became. It was all about what he could get. How high he could go and how quickly he could get there. Kennedy and the twins got pushed to the side.

"Not all men are jerks, Ken."

She rolled her eyes. "Don't you start too."

He chuckled. "I'm not. Just cautioning you not to rule out ever entering into another relationship because Pete's an idiot."

Kennedy offered him a short nod. "Noted."

His brow wrinkled as he stared at her for a long moment, then he turned away. "So, what's with the chaperone?"

It was Kennedy's turn to frown. "Chaperone?" Her face cleared as she remembered Marshal Paulson pulling in behind her. "Oh, that. It's no big deal."

"Oh, now I know it's a big deal. What's going on?"

She waved a hand, not wanting him to worry. "Nothing. There were some threats made against the judiciary, so the Marshals put a detail on me. I'm not housebound or anything. They're just being cautious."

Ben's frown dipped low, and he crossed his arms. "The

Marshals don't put security details on judges unless there's a serious threat. What happened?"

Kennedy huffed. He wouldn't let this go until she told him the entire story.

A car door slammed below, distracting them. She glanced toward the parking area, but couldn't see anything past the end of the house.

"That's probably Finn." He shook a finger at her. "We're not done." He turned to go back into the house.

"Don't shake that finger in my face. I'll bite it, just like I did when we were kids." She followed him inside.

He tossed her a playful smile over his shoulder. "Do you remember what I did to you when you bit my finger?"

She laughed. "You threw me over your shoulder, then took me down to the stables and made me muck stalls."

His smile widened. "Exactly. There aren't any stables here, but there will be fish. I'll make you clean them all."

Kennedy's mouth twisted, and she scrunched her nose. "Yuck."

Laughing, he led her down the hallway and back to the great room. They reached the main floor just as the doorbell pealed through the house. Ben went to answer the door while Kennedy hung back. The others turned from their positions around the island to see the newcomer.

Grasping the knob, Ben opened the door. "Hey, Finn. Come in." He stepped back.

Silhouetted by the bright sunshine, a tall male figure loomed in the doorway. When Ben moved, he crossed the threshold, bringing his features into clarity. Kennedy gasped as she got her first look. She knew that face.

# EIGHT

F inn stepped into the house and blinked, clearing his vision from the bright sunshine. The interior of the log and stone building was just as impressive on the inside. When he'd cleared the trees and caught his first glimpse of the house, he thought he took a wrong turn somewhere until he saw Ben's SUV parked around the side.

"Thanks for inviting me. This place is huge." His eyes went to the rafters three stories above. He'd hate to be the one who had to clean this place.

A soft gasp drew his attention. He looked down and past Ben to the source. His brow furrowed as his mind registered the identity of the dark-haired woman standing there. "Judge Davidson?" As soon as he said her name, her identity clicked. He glanced at Ben. "I take it you two are related?"

"She's my sister. You've already met?"

Finn nodded. "We nearly collided in the hallway yesterday." This was an unfortunate turn of events. He'd been hoping this weekend would not only help relax him but also take his mind off the beautiful judge. She hadn't been far from his thoughts all week; then after their near-collision yesterday, she'd been at the forefront of his mind. No matter how hard he tried to bury thoughts of her, she refused to stay away. At the very least, he wanted to figure out why.

Though seeing her in those jeans and that snug t-shirt gave him a good idea what it was that held his attention. She was tall. Though not overly curvy, she was well-muscled. He liked a woman who didn't shy away from exercise.

"Oh. Well, that saves one introduction, I guess." Ben smiled, then turned to the rest of the people in the room, introducing Tristan and Jake's wives. Everyone else Finn already knew.

Voices upstairs filtered down. He glanced over to see two teenagers enter the gallery area, heading for the staircase. Bickering, the boy ran ahead of the girl, rolling his eyes. Finn heard Kennedy sigh.

"One day. That's all I want," she muttered, looking at Ben.

He grinned. "They're teenagers."

She huffed and stepped away, intercepting the kids as they came toward everyone. "What are you arguing about? We've been here ten minutes."

The boy crossed his arms and glared at the girl, who rolled her eyes and sighed dramatically.

"Who comes to a place like this and just wants to sit inside on their phone? I asked him what he wanted to do this afternoon, and that's what he said. I mean, seriously?" Paige's hands flew as she talked.

Finn bit back a smile. He liked her spunk.

Kennedy inhaled a breath, staring at the boy. "You're not sitting inside the whole time. We came here to have fun." When he opened his mouth to speak, she held up a hand. "I get that playing games on your phone or watching videos is fun for you. We're here for a different kind of fun. An active fun. You wanted to see your aunt and uncle." She gestured to Ben. "You can't do that with your nose buried in a screen."

The boy dropped his arms and looked up, but Finn saw a look of acceptance cross his face.

"Fine." The kid looked at Kennedy.

"Good." She nodded, then glanced at Finn. "Sorry. That was not the best first impression. These are my kids, Paxton and Paige."

Finn waved and smiled at the teens. "Hello."

"Kids, this is Finley Porter. He's a friend of your uncle's. He and I also work together. Sort of."

Paige gave him a wide-eyed look. "You're a judge?"

"No." Finn's smile widened. "I just work in the federal complex. I'm an ATF agent."

"Whoa." Paxton's eyes grew round. "That's cool."

"It can be. Most of the time it's rather dull, though. Lots of paperwork." He glanced at Kennedy and winked. A pretty blush stole over her cheeks.

Ben snorted. "That's the hallmark of any law enforcement job nowadays. I know I certainly drown in it."

A soft chorus of agreement went through the group.

"But we love it, so we deal," Jake said.

Finn agreed. Paperwork sucked, but he couldn't imagine doing anything else with his life.

Movement drew his gaze to the right. A shorter, dark-haired woman came down the stairs from the second floor, a pensive expression on her pretty face. When she hit the bottom, it cleared, and she pasted on a smile.

"Well, hello." Her gaze encompassed him as well as Kennedy and her kids. "Seems like I missed some things while I was dealing with my peckerhead of a fiancé."

Finn coughed, covering the surprised look on his face. The kids had no qualms about theirs, though. Both giggled. Kennedy rolled her lips in and blinked.

Ben chuckled. "Guys, this is Brooke McGinty, our hostess. Brooke, my sister Kennedy and her kids, Paxton and Paige."

He motioned to them. "And my colleague, Finn Porter." He pointed to Finn.

She waved. "Welcome. I'm hungry. Y'all hungry? I was in the midst of making lunch when good ol' Johnny called." Her eyebrows pinched, and she walked around them all toward the kitchen.

Finn frowned as he turned to watch her. Something told him her relationship wasn't in good-standing. He shared a look with Ben.

"Johnathan backed out, didn't he?" Gemma asked.

Brooke nodded, mouth flat. She walked to the stove without another word and opened the oven. Steam billowed out, and she grabbed a set of oven mitts, removing the two sheet pans inside. "I hope everyone's hungry." They clattered as she set them on top of the stove.

The smell of cooked sausage and roasted vegetables hit Finn's nose. "That smells great."

Murmurs of agreement went through the crowd.

"We finished the rest of the prep." Gemma motioned to the platter of fruit on the island.

"I appreciate it." Brooke snagged a spatula and a set of tongs from a drawer and set them beside the pans. "Everyone, grab a plate and dig in. I've got a fun afternoon planned, but we can't start until we eat."

Like the others, Finn got in line to dish up a plate of food. They all loaded their plates, then sat at the large dining table that filled one corner of the great room. He speared a piece of sausage and popped it into his mouth. The flavors burst over his tongue, prompting him to eat more.

Several minutes into the meal, Finn leaned over to Ben, who sat next to him. "I'm impressed. You got the whole gang here. How did that happen?"

Ben grinned. "I'm the boss, and I make the schedules. Once Cullen told me his, I just worked around it. We almost lost Carter and Mara, though. They planned to go see his mom in Charleston for Mother's Day, but I guess she had something come up and asked them to come another weekend."

Finn frowned. "Mother's Day is next weekend."

"I know, but Carter's on duty then, so they wanted to go this weekend."

"Oh. Makes sense." He stabbed a slice of pepper and ate it. "I need to get my mom something. What did you buy for yours?"

"We always take her out for brunch and get her a gift card to one of her favorite stores."

"I wish I was close enough to take her out to eat. But I like the gift card idea. There's a boutique back home she loves." He'd have to call his dad and have him pick up a gift card to the shop, then send him a check to cover the cost. She'd love it.

"When were you home last?"

"Christmas. But it was only for a couple of days. I'm hoping I can get home for a little longer this summer."

"Where are you from?" Paige's voice broke into their conversation.

Finn turned to look at her across the table.

She blushed. "Sorry. I couldn't help but overhear."

He smiled. "You're fine. I'm from Florida. My parents live in St. Augustine."

"I like Florida. I've never been to St. Augustine, though."

"It's a neat town. Lots of history."

"It's the oldest city in the U.S., right?" Paxton asked.

Finn nodded.

"That's cool."

"Do you like history?" Finn tipped his head, sensing the kid was interested.

The boy lifted a shoulder. "It's okay. My favorite subject is math."

Surprised by that admission, Finn's gaze flicked to Kennedy. She looked on, her expression carefully unreadable, which told him a lot. She kept herself guarded. Paxton's attitude said he did too. "Well, I'm glad there are people out there who do. They make the world run by becoming engineers and scientists. I am not one of those people." He chuckled.

"What was your favorite subject in school?" Paige asked.

"In high school, I liked English. In college, it was psychology. That's what my degree is in."

Her head bobbed, and she speared a piece of strawberry with her fork. "Neat. I like chemistry. Mixing things together to make other things is fun." She ate the fruit, a bit of a wicked gleam in her eyes.

Finn glanced at Kennedy again, a smile flirting with his lips. She still listened with a blank look.

"I liked that part of chemistry too," he told Paige. "Especially the experiment where you make fire with water. That was cool. I didn't like the math calculations part, but the mixing and experimenting part? Oh yeah."

"So, is that why you joined the ATF?" Kennedy asked.

He looked at her, surprised she'd injected herself into the conversation. She'd looked like she wanted to go hide in the corner. "Partly. I sent applications to all the federal agencies. They and the FBI called about the same time. I thought the ATF sounded more interesting." He lifted a shoulder, eating another bite of his food. "Why did you go into the judiciary?"

"Same reasons, different career. It was more interesting to me than just being an attorney. I like the impartiality aspect of it. The interpreting of laws and making sure they're followed. That's more interesting to me than trying to argue for or against them."

He nodded, understanding her point. "It's more structured too. You're working within a framework."

She tipped her head side to side. "Sort of. We still have the framework as attorneys. When I practiced law, I could push those boundaries, though. It was up to the judge to keep me and my counterpart inside them." She shrugged. "I like making sure people follow the rules. It's what keeps our judicial system fair. I just wish everyone felt the same. Then it might actually work the way it's intended."

"You think our system is broken?"

"Don't you?" She looked directly at him.

He tipped his head briefly and nodded. "I guess, but maybe not in the same way you do."

"Oh? How so?"

"My issue is when someone I know is guilty goes free. Or vice versa. That's where I think the system is broken."

"A lot of times, though, those things happen because someone didn't follow the law." She pointed her fork at him, then used it to pick up some fruit and eat it.

He couldn't argue with her there. "True. I just wish the criminal code was simpler."

"You and me both." She smiled.

"So, do you have any siblings?" Paige changed the subject.

"I have a brother. He's younger. He lives in St. Augustine too."

"Oh? What's he do? Is he a cop, like you?"

Finn shook his head. "No. He's a fisherman, like my dad."

Paxton's head lifted at that, and he frowned. "How did you end up as a fed?"

With a shrug, Finn lifted a forkful of sausage. "It just interested me. Don't get me wrong, I like fishing, but it wasn't what I wanted to do for a career."

"That's cool. My dad keeps pushing me to be a lawyer. Like him." Pax wrinkled his nose. "I don't want to be anything like him."

Kennedy stiffened beside Paige, that carefully blank mask descending over her face again. Except over her eyes. Those telegraphed loud and clear that Finn needed to watch what he said next.

He cleared his throat, keeping his voice and his posture light. "Well, I'd say it's up to you. But it's also something you need to discuss with him. And with your mom." He nodded to Kennedy.

"Mom's cool with whatever we want to do," Paige said. "Dad doesn't get a say."

"Paige." Kennedy's voice held a note of warning. The look she leveled on the teens asked them to change the subject.

"Well, he doesn't." Paige shot her mother a defiant look. "I'm glad we moved away. It's easier to ignore him when he's being a dumbass."

"Paige!" Kennedy's eyes widened.

"Sorry," the girl mumbled. She forked some fruit into her mouth and looked out the window.

Paxton chuckled. "At least it's not me who's in trouble this time."

Kennedy let out a tired sigh and closed her eyes briefly. "I'm sorry." She looked at Finn.

He waved his hand. "Don't be. I have two nephews. They're a little younger than them—eleven and thirteen—but they're both honest as the day is long too. I find children refreshing. Even as teenagers"—he gestured to Paxton and Paige—"they have little time for artifice. It's nice when you deal with people who want to lie to you all the time. I don't need to guess what's on their minds." He nodded at the twins.

Kennedy pushed the remaining food on her plate around with her fork, nodding. She glanced up. "Still, there's honesty and then there's *honesty*." A smile toyed with her lips as she looked at the teens.

Some of the tension faded from Paige's shoulders at the softer look on her mom's face, and she smiled back. "I just tell it like it is. Finn's right. Talking around the truth takes too long."

Kennedy blinked at the girl, then looked at Finn. "I'm glad you find them refreshing."

He laughed, making her smile. The sight sent a warmth through him. This was going to be an interesting weekend.

# NINE

"A canoe race?" Gemma stared at Brooke. The other woman had led them through the yard to the boathouse next to the dock—after making them all change into clothes they didn't mind getting wet. "That's your fun afternoon plan?"

Brooke's brow wrinkled. "Well, yeah. What did you think it would be? We're on the river, Gems."

Kennedy rolled her lips in to keep from laughing at the look of consternation on her sister-in-law's face.

"What are we supposed to do with the babies?" Gemma jostled the infant in her arms, then nodded to Laurel, who held her son, Wyatt. Meredith babbled and patted Gemma's face.

"Oh!" Mack raised her hand. "I'll watch them. I probably shouldn't be paddling a canoe right now." She pointed to her heavily pregnant middle, then put a hand on it. "Besides, with a life vest on around my belly, I'm not sure I could get my arm across my body to paddle. Me sitting out will even up the teams too. Then you all just need to decide how you'll pair up."

Brooke frowned. "Why wouldn't we just do it by couple? I can take your place, and Kennedy can ride with Finn."

"Right, but what about Paxton and Paige? Is it fair to put two fifteen-year-olds up against a fleet of adults?"

"Hey!" Paige stepped forward. "Pax and I will kick all y'all's butts." She looked at her brother. "Right?"

"Heck, yeah." The boy propped his hands on his waist and cocked out a hip, the look on his face daring anyone to contradict them.

Kennedy crossed her arms and lifted a hand to cover her mouth, hiding her grin. Honestly, they had a chance. Both kids were strong and worked out regularly as part of their conditioning for sports—Paige for cheerleading and Paxton for soccer. They also had the stamina of youth.

"Oh, it's on." Ben looked at Kennedy. "I don't know about you, but I'm not about to get beaten by them."

She dropped her hand and let her smile show. "Nope." They'd gloat forever if they won.

"Uncle Ben, you're going down." Pax pointed a finger at the ground. "You, too, Mom."

Kennedy laughed. "Oh, we'll see. My partner looks pretty buff."

Finn, being a good sport, lifted an arm and flexed. Kennedy swallowed hard and looked away. She hoped he left his shirt on while they did this race, or she would be worse than useless.

Pax snorted. "Whatever, man." He turned to Brooke. "Let's do this."

She clapped her hands once. "All right. The canoes are in the boathouse." She pointed at the structure and moved toward it, taking a key from her pocket.

Kennedy hung back with the other women while the men followed Brooke inside to retrieve the canoes and paddles. When they were out of the way, Gemma motioned the ladies inside, and they gathered enough life jackets for everyone. In minutes, they were all suited up and had the canoes at the water's edge.

"So, how do we do this?" Piper took the paddle Cullen held out to her and peered around him at Brooke. "Are there markers in the river?"

"Sort of. The dock is the starting point. We line up across the channel, then race with the current to the sand bar down river. It's not that far. A few hundred yards around the bend." She pointed downstream where the water curved out of sight.

"Sounds good." Piper spun the paddle, then lifted it. "Let's win this, babe." She glanced at Cullen with a saucy smile.

"Wait." Paxton held up a hand. "What's the prize for winning?"

"Ah, yes." Brooke grinned. "I figured you all"—she pointed at the men—"would be competitive and need something to shoot for besides bragging rights. So, I bought these." She put her hand in her pocket and withdrew two keychains. "They say, 'I paddle hard.'" Her face scrunched, and she glanced at Kennedy. "Sorry. I didn't know we'd have teen competitors when I bought them." She looked at the twins. "I'll be happy to take you into town and let you go hog-wild at The Dairy Shed."

The teens glanced at each other, then nodded.

"Ice cream is acceptable if we win," Paige said.

"Not if." Pax held up a finger. "When."

Ben clapped a hand over the boy's shoulder. "You talk a big game, Pax." He leaned in and lowered his voice. "Bring it."

Laughing, Kennedy walked past them. "Stop trash-talking and get in your boats."

For the next few minutes, laughter rang out, interspersed with a couple of surprised shouts as the boats wobbled as they all got in. Maverick barked from shore, wanting to join the fun, but Carter made him stay with Mack and the babies.

Kennedy held the sides of the canoe as it tipped, taking Finn's weight when he climbed in behind her. Once it quit rocking, she glanced over her shoulder. "Are we set?"

He nodded and lifted his paddle, wrapping his strong fingers around the wooden handle. "I think so. Let's go get in line."

"Okay." Turning around, Kennedy dipped her paddle in the water. She felt the canoe surge as Finn added his. They spun a bit to the left. Water splatted the back of her life vest as he moved the paddle to the other side, correcting their course.

It took them a few minutes, but they found a rhythm and paddled to the middle of the river, taking their place in the line. Kennedy glanced at the dock. Mackenzie stood at the end, Maverick beside her. Beyond her, the babies laid on a blanket in the grass under a tree, playing with toys. Before they had jumped into the canoes, Brooke gave Mack a whistle. When she blew it, it was their signal to start.

Kennedy glanced from one side to the other. All the boats were lined up, fighting the current to stay put. She looked at Mackenzie, hoping she blew the whistle soon, or they were going to be too staggered for it to be fair. The river had a strong current. Stronger than it looked from the surface.

Mack didn't make them wait. Moments later, she blew the whistle. Kennedy dipped her oar in the water and pulled. Finn's powerful strokes sent them flying forward. They spun again to the side, and she paddled quickly, bringing them straight. When her attempts couldn't keep up, he switched sides, and they soon settled into a rhythm.

A quick glance around told Kennedy they were in the lead, but the twins were keeping up. Gemma and Ben, and Carter and Mara weren't far behind. Jake and Brooke and Cullen and Piper had spun sideways and were busy trying to right themselves. Tristan and Laurel had suffered a similar fate, but were making little headway. Laurel had dissolved into laughter. Tristan's curses, interspersed by deep laughs, echoed off the water as he tried to right their course.

Rounding the bend, the twins surged ahead. Kennedy's arms burned. She knew their youthfulness would give them an edge. Clenching her teeth, she paddled harder. They wouldn't win without a fight. Ahead, she saw the sandbar.

Paige shouted to her brother and pointed. Kennedy heard him acknowledge her. When she looked over, the fierce expression on his face told her how much he wanted to win. For a moment, she thought about backing off. But she didn't want him to accuse her of letting them win, so she dug deep and kept paddling hard.

"They're gonna win," Finn said.

"Paddle harder. I'll never hear the end of it if they beat us."

He groaned. "My arms are on fire."

"Mine too." Sweat also trickled down her brow and the back of her neck.

The sandbar loomed larger. A boat-length ahead, Paxton and Paige bumped the riverbed, coming to a halt. Both teens let out a loud whoop as they looked back and realized they'd won.

Kennedy and Finn ran aground a moment later. With a groan, Kennedy pulled her paddle in and slumped. "Oh my God, I can't feel my arms."

"Me either. That was intense." Finn's oar clattered on the canoe bottom. He heaved a breath, then stood, hopping into the shallow water.

With a groan, Kennedy followed, taking his hand when he offered. She helped him pull the boat out of the water. Next to them, the twins celebrated, doing a dance as they watched the rest of the boats come ashore.

"Do you think we should tell them they still have to carry

their boat back to the boathouse?" Finn propped his hands on his hips, watching them.

Kennedy laughed. "Soon enough. Let them gloat for a bit." Her smile faded as she sobered slightly, staring at them. "This is the most animated they've been in a while." She looked at Finn. "Moving's been rough."

Sympathy shone from his gray eyes. "I'll bet." He tipped his head toward the twins. "Come on. Let's go congratulate them." Not waiting for her, he turned toward the kids, walking away.

Smile returning, Kennedy trailed after him.

# TEN

The murmur of voices and laughter accompanied the chirping birds as the group walked back to the house. Finn's arms and shoulders still burned, and he knew they'd be sore tomorrow. But it would be a good sore. The race had been fun, even though they lost. Paige and Paxton's enthusiasm made up for it.

Clearing the trees rimming the yard, he glanced around. His gaze stopped on the woman standing by the driveway, watching them approach. He'd noticed the car with government plates when he pulled in earlier, but hadn't done more than speculate about to whom it belonged before becoming engrossed in the day's activities. Now, though, he couldn't help but wonder why a U.S. Marshal was here. He knew Taylor Paulson well. They'd worked together on many cases over the years.

His eyes strayed to the woman walking in front of him, carrying her half of the canoe. Could Paulson's presence have something to do with Kennedy? One of the Marshals' duties was to protect judicial officials. It made the most sense for why she was hanging around. But why? Kennedy had been on the job a week. What could have happened in that time frame to necessitate protection? He didn't know, but he'd find out.

They neared the boathouse, giving them all a last burst of energy. Finn wasn't the only one ready to put his canoe away and give his body a break. The twins had demanded their reward as soon as Brooke's feet touched the sandbar, and to be honest, ice cream sounded great right about now. He was hot and sweaty and tired. The sweet treat would go a long way toward cooling him off and perking him up.

"So, who won?" Mackenzie wandered up with a smile, holding Wyatt. Meredith napped on the blanket under a tree. Maverick barked as he was reunited with his handler. Tail wagging, he hopped as Carter and Mara came down the bank.

Jake pointed at the twins. "The young ones."

Mack laughed. "You guys all got beat by a couple of teenagers?"

"Don't laugh." Piper shook a finger at her friend. "They were like a rocket. From the second you blew that whistle, they flew down river." She shook her head. "And look at them." She pointed to the twins, who skipped ahead toward the boathouse to stow their canoe. "I don't know where they get all their energy."

It was Kennedy's turn to chuckle. "It's a teenager thing. They're slow to start in the mornings, but once they wake up, it's go, go, go until they crash at night."

Piper shook her head again. "If you ever figure out how to bottle their energy, pass it along."

Smiling, Kennedy nodded. "Will do."

Finn wouldn't mind a bottle of that, either. He was fit, but the teens' energy levels were something else. It had been a long time since he'd been in their shoes. Some days, he felt every one of his thirty-eight years.

The group filed toward the boathouse and stowed their canoes and gear. Once everything was put away, they headed for the house to change into street clothes so they could go to town. Finn followed Kennedy and the twins upstairs, where they split off. He put on the clothes he'd arrived in and grabbed his wallet and keys from the dresser, then exited his room.

From the stairs, he could hear Paige and Paxton racing down, debating what kind of ice cream to get. Finn shook his head. Knowing teenagers, they'd probably get every flavor their mother allowed.

The door across from his opened, and Kennedy stepped into the hall.

"Oh, hi." She smiled.

He lifted a hand. "Hi." She looked nice in her jean shorts and t-shirt, but he missed the workout tank and board shorts she had on for the canoe race. They'd showed off the play of her muscles.

Fire stirred in his blood. Maybe it was a good thing she was more covered up. Now he wasn't tempted to reach out and feel her muscles moving beneath her soft skin.

She fell into step beside him, and they made their way toward the stairs.

"So, how long is Marshal Paulson your shadow?" He took a stab that his hunch was correct about why Taylor was here. It also served to distract his mind from thoughts of her lithe body.

Kennedy blew out a breath. "No idea." She glanced at him. "Did you hear why I have a protection detail?"

"No."

"Javy Gonzales."

"What? I thought he was cooperating with us."

"He is. He gave up Gustavo Herrera."

"Oh, man. I hadn't heard that." Nick had told him very little about what was happening with Gonzales, even though he'd promised to keep him in the loop. Finn had been too busy to stop by and ask, either. He'd also tried to secure a meeting with Gonzales, to question him about the illegal weapons, but his attorney had stonewalled him. It was frustrating and maddening. He couldn't wait until this case was finished.

"They just put me under protection yesterday. In fact, when I ran into you, it was right after Taylor informed me I now had a shadow."

That explained a lot about that meeting. He knew she'd seemed preoccupied. "So, what do they know?" The image of the man he followed and lost the day he saw her at Cuppa flashed through his mind. He couldn't help but wonder if that guy was involved in the threat against her. He needed to mention it to Taylor.

Kennedy shrugged as she stepped down onto the first stair. "Just that Herrera's men are trying to disrupt his trial. She said they're coming after the judges because we're easier to get to than Gonzales. They've already proven that. Elijah Jedynak's accident wasn't an accident."

Finn's mouth flattened. He didn't like the idea of Kennedy having a target on her back. He didn't like the idea of any of the judges being targets, but it bothered him more with Kennedy. Why that was, he didn't know. Maybe because he was getting to know her in ways he didn't know the other judges. He'd never spent a weekend with any of them and their families. Nor was he friends with any of their family members.

"What's being done, other than to put a security detail on you?"

She shrugged. "I assume they're trying to root out the people behind the plot. The U.S. Attorney's office needs to make Herrera's trial a speedy one. The sooner Gonzales testifies and he's convicted, the sooner I can stop looking over my shoulder."

"I hope it's quick too. That man needs to spend the rest of

his life in jail for the things he's done. If you need anything, you can call me. I'll make sure to give you my number before we all leave tomorrow."

"I appreciate that. I think I'll be okay, though. Between the Marshals and my brother, I'm covered."

Finn's head bobbed once. He stepped off the stairs and turned to face her. "Still, you can never have enough backup."

She tipped her head. "Fair enough. Okay."

"I also think everyone should be aware of the situation before we go into town. Do they know?" He nodded toward the group gathering near the picture window.

Kennedy shook her head. "Ben asked why the marshal was here, but we got interrupted before I could give him more than just a few details."

"You need to before we leave. Do your kids know?"

"Yes. They were bound to notice a strange car following us, and that's not something I'd keep from them."

"Good. Do they have their own protective detail?"

"No. Taylor said there's no indication the threat includes our families. The twins can't drive yet, so I don't really have to worry about them going off alone."

He arched an eyebrow. "Are you sure? They seem like the type who would go for a walk if they really wanted to go somewhere."

A smile bloomed on her face. "They are, but we've only been in town a little over a week, so they don't know where much of anything is at the moment. And they don't have any close friends yet, which helps."

"True." He held out an arm, motioning her forward.

She wrinkled her nose, but walked toward the group. "I don't want to do this. Everyone looks so happy. This news will put a damper on everything."

"Maybe, maybe not. It's a group of cops—well, mostly." He nodded to Cullen and Piper. "But everyone here is connected to law enforcement in some capacity. They'll understand. And they'll want to know, rather than be blind-sided if something happens. I can also guarantee everyone's noticed your shadow."

She huffed. "Fine." Reaching the group, she waved her hands. "Can I have everyone's attention, please?"

Their voices quieted as they all turned to look at her.

"I'm sure you all noticed the woman in the suit standing in the yard. She's a U.S. Marshal assigned to protect me." Kennedy gave them a quick rundown of what was going on.

Finn watched expressions turn serious, some even morphing to anger. Piper looked like she could march straight to federal holding and throttle Herrera. He didn't blame her after what the man did to her.

Ben was the first to speak once she finished. "This guy just doesn't want to disappear. Okay." He glanced at the others. "I think we should stay armed this weekend. Just to be safe. Probably once we get home too. Piper, Cullen, you two should be extra careful. I'll talk to Marshal Paulson about what the threat is to you."

Piper scrunched her face. "I'll be so glad when this is all behind us and that asshole is rotting in jail."

Cullen murmured an agreement.

Finn concurred. "Let's get our weapons and head out." He motioned toward the stairs. "We've delayed the twins getting their reward long enough." He offered them a smile.

Pax quirked a brow. Paige smiled back.

Giving Kennedy a quick look, he turned away, the image of her pinched expression sticking with him. It would be a frosty day in hell before he let anything happen to her.

# ELEVEN

Shadows stretched across the yard in the low light. The moon peeked through the trees, competing with the glow from the fire burning on the small beach. Kennedy stifled a yawn. She should probably head inside to bed. Some of the others already had. Only Cullen and Piper and Finn were left. Kennedy had only stayed because the kids didn't want to go in yet. She knew they were old enough to stay out here alone and to put themselves to bed, but with the threat looming, she wasn't comfortable letting them out of her sight, even in a place where she felt safe. Anyone could be lurking in the shadows, and they would never see them in the darkness.

Another yawn stretched her jaw. She covered her mouth and blinked away the moisture that gathered in her eyes. She'd give the kids another ten or fifteen minutes, then they were going in. Hopefully, she could last that long.

Piper echoed her yawn. "Sheesh. I feel like an old lady. It's only what, ten?" She shook her head. "Who knew canoeing could take so much out of a person?"

Cullen patted her thigh, glancing away from Finn. They'd

been deep in conversation about something science-related. Kennedy had quickly learned Finn was a bit of a geek. He had a lot of useless, but interesting, knowledge floating around in his head. Like how chocolate was made, or how to tell the composition of a fire. They'd all gotten a lesson on that one when Brooke lit the fire earlier.

"I'm ready to go to bed." Piper covered Cullen's hand with her own. "Are you?"

"Sure. My old bones could use a soak first, though." He waggled his eyebrows at her. "You wanna try out that big jacuzzi tub I saw in our bathroom?"

Piper shot out of her chair. "Hell, yes." She looked at the others, offering a quick wave. "Night, all."

Smiling, Kennedy waved back.

With a chuckle, Cullen took her hand and led her away.

Covering yet another yawn, Kennedy glanced at her kids. They had positioned themselves in the fire's glow and were making puppet shadows in front of a tree, laughing as they tried to guess what the other made. Some of them were quite inventive.

Needing to move, Kennedy got up and wandered down to the water's edge. The river lapped gently against the sand and rocks, a soothing accompaniment to the crackling fire behind her. She wished she could stay here. This place was so peaceful. Her new house was great, but even her quiet neighborhood had city noise. Here, she could actually shove aside the stress of her job. Being here also made it easier to forget the U.S. Marshal sitting watch. Surrounded by family and friends, Kennedy didn't think about trials or bad guys. She just enjoyed life.

Paxton's loud laugh brought a smile to her face. This place had been good for them too. Being with family had helped remind them this move wasn't all bad. Just different.

"They're certainly having fun."

Finn's voice washed over her, eroding a modicum of her peace. That zing of excitement that always went through her when he was nearby heightened her senses. She didn't necessarily mind how he made her feel, but it also wasn't welcome. Kennedy didn't need the complication of a man in her life. Her body felt otherwise, though, hence the excited flutters in her belly. Sex was a distant memory. So was kissing. And he was the first kissable man she'd been around since her divorce.

She looked over at him as he came up beside her, then glanced past him at the twins, a ghost of a smile on her lips. "Yeah. It's nice to hear that laugh again."

"Give them time. They'll adjust."

"Oh, I know. It's just hard watching them be upset. Paige has taken it better than Paxton. But she's bubblier than her brother and makes friends more easily. I'm just glad we have the technology we do. Their phones allow them to keep in contact with their old friends. Pax has already made plans to have his best friend spend part of the summer with us."

"Good. Maybe he'll make some new friends in the last few weeks of school, and they can all hang out. It'll help bridge the gap between old and new."

"That's not a bad idea. I'll mention it to him."

"So, what about you?"

A wrinkle formed between Kennedy's eyes. She looked away from the twins to frown at Finn. "What about me?"

"Have you made friends?"

"I'm an adult. It's a little different for me. I can survive longer without social interaction."

He shrugged. "Adults still need friends."

She cast him a sly look. "Are you offering?"

Finn chuckled. "Maybe." One shoulder lifted again. "I figure you're going to see me, anyway, because of my friendship with Ben. We'll see each other at work too. Might be a little awkward if we barely acknowledge each other."

Kennedy laughed. "You're not easy to ignore."

He grinned. "Good. I don't want you to ignore me."

She hummed and glanced away. The flirting felt nice, even if it couldn't go anywhere. "So, what does being your friend look like? Beers and a game on the weekend? A stroll in the park? More canoeing?" She held a hand out, palm up, and gestured to the river.

He chuckled. "It can be any of those things. But how about we just start with saying hello when we pass each other? Maybe get coffee every so often?"

She scrunched her nose. "Coffee would be nice—once I'm off house arrest."

A smile made his dimples pop. "I'll bring it to you until then."

"Oh, my interns will love you."

Another low chuckle rumbled from his chest. "Glad I can be of service."

Kennedy's smile was interrupted by another yawn. She covered her mouth. "Oh. Sorry." Waving her hand, she sent him a rueful smile. "It's been a long day. Good, but long."

"Yeah. We should probably put this fire out and head inside." He nodded to the fire, then looked at the twins. "They're having a great time, though."

"I know. I hate to end it. But Brooke mentioned boating and fishing for tomorrow's activities. We can't sleep late."

"True. Do you want me to break it to them?"

It should surprise her he would want to do that. He'd only known the kids a day. But she'd caught him in conversation with Pax on more than one occasion. Finn was good with kids —at least her kids, anyway. And they seemed to like him, for which she was happy. As he'd said, he would be around, thanks to his friendship with her brother.

"That's okay. I'll do it. How about you put out the fire?"

He gave a short nod. "Sure."

With a quick smile of thanks, she turned away before he could flash her that dimpled grin again. It didn't matter, though. It was still burned into her retinas. For the second night in a row, she knew she was doomed to dream about him.

# TWELVE

Kennedy cracked her door open, tiptoeing out, not wanting to wake anyone else. Despite the fresh air and their busy day, she hadn't been able to sleep. At the first rays of sun peeking through her window, she'd awakened and been unable to fall asleep again.

Closing the door with a soft snick, she turned and headed for the stairs, descending to the main level on light feet. The house was quiet. She wasn't even sure Ben was up yet, and he was an early riser.

She rounded the banister, aiming for the kitchen and the fancy coffee machine, but movement in the sitting area drew her attention. Pausing, she glanced over to see Finn on the couch, tying his shoes.

"Hey." He glanced up and smiled.

Kennedy's heart thumped. It was too early for his gorgeousness. Her defenses were down. "Hey. Do you always get up this early?"

He shrugged, pulling his laces into a bow, then straightened. "Usually. I like to run or go to the gym before work."

A run sounded great. With the move, she'd only run on

her treadmill and was itching to run outdoors. She'd figured it would have to wait, though. Until she didn't have a detail following her. She doubted Taylor would want to run in her suit. But maybe the marshal would let her go with Finn. "Would you like some company?"

"Sure."

Kennedy smiled. "Give me a few minutes to change and to tell Taylor."

He nodded. "I'll get my weapon."

Some of her enthusiasm died. She figured he'd want to go armed if she went, but it was a sobering reminder to hear it said aloud. "Sounds good." Changing direction, she went back upstairs to her room. Quickly shedding her olive green linen shorts and white t-shirt, she put on a pair of leggings and the tank top she wore yesterday for the canoe race. Tying her running shoes onto her feet, she went downstairs to find Taylor.

Glancing around the great room as she headed for the door, she didn't see Finn. Maybe he was waiting outside. Kennedy stepped onto the back deck, then descended the stairs. Rounding the corner of the house, she saw Finn. He stood next to Taylor's car, talking to her through the open window.

Taylor spotted her and waved. Kennedy jogged over. "Good morning."

The woman smiled. "I don't know about good, but it's morning."

Kennedy frowned. "Why isn't it good?"

"Because it's morning." The marshal lifted a large coffee cup from the cup holder in the center console and took a drink.

"Oh." Kennedy chuckled. "Do you want to run with us? It might wake you up?"

Taylor waved her hand. "No. I have never—other than during training—exercised in the morning. I'd rather sleep."

Normally, Kennedy would too, but since she was awake, she figured, why not? It always energized her.

"I already talked to her about going out alone with you," Finn said. "I figured we could run along the riverbank. She and her colleagues have been watching the road all night. Unless someone hiked in from miles away, we're safe."

"Sounds good to me. Are you ready?"

He nodded, then glanced at Taylor. "I have my phone. Call if you need to."

"I will. You do the same."

"Will do." He turned to Kennedy. "Let's go."

Gravel crunching underfoot, Kennedy spun on her heel. Side-by-side, they jogged toward the river.

"So, how far are we going?" She paused near the firepit and leaned to the side in a deep lunge.

"I usually go about five miles. On this terrain, though, and with the trouble surrounding you, we could do less. Three?" He followed her lead, stretching out his muscles.

"Sure. A mile and half down and then a mile and a half back?" She leaned the other way, then straightened and brought her leg up behind her.

"Yep." Finn lifted his wrist and opened an app on his watch. "Ready?"

Kennedy nodded.

"Then, let's go." He tapped the screen, then took off at a quick jog.

The trail along the riverbed was only wide enough for one. He motioned for her to go ahead, for which she was glad. She had a feeling he'd leave her behind if he went first. Not intentionally. Just because his legs were longer and he ran faster.

Kennedy settled into her pace, watching her footing on the

uneven ground. The trail curved and dipped as it followed the river. After about five minutes, they reached the end, and she paused. "We must be at the edge of the McGintys' property."

Finn stopped beside her and glanced at his watch. "We've only gone eight-tenths of a mile. Do you want to head back?"

"We could. Then maybe go down the road a little ways?"

"That works." He lifted his shirt and wiped the sweat from his forehead.

Kennedy's mouth watered. Dear Lord, the man was buff. She spun around and took off up the trail, needing to put the sight behind her. It was too distracting. She'd come here to relax. Not get tied up in knots because of a sexy ATF agent.

Too caught up in her thoughts and not paying attention, her foot snagged on a rock, and she pitched forward. She tried to catch herself, but her other foot glanced off the side of another stone, twisting, and she went down. Her knees hit the dirt, sending shockwaves of pain up her legs. Pebbles dug into her palms, scraping them as she slid. Landing on her belly, she laid there for a moment.

"Kennedy!"

She heard Finn's shoes scuff the dirt as he ran toward her. With a groan, she rolled over as he reached her.

"Are you all right?" He crouched next to her and wrapped a hand around her upper arm, helping her sit up.

"I think so." She grimaced. Her hands and knees stung, and her ankle throbbed. "Help me up."

He stood, putting one hand under her elbow and the other around her back as he pulled her to her feet.

Kennedy put weight on her feet, then let out a soft cry and raised her left foot. "Damn rocks. Ow."

The surrounding landscape whirled and her feet left the ground as Finn scooped her into his arms.

"Oh! What are you doing?" She grabbed his shoulders, looking at him with wide eyes.

"Taking you back to the house." He started walking. "We'll look at your injuries there. I can't do much about them out here."

"I'm fine. I just tweaked it. If you put me down, I can walk it off."

He looked at her. "Just sit back and enjoy the ride."

Kennedy huffed. "Are you always this bossy?"

A smile slashed over his face, showing off his dimples. "Only when I need to be."

"Now is not one of those times."

"I beg to differ. If I'd waited for you to test your ankle, you'd have probably decided to hobble back. That could have hurt it worse. Or we'd have been out here so long, Taylor would come looking for us. I'm saving us all some trouble by carrying you."

She stared at him and blinked, trying to follow his logic.

He cast a glance her way, then looked ahead. "What?"

"The defense attorneys hate you, don't they?"

Finn barked out a short laugh. "Probably. My mom always told me I should have been a lawyer."

"Why didn't you listen to her? It's still law enforcement."

"I know. But I like the action. I didn't want to be stuck behind a desk." He rolled his eyes. "Though I do that enough. Damn bureaucracy."

Kennedy chuckled. "I feel you on that." She glanced around, watching the scenery. It couldn't distract her from the feel of his arms around her or the press of his chest to her side. An image of the rock-hard abs he flashed her just minutes ago entered her mind. She needed a change of subject.

"So, tell me about your family. You mentioned they're fishermen. Does that include your mom and your sister-in-law? Or is your brother not married? You mentioned kids, so I just assumed..." She clamped her lips together to stop the rambling.

"He's married. Katelyn's a teacher. Middle school science. My mom runs a food truck."

She glanced at him in surprise. "Really?"

He nodded. "Dad sells some of his catch to canneries, but the rest, Mom turns into all kinds of things. Her fish tacos—" He tipped his head back and let out a soft moan. "I miss her fish tacos. And her shrimp kebabs."

Kennedy's stomach grumbled, and she laughed. "Stop. You're making me hungry. I didn't eat breakfast before we left."

He grinned. "Neither did I." His stride lengthened.

"Where did you go to college?" She asked, hoping the conversation would keep thoughts of food at bay. Now that he'd mentioned it, she was starving.

"The University of Florida. You?"

"The University of Virginia. And Georgetown for law."

"Really? I figured you'd have gone to one of the fancy Ivy League schools for your undergrad too."

Kennedy shrugged. "I thought about it, but I wasn't entirely sure law was what I wanted when I graduated high school."

"Oh? What was the other option?"

"Don't laugh."

A slow smile spread over his face. "Oh, now I'm intrigued. What was it?"

"Marine biology."

His eyebrows shot up. "That is vastly different from law."

"I know. But I spent a lot of time on the water growing up. My dad owned a yacht and a sailboat. Ben, our brother Howie, and I probably spent more time on the water in the summers than we did at home."

"Same. Not the yacht and sailboat part. But the water part. That was my summer job from the time I was seven or eight all the way through college. I haven't been on a boat, though, in probably ten years."

"Seriously?"

"Yeah. I've let work get in the way. I don't go home as much as I used to."

"You sound like you have good relationships with your parents and brother, though. Do you talk to them a lot?"

"I do. But as my career has progressed, so have my responsibilities and my caseload." He shook his head. "There isn't enough time for everything."

"Burnout's real, you know." She shook a finger at him.

A corner of his mouth kicked up. "Why do you think I'm here this weekend? Something needed to give. The Herrera case has driven me to the brink."

Kennedy's mood soured. "It's driven everyone to the brink."

Finn snorted. "Truth. So, your kids like math and science, huh?"

She blinked at the change in subject, but was glad for it. She didn't want to talk about Herrera. "Yeah. I don't know where they get the math thing from. Neither their father nor I excel at it. But Pax can do some crazy equations in his head. And Paige, she's always loved science. I bought so many of those little DIY experiment kits when she was younger. Now she brings me articles from the internet and asks me to get her supplies. I'm kind of dreading when she gets a job and a car. She won't need my money to buy her own stuff. There's no telling what I'll come home to."

Finn chuckled. "They are live wires, that's for sure. But that's not a bad thing. It'll set them up well for adulthood."

"I keep telling myself that." She met his gaze, smiling.

The trees gave way, and they entered the yard. Finn walked through the grass to the house, mounting the steps like she weighed nothing and he hadn't been carrying her for half a mile. Kennedy turned the doorhandle and let them into the house. All eyes swung toward them, and a moment of silence reigned before there were several exclamations of worry.

"Mom, are you okay?" Paige asked, her hazel eyes wide.

"What happened?" Ben got up from his seat at the table.

"I'm fine." Kennedy waved a hand.

"She tripped on a rock and twisted her ankle." Finn strode past everyone to the couches in the sitting area.

"I'll go get the first-aid kit." Brooke took off down the hall.

Kennedy sighed as Finn set her down. She used the toes of her right foot to nudge off her left shoe. Rolling her ankle around, she didn't feel any twinges. "He's made a fuss for nothing." She glanced at Ben. "It feels fine. He wouldn't let me walk it off. Just scooped me up and started walking." She pulled her sock down, then looked at Finn. "See? Not even swollen."

He shrugged. "Better safe than sorry."

Brooke returned with the first-aid kit. Finn took it and sat beside Kennedy. "Let me see your hands."

Dutifully, she held up her hands, palms skyward. After his refusal to let her walk, she figured it would be easier and quicker to just let him clean her up. Then they could get on with their day.

Rifling through the box, Finn found some antiseptic wipes. He tore a few open and cleaned the dirt from her palms. She had a few scrapes, but nothing serious.

"How are your knees?"

"Bruised, but not bleeding. I'm fine." She pulled her hands back. "Can you stop fussing over me now?"

His mouth flattened. "I suppose. Are you sure your ankle is okay?"

Kennedy stood. Her ankle twinged just the slightest bit, but she kept her expression blank. She was done being mollycoddled. "It's fine." She looked at Brooke. "What's on the agenda for today?"

A knowing smile spread over the smaller woman's face. "Not hiking."

Kennedy grinned. "Good."

Ben chuckled. "Okay. How about we all finish breakfast, then go outside? Brooke, you mentioned fishing yesterday. Is that still the plan?"

She nodded. "I'd like to do a fish-fry for dinner."

Tristan clapped his hands together. "I could go for a good fish-fry. That sounds great."

Kennedy nudged Finn's shoulder and smiled. "Did you inherit your mom's cooking abilities?"

His mouth tipped up. "I can't replicate her fish tacos, but I can hold my own."

Her smile widened. "Perfect. But I think the better question is, did you really go into law enforcement because you're a terrible fisherman?"

He narrowed his eyes. She laughed and walked toward the kitchen.

"Those are fighting words." He pointed at her and followed behind.

She tossed him a saucy smile. "Guess you'll have to prove it."

# THIRTEEN

Finn laid a hand over his stomach and sat back. He was stuffed. Between the fish, fresh vegetables, and the s'mores, he didn't think he had an ounce of room left in his stomach. He probably should have said no to the last s'more, but the fullness hadn't hit yet. Now he didn't want to move, even though he knew he should go inside and go to bed. One by one, the others had trickled inside. Even the twins had gone in about five minutes ago.

He couldn't blame them. They'd gone hard today. If they weren't fishing, they were swimming or running around the yard with Maverick. Kennedy was right—they really were Energizer bunnies.

"Why are you still out here?"

Startled, he glanced over. "Where did you come from?"

Kennedy sat down beside him. "I saw the fire still burning and came out to put it out. I didn't know anyone was still out here. I thought the twins forgot to smother it."

"Nope. I just haven't been able to convince my muscles to move and take me upstairs yet."

She smiled. "It is a nice night." She glanced up.

Finn's eyes followed her gaze. Millions of stars twinkled in the inky sky. Away from the city lights, not even the moon could drown out their brightness. He closed his eyes, feeling the warm breeze. Maybe he'd just sleep out here.

Kennedy yawned.

Sighing, Finn got up. "Come on." He held out a hand.

"Oh." She took it and let him pull her to her feet. "Are you sure you're ready to go in?"

"Yeah. We both need to get to bed."

"I still can't believe we let the twins talk us all into staying tonight and going back early tomorrow."

He grinned, bending to pick up the pail and scoop dirt over the fire to put it out. "They're very persuasive."

"They just wanted s'mores."

Finn laughed. "And the adults didn't?"

"True. But we're all going to curse them out when we're up at five o'clock to go home and change before work."

"But it was worth it." Straightening, he stepped toward her.

"Hmm. You think?"

He nodded. "Yeah."

She lifted her face, looking up at him. The soft smile toying with her lips sent a shaft of need through Finn, surprising him. There'd been something simmering beneath the surface all day, but this was different. Even when he carried her and she'd been pressed close, the awareness he'd felt then didn't compare to this. That had just created a hum in his body. Any desire had been drowned out by his need to keep her safe and make sure she was all right.

But now? There was nothing to keep his feelings in check. She'd captivated him.

In the low light from the moon, he saw a pretty blush steal over her cheeks. He shuffled a little closer and raised a hand to touch her face. Her eyes fluttered shut as he skimmed her soft skin. Like a magnet, she drew him in, and he leaned closer.

A light bobbing around the corner of the house caught his eye a moment before he would have kissed her. In a single move, he hooked an arm around her, spinning her behind his back as he stepped forward. His hand went to the gun strapped to his waist under his t-shirt.

"What in the world?" Kennedy muttered from behind his back.

Finn shushed her. "Federal agent. Who's there?" he called.

The light paused, then swung toward him. Finn tensed, wishing he had body armor. Or at least something to hide behind. They were in the open here.

"It's Marshal Getty." The male voice carried to them across the yard, and the light resumed its bounce, but grew closer now.

Finn's shoulders relaxed, but annoyance hardened his features. The marshal had interrupted something he wasn't sure he could get back now.

Kennedy let out a long breath and came up beside him. They walked toward the light, meeting the marshal in the yard.

"Sorry. Didn't mean to startle you. I thought everyone had gone inside. I'm just doing my perimeter sweep." The marshal pointed his light at the ground, but the powerful beam lit up the area.

"We were about to go in," Finn said, recognizing the man who took over for Taylor at night.

Getty nodded. "Well, have a good night, then."

"Thank you." Kennedy offered him a tight smile, then walked around him, headed for the house.

Finn gave the man a nod, then hurried after her. "Kennedy."

She held up a hand, waving it, and didn't turn around.

Dammit. Finn ground his back molars and followed her inside. She crossed the darkened great room and went up the stairs. He stayed on her heels. On the third floor, she stopped outside her room and looked at him.

"Goodnight."

"Ken—"

He didn't even get all of her name out before she held up her hand. "I hope you sleep well. It was nice getting to know you this weekend."

Finn bit back a sigh. Any chance he had to pick up where they left off before Getty interrupted was gone. She'd thrown up her walls and locked the gates. "You too. If I don't see you in the morning, have a safe trip back to Asheville. I'll see you at work. Bring you that coffee I promised."

She nodded, her careful mask still in place. "Goodnight." She twisted the doorknob and disappeared inside her room.

He let out a short huff, then shook his head, crossing the hall to his bedroom. Opening the door, he stepped inside. Maybe it was a good thing Getty interrupted them. A kiss might have ruined the tentative friendship they'd developed. Finn might be open to more, but Kennedy wasn't.

Not that he wanted more. Did he?

Groaning, he scrubbed his hands over his face. That wasn't a question he was ready to answer tonight.

# Fourteen

Finn's desk phone trilled, pulling his attention from the report he was working on. He sighed, wishing he was back on the river with his friends. This week had been crazy. It had been one thing after another. He hadn't finished a task all week without getting interrupted. It looked like his Friday was shaping up to be no different.

Kennedy's face floated through his mind. He'd settle for just spending time with her. Even five minutes. He'd yet to make it to her office with the coffee he promised her.

Gaze flicking to the caller ID, Finn noted the out-of-area area code and frowned, thoughts of Kennedy moving to the backburner. He snagged the receiver and lifted it to his ear. "Special Agent Porter."

"Agent Porter, this is Special Agent Ricki Crimshaw. I work out of the El Paso ATF office. I think I have some information you'll be interested in." The female voice on the line carried a hint of no-nonsense.

"Oh? What kind of information?"

"TSA intercepted a shipment of guns at the El Paso airport. The address it shipped from is out of Asheville. We processed the crate and got a fingerprint. When we ran it, it came back to someone you already have in custody. Javier Gonzales."

Finn sat up. "Seriously?" His heart thumped in his chest. This could be what he needed to root out the gun shipments coming from the cartels.

"Yep. I'm sending you what I've got. When you talk to him, I'd appreciate any info you get on people connected to him here. I'd like to disrupt the cartel's weapons route. It'll give our guys a little bit of breathing room before someone fills the gap again."

Some of Finn's enthusiasm faded at her accurate depiction of how the cartels worked. There was always someone waiting in the wings to pick up the reins. "Will do, Agent Crimshaw. Thank you."

"You're welcome. Talk to you soon." She hung up.

Finn stared at the handset for a moment before he dropped it back in its cradle. Gonzales had been cooperative, but Nick told him earlier this week that he'd recanted his statement against Herrera. Apparently, the judges weren't the only ones with targets on their backs. Someone had attempted to kidnap Gonzales' ten-year-old daughter on her way home from school the other day. Javier had immediately clammed up and recanted everything he told investigators. Maybe this new information would get him to open up again. Finn needed a meeting with the man.

His computer dinged with an incoming email. Finn opened the program and saw a message from Agent Crimshaw. He clicked on the attachment, bringing up the case file, and started reading. A low whistle escaped through his teeth. They had him dead-to-rights. His prints were on a gun inside, as well as a piece of the packing material. Finn's eyes went wide as he noted they also found heroin residue inside the crate.

"Jesus. Did he want to get caught?" Shaking his head, he reached for the phone to call Joe Caster. The U.S. Attorney's office needed to file new charges against Gonzales.

The line rang a handful of times before Caster picked up, sounding distracted.

"This is Caster."

"Hey, Joe, it's Finn Porter. Remember asking me what info I had on Javy Gonzales?"

A short pause met his words. "Yeah. You didn't have anything concrete."

"I do now." He explained what Agent Crimshaw found in Texas and the file now sitting on his computer.

"Holy crapola. This is great. He recanted everything he told us about Herrera, you know."

"I know. Sharpe told me. Maybe we can get it back with this. I'm sending you the file now." He clicked "Forward" as he talked and entered Caster's email address. "I'm going to call his attorney next and set up a meeting. What kind of deal do you think he could get if he rolls on Herrera?"

Caster blew out a long breath. "It's hard to say until I look over what you've got. But without a deal, he's looking at probably a minimum of fifteen years for the guns. He's already looking at that much for the heroin the DEA caught him with."

"Okay. The El Paso office found heroin residue in the crate. What sort of difference does that make?"

"Oh, hell. A lot. I was going to say knocking half the total sentence off wouldn't be unreasonable, but with that? In his case, it could double the minimum sentence. Now we're talking forty-five years total. I'm not sure we can go less than thirty."

Finn gritted his teeth. "That's not much incentive. What if he gives up the El Paso network too? He'll ask for immunity; you know he will."

"I know. He won't get it. I need to talk to my boss. We offered him seven when he gave up Herrera. I'm not sure how low we can go. He's not a little fish, and he's got an extensive record from his younger days."

The wheels turned in Finn's mind. He needed to figure out a way to get Gonzales to cooperate. Again.

"You also have to consider he's burned some credit by recanting his testimony. That attempt on his kid really threw a wrench in the works. Enough that the Marshals have backed off their protective details on all the judges except for Stechschulte's office. I heard they put their witness under protection, though."

Finn had heard that too. Two days after they returned from their weekend gathering, Gonzales recanted. That put Piper square in the hot seat. Her allegations of kidnapping and attempted murder were now the heftiest charges against Herrera that actually had the ability to stick. Nick told him that she and Cullen decided to take a vacation and give the authorities time to get a handle on the threat. What he hadn't heard, though, was that they'd removed the detail from Kennedy. That bugged him. He needed to go down and check on her. So far, he'd been a terrible friend. But his hectic caseload wasn't the only reason he hadn't brought her coffee this week. She stirred something in his blood. Time and distance meant he'd had plenty of opportunity to think, and doubts had crept in. He wasn't sure he wanted to fan that particular flame. Women—especially divorced ones with kids—complicated things.

But right now wasn't the time to think about things like that. He had a more pressing concern.

"I'm glad they put a detail on Piper. It bugged me they didn't before. Hopefully, you guys can get this case to trial quickly and give everyone their lives back."

Caster snorted. "With as many moving parts as this thing

has? Don't hold your breath. But I'll do my best. Go talk to Gonzales. Give me something to work with."

Finn echoed Caster's words back to him. "I'll do my best."

"Sounds good. Let me know what you find out."

"Will do. Bye." He hung up.

Rapping his fingers against the desktop, Finn stared at the wall. He replayed the conversation. Something Caster said niggled the back of his mind.

*The kid.*

Gonzales loved his children. Finn could use that. He lifted the phone again and called the man's attorney. They wouldn't stonewall him this time.

"Baez, Carrara, and Tremoyne. This is Monique."

"Hi, Monique. This is Special Agent Finley Porter, ATF. I need to speak to Mr. Baez about his client, Javier Gonzales."

"I'm sorry. Mr. Baez is out of the office. I'd be happy to take a message, however."

Finn rolled his eyes. "Look, I know he's there, and you've been told not to connect any calls from law enforcement to him. But it is in his client's best interest if he talks to me."

There was a short pause. "I'm sorry—"

"Just ask him."

She let out a soft huff. "Fine."

Music played in his ear as she put him on hold. He resumed tapping his fingers on his desk while he waited, eventually reaching for a pen and twirling it through his fingers. The man had probably decided to take his call, but was deliberately making him wait. He hated defense attorneys. Especially the ones who represented people like Gonzales and Herrera. They were no better than their clients. Just savvier about not getting caught.

The music cut out, and a moment later a male voice took its place. "This is Ed Baez."

"Hello, Mr. Baez. This is Finley Porter, ATF. I'd like to set up a meeting with your client, Javier Gonzales. We have some things to discuss."

"Agent Porter, as my office has already told you, my client has nothing to say to you."

"That was before my colleagues in El Paso intercepted a shipment of weapons with his fingerprints all over it."

Silence met his words. He had to give the lawyer credit. Other than the pause, there was no audible reaction.

"I'm sorry. I'm sure you must be mistaken."

Finn could almost picture the man sitting ramrod straight in his chair, staring down his nose, like Finn was some annoying rodent to be shooed away. Well, he wouldn't be shooed away. Not this time. "Nope. Results are clear as day. His prints were in two places. They also found heroin residue in the crate. Do you think he'd like to talk to me now?" A corner of his mouth kicked up, knowing he had the attorney by the tie.

Baez cleared his throat. "I'll call the jail. Does three o'clock this afternoon work?"

Glancing at his watch, Finn did some quick calculations in his head. Federal holding in Butner was almost four hours away. But it was only nine-thirty. That was more than enough time. "It works just fine. I'll see you then." Finn set the receiver down, ending the call. His smile blossomed until it covered his face. Time to get this case back on track.

# FIFTEEN

Metal clanged as the cell door separating the visitor's intake from the interview area of the prison shut behind him. Finn followed the guard down the hall to a room, thanking the man as he let him inside. From the far side of the table, Javy Gonzales and his attorney watched him.

"Gentlemen." Finn sat in the chair across from them, setting down the leather portfolio he carried. He flipped it open and withdrew a pen from the holder along the edge, clicking the end. "Mr. Gonzales, has your client informed you of the new charges you're facing?"

"Let's get something clear, before we begin, Agent Porter." Baez held up a hand. "You will talk to me. My client has nothing to say. He's here to listen to what you have to say, that's all."

Finn hummed. He clicked the pen again. For now, he'd play along. "Have you informed him of what we talked about?"

Baez nodded. "I also contacted Mr. Caster's office to confirm your story. Formal charges are coming."

Finn put a hand over his heart and gave the man a wounded look. "You doubted my honesty? I'm hurt."

"Cut the crap." Gonzales spoke up. "Tell me what you want."

"Javy—"

Gonzales waved a hand, silencing the attorney. He pierced Finn with a hard stare.

Any levity Finn felt disappeared. It would not pay to underestimate Gonzales. An intelligence swam in his dark eyes. Which begged the question of why he let something with his prints on it enter the shipping system in the U.S.

"I'll cut to the chase, Mr. Gonzales. We have enough to put you behind bars for forty-five years, minimum. We have solid proof of you running drugs and weapons. Now, I can't guarantee you the seven years the U.S. Attorney's office offered you before, but Mr. Caster expressed a desire to work with you —if you give up not only Herrera but also your contact in El Paso."

Hesitation entered Gonzales' eyes, and his jaw worked. He glanced at his attorney, who leaned over and whispered something in his ear. Javy's jaw clenched and unclenched once more. He whispered something back.

Finn clicked his pen, giving off an air of nonchalance as he waited. Inside, his stomach twisted, knowing he might only have one shot to get Gonzales to talk.

The two men sat up.

"My client is willing to talk for complete immunity."

"Yeah, no." Finn sat forward, eyes fixed on Gonzales. "Look, the choice you have is a simple one. You can keep your trap shut, go to trial and end up in jail until you're what? Eighty? Or, you can talk to me. Give me everything you know about Herrera, the cartel here in Asheville—hell, even the region, if you know anything—and whatever you know about the people on the other end in El Paso, and maybe, you'll get to see your daughter get married one day."

Javy's gaze narrowed. "That's a nice sentiment, but if I talk, she won't live to see her wedding. She won't live to see the end of fourth grade. And what about my son? Or my wife? If I talk, they're all in danger. I want protection for them. Something you all failed to give them last time."

Finn's mouth flattened, recognizing the accuracy of that statement. That attempted kidnapping should never have happened. "This time, I think the Marshals' office will be prepared to offer them protection." Mentally, he crossed his fingers. He hadn't actually talked to them about that yet and had no idea if it was true. But he'd argue for it until he was blue in the face. They needed Gonzales' testimony.

A light entered Gonzales' eyes, one that made Finn narrow his gaze. There was more going on behind the man's controlled façade than he'd thought. The drug lord had his own plan.

Gonzales glanced at his attorney. The man stared at his client for a long moment before turning to Finn.

"We would need that in writing before my client would divulge anything."

Finn gave a mental fist pump. He knew he was playing into what Gonzales wanted, but if he also got what he wanted, he didn't care. "All right. I will talk with them as soon as I leave here."

"And once I leave prison. I want to be put with them." A hint of pain colored Gonzales' dark eyes.

Holding his gaze for a long moment, Finn finally nodded. "I'll see what they say."

Gonzales gave a sharp nod. "You do that, Agent Porter, and we'll talk. I will tell you whatever you want to know." He glanced at Baez. "I'm ready to go back to my cell now."

Knowing he would get no more out of Gonzales until he

had a deal in hand, Finn closed his folder and stood. "Thank you for your time, gentlemen. I'll be in touch soon." A fierce resolve carried him on light feet to the door. Gonzales' testimony could bring down a significant chunk of the Vargas-Ruiz cartel. Now, he just had to convince the Marshals and the U.S. Attorney's office to give the man what he wanted.

"Agent Porter."

Finn paused at the door, glancing back when Gonzales called his name.

"Herrera—he hasn't forgotten."

A frown creased Finn's forehead, and he turned around, curious. "Forgotten what?"

"About your judge friend. Or your witness."

Baez elbowed Gonzales in the side. "Javy—"

Gonzales glared at him, silencing the man once again, then looked at Finn. "I might be a career criminal who's done my fair share of awful things, but I'm not a heartless man, Agent Porter. And the truth is, this life—it wears on you after a while. I want out. And I don't want anyone else to get hurt. Herrera is a cold, ruthless son-of-a-bitch, who likes to hold a grudge. Just because I'm silent for now doesn't mean he's forgotten about the other judges. I guarantee they're still in his sights. And probably their families too. His philosophy is if he's going down, everyone is going with him. No one—and I mean no one—involved in this is safe. That includes me, my family, and anyone connected with me, even if only inci-dentally."

Finn studied the man for a long moment. "If that's the case, why did you recant? It wouldn't matter if you went through with testifying. Your family would still be in danger whether you talked or not, if what you say is true."

"Yes, but—" Gonzales glanced at the table, his jaw working a moment as he weighed his words. He looked up.

"Recanting gave them time. Gustavo's a psychopath. He likes playing with his prey."

Finn knew that, but hearing someone in Herrera's inner circle say the same thing sent a shiver down his spine. What all had Herrera done that they didn't know about?

A sardonic smile lifted one side of Gonzales' mouth. "He thinks he's made me feel like I did the right thing. That I've kept my family safe by keeping my mouth shut. But his psychopathy is also his greatest weakness. It makes him arrogant, and he fails to realize he's not as smart as he thinks. I've been able to read him for a long time. I know how he thinks." He lifted a shoulder. "Maybe that makes me a bit of a psycho too. In any case, it's me who's playing him. I will get my family to safety. I promise you that." His eyes hardened, and he pierced Finn with a cold stare.

That feeling that underestimating this man would be a terrible idea punched Finn in the gut again. Herrera wasn't the only killer they needed to worry about. Gonzales was just as capable—under the right circumstances.

"I will do my best to help you with that." Finn's quiet voice held a wealth of promise. He didn't want to see Gonzales' family hurt, either. "If your testimony is as good as I think it is, I doubt the Marshals will have a problem making sure they're safe."

"You bring me their promise, Agent Porter. Until then, I've said all I'm willing to say."

With a final long look, Finn nodded, acknowledging the promise in Gonzales' eyes as well as giving the man his own. He turned and knocked on the door. "Guard."

A moment later, the door swung open. Finn walked out without a backward glance. They'd said all they needed to say for now.

Long strides led him down the hall and through the door to the visitor's intake area, where he signed out and collected his phone. Exiting the facility, he lifted his phone, unlocking the screen and finding Kennedy's number in his contacts. His thumb hesitated over her name. She was likely in court and wouldn't answer.

He swiped away from his contacts and dialed the switchboard at the ATF offices.

"Alcohol, Tobacco, and Firearms, Asheville division. This is Nan."

"Hey, Nan, it's Finley Porter. Can you connect me to the judges' office manager, Suzie MacKinnon?"

"Sure. One moment."

The line clicked, then rang as she transferred him. He kept walking toward his car.

"District Court. This is Suzie."

"Hi, Suzie, it's Finn Porter. Is Judge Davidson in, or is she in court?" His car beeped as he unlocked it.

"She's in court. Would you like to leave a message?"

Finn opened his door and got in, debating. "Actually, no. I'll try to catch her later. Thanks, though." He'd rather she hear what he had to say from him and not read it on some note. He also didn't want to start a panic in the judges' office.

"Of course. I'll let her know you called."

"That works, thanks."

"You're welcome. Have a good day."

"You too." He hung up, then switched to his contacts. Tapping Kennedy's name, he lifted the phone to his ear again. He knew he'd need to leave a message, but he didn't want her to leave the building today, unaware of the danger. It rang several times, then rolled to voicemail.

"Kennedy, it's Finn. So, I just had an interesting chat with Javier Gonzales. I know the Marshals pulled their detail off of you, but I'm not sure the threat is gone. Please be careful going home this evening. I'm going to call Marshal Paulson on my way back to Asheville and discuss with her what I learned.

Text me your address when you get this, and I'll come by tonight so we can talk."

He pulled the phone away and hung up, then immediately dialed Taylor's office. "Please be in," he muttered, starting the car. The phone connected to his vehicle and rang through the interior once before Taylor's voice came on the line.

"Marshal Paulson."

"Taylor, it's Finn. Has there been any chatter about hits out on the judges? Other than those on Stechschulte and her team?"

A brief pause met his question. He could picture her frowning.

"Are you upset we pulled the detail off your friend?"

"Yes, but that's not why I'm asking. I just met with Javier Gonzales. He indicated Herrera hasn't canceled anything. That he's just waiting until we think it's all clear."

She scoffed. "Criminals lie, Finn."

"I know, but I don't think he was." He quickly explained what Agent Crimshaw's team found and the new charges Gonzales would soon face.

"Well, that's just great. You're sure he's going to talk?"

"That's another thing."

She groaned. "What?"

"He wants his family to go into WitSec."

Taylor sighed. "Finn—"

"I think you need to seriously consider it. He said he wanted out of the life. He's willing to sing like a bird and bring down not just Asheville's cartel sect, but also El Paso's. We could do some serious damage to their operations with his testimony."

Another beat of silence passed. "You're sure his info is good?"

Finn went with his gut. "Yes. You weren't there. You didn't see the look in his eyes. He knows the stakes, knows he's been caught, and that this is his chance to get out and to keep his family safe while he does so."

"Damn. Okay. I'll talk to Ty," she said, mentioning her boss. "Does he have formal charges yet?"

"I'm not sure. Caster was working on them. Probably soon, if they haven't come through yet."

"All right. I'll talk to my boss, then coordinate with him and see what kind of deal we can come up with. You just made my life a lot more difficult."

Finn chuckled and put the car in gear, pulling out of the lot. "Mine too. Let me know what you come up with. And please reconsider the security details."

"I already am. If he testifies, we'll need them, but I'll have to convince Ty. He wasn't a fan of them in the first place. But I'll see what I can do. No promises."

Finn's mouth flattened. "Do your best. I have a bad feeling about this."

"I'll do what I can. Talk to you soon."

"Yep. Bye." He tapped the phone icon on his steering wheel to hang up. A sign for a gas station loomed, and he switched lanes. He needed coffee to keep his voice going. Taylor was only the first call of many on his drive home.

# Sixteen

The doorbell pealed through the house. Kennedy looked up from her book. She closed it, only remembering after she did so that she didn't mark her page. Sighing, she set it on the coffee table and got up. It wasn't like she'd really been reading, anyway. Too many thoughts ran through her head, and they were all centered around the voicemail Finn left. That better be him ringing her doorbell. She wanted answers.

Staying to the side, she peered through the windows beside the door. The textured glass kept her from making out who it was, but she could tell it was a man. She took her phone from her pocket and dialed Finn's number. Ringing erupted on the other side of the door.

"It's me, Ken." His voice came through the door, even as his phone continued to ring.

Kennedy ended the call and twisted the locks, opening the door. He stepped in and relocked it.

She crossed her arms and rocked forward on the balls of her feet. "Hey."

"Hi. Thanks for texting me your address."

"I figured you'd just call Ben and ask for it if I didn't. I don't want to involve him. He'll just worry, which will turn into him bugging me all the time."

A smile toyed with Finn's lips, making one dimple appear. "He just wants to look out for you."

"I know, but that doesn't mean I want him to hover. I'm a big girl." She waved a hand. "Come tell me what you know." She spun on her heel, leading him deeper into the house to her office. The kids wouldn't inadvertently overhear them in there. She didn't want to keep them in the dark, but she wanted to tell them in her own way.

Inside, she shut the door, then flopped onto the couch. He sat down beside her.

"Where do you want me to start?"

"Tell me what you can without divulging anything about Gonzales' case. Charges he's facing are okay, but no details."

"Wow, you don't ask much." He blew out a breath, brows dipping. "Okay, let's see. He and I had a chat. He's got some new charges pending for arms trafficking. The threat to you is still there and it may not be limited to just you. The twins could be targets as well."

Kennedy's eyes went wide, and she let out a soft gasp.

Finn held up a hand. "Gonzales isn't the threat. It's all Herrera. I talked to Taylor Paulson, and even with what I told her about—things—her boss isn't convinced, so they're not reinstating your security detail."

Apprehension brought her to her feet. She paced to the window and glanced out at the backyard, a million thoughts running through her mind. She was beginning to wonder if this job was worth it. Surely, it couldn't always be like this? It had to be a fluke that her first couple of weeks were so eventful.

"I told her I thought it was the wrong call, but her hands are tied."

She crossed her arms and lifted a hand to her mouth,

chewing on her thumbnail as she continued to stare outside. "Do you believe there's a danger?"

"It's all hearsay, but knowing what I do about the players involved, yes. I believe the threat is real."

She turned back to him. "So, what now? How do I keep my kids safe?"

Finn stood and crossed the room to stand in front of her. The hair on Kennedy's arms rose at his nearness. She started to sway toward him, but the rational part of her mind spoke up, reminding her that getting involved with a man at this juncture of her life was a bad idea. Gritting her teeth, she stiffened her spine and stayed put.

"I'm going to take some time off and become your shadow —or theirs. Or both. Herrera and Gonzales fall under the purview of a task force headed by the DEA. My part in that is small, and I can handle most anything without being in the office, so long as I have my laptop and an internet connection."

Startled, she blinked up at him. "What? I can't ask you to do that, Finn. We're not your responsibility to protect. And what about the other judges involved in the two cases? Who will protect them?"

"I'm not sure, but I asked Taylor to at least make everyone aware there could be a threat. It would be irresponsible to not do that much. As for you and the twins, I did a lot of thinking after I talked to Paulson just before I came over here. I know you're not my responsibility, but that doesn't change the fact I feel the need to make sure the three of you are safe. I couldn't live with myself if something happened to any of you and I had the power to prevent it."

Kennedy rolled her lips in and nodded, glancing away. "Mmm-hmm, I see." Anger sparked. She didn't want to be an afterthought of a guilty conscience.

"What? Why are you frowning?"

She glanced at him, letting her anger shimmer in her eyes. "You can save your leave. My kids and I don't need your sympathy. I hereby absolve you of any guilt should something happen."

His frown deepened. "Wait, I'm confused. Why are you so upset? I'm trying to help."

"To assuage your own conscience. I don't need your pity, Finn. That's no better than my brother hovering."

"Whoa, hold up." He raised a hand. "I don't pity you, Kennedy. Yes, I would feel awful if something happened to you and I did nothing to stop it, but I'm not doing this for me. At least not in the sense you believe. I care about you. And the twins. We're friends, and friends help each other."

"Oh, is that what we are? I seem to remember someone saying he'd bring me coffee and then he never did." She knew she was being a bit petulant, but dammit, he'd struck a nerve. She'd had enough empty promises to last her a lifetime. Plus, she'd been looking forward to seeing Finn this week—despite telling herself she was better off not starting anything with him—and then he never visited.

"Aha!" He pointed a finger at her.

Kennedy clenched her teeth to keep from snapping at it. She was not a fan of having someone's finger in her face. Pete did that whenever he wanted to make her feel like his actions were her fault. Instead, she batted it away. "Don't stick your finger in my face."

He dropped his hand. "You're not mad because you think I have some misplaced guilt. You're mad because I haven't been around." He narrowed his eyes and bent closer. "And now that I want to be around, you're upset because it upsets you to have me close by."

"That is ridiculous." She turned her nose up and looked askance, not willing to admit how close to the truth he was. "I'm mad because you said you'd do something and didn't.

And how did we go from your guilt to my feelings about you?"

"So, you admit you have feelings for me?"

Her eyes grew round. She tipped her chin higher. "I'm not even debating you on that. I told you why I'm upset."

"I'll give you that I should have stopped by before now, but I don't buy that as the only reason. No, there's more to it, and it's a logical conclusion that you're fighting some attraction to me."

She lifted one eyebrow and cocked her head. "Do you hear yourself? Could you be any more arrogant?"

A wicked smile slashed over his face, bringing out those dimples. Heat gathered in her belly and on her cheeks, but she refused to look away. She wouldn't give him the satisfaction. Arrogant jerk. Her traitorous body needed to shut up and listen to her brain. Finley Porter was heartache waiting to happen. His arrogance reeked of the same brand as her ex-husband's.

*Liar.*

Kennedy's frown deepened as her inner voice injected itself into the debate.

*He's nothing like Pete. He actually listens to you and the kids.*

She bit back a huff and told the voice to shut up.

"It's not arrogance, sweet cheeks. I'm just stating the obvious." His smile widened. "And you want to know something? It's mutual."

Her cheeks flamed hotter, the heat spreading south. What? Her mouth went slack. He couldn't be serious. What was she supposed to do with that information?

Some of his mirth faded as she stared at him agape. Those gray eyes shone with an understanding, and his words confirmed it.

"Look, I'm not trying to make you uncomfortable or start

something. I don't think either of us is really looking for a relationship. But, Kennedy, I can't sit by and leave you unprotected. Both for your sake and for mine."

The serious tone to his voice kicked her brain back into gear. The rational part that had taken a hike. "Dammit, Finn. I do not need this. Not the danger or you." She scrubbed her hands over her face, groaning. "I just want a normal life, free from drama." She dropped her hands. "Fine. If you want to follow me and my kids around, do it." A frown darkened her face. "But how are you going to do that twenty-four-seven? You have to sleep."

Some of the mischievous twinkle returned to his eyes. "Well, I was kinda hoping you'd let me crash inside."

Her eyes widened. Finn in her house? Overnight? And first thing in the morning when she didn't have her wits about her yet? Oh, boy.

He raised his hands, palms out, waving them slightly. "I can totally camp out in my car in your driveway, but I figured I'd keep better watch if I'm inside and can hear a window break or someone moving around who shouldn't be. And I don't even need a bed. The couch will work. Either in here, or in the living room."

Kennedy bit back a growl. Why did he have to be so logical? His reasoning totally made sense. And she'd feel safer if he was in the house. "I have a guest room." She sighed. The kids were going to freak out. Having Finn in the house made things seem much more serious than a U.S. Marshal outside, watching the house. "When did you want to start this?"

"Now."

"Oh. Right. I guess that makes sense." She bit back another groan. Where did her brain go? You'd never know she was a federal judge.

"I need to go home and pack a bag. I came here straight from the office. Do you want me to talk to the kids with you?"

"No. I'll talk to them while you're gone." She'd get a more genuine response from them without him there to make them guard their emotions.

"Okay. Let them know that I'll be happy to answer any questions they have." He backed away. "I'll be back soon." Turning, he took a step toward the door.

"Finn."

Pausing, he glanced back, a question in his gray eyes.

"Thank you. I never meant to sound ungrateful to you. I appreciate your willingness to use your vacation days to keep my family safe."

His expression softened, and a ghost of a smile flitted over his lips. "You're welcome." He stepped toward the door. "I won't be long."

Kennedy pressed her lips together, nodding. He turned and left.

Her breath left her on a short sigh, and she hung her head, giving herself a moment to let the emotions run free so she could acknowledge them. Later, when she was alone in bed, she'd process everything going on. Right now, she just wanted to recognize how she felt.

Grabbing hold of a few of the stronger feelings, she pushed them each into a box in her mind to deal with them later. Once she had a handle on herself and felt a little calmer, she followed Finn from the room, making sure the front door was locked before she wandered upstairs to find the twins.

She poked her head into Paige's room first. The girl looked up from where she sat on her bed, headphones on. When she pulled them off, Kennedy heard music playing.

"Yeah, Mom?"

"I need to talk to you and your brother. Can you come out here?"

"Sure." She paused her music and set her phone and headphones on her bed, getting up. "What's this about?"

"I'll explain in a minute." She walked across the hall to Paxton's room, knocking. When he didn't answer, she poked her head in. He sat at his desk, headphones on, playing a computer game. "Pax."

He saw her and pushed one earphone off. "Yeah? I'm playing with Grady." He pointed at the screen as he mentioned his best friend.

"Can you take a short break? I need to talk to you and your sister. You can get right back on."

"Uh, yeah. Hang on." He turned away, pressing a button, then talking into the microphone hanging in front of his mouth. "Hey, man. My mom needs me for a minute. I'll be back in a few." After a short pause, he removed the headphones and stood.

Kennedy motioned for him to sit. "We can talk in here." She pushed the door wider, stepping inside and motioning for Paige to come in. They perched on the edge of the bed, and he swiveled to face them.

"What's wrong? You look upset." Paxton frowned as he stared at her.

Not wanting to upset either of them, Kennedy schooled her features as best she could. She wanted them to be aware of the danger, but she didn't want them to see her worry. That was for her to bear. And if she needed to talk and get things off her chest, she had a feeling Finn would listen. The twins didn't need that burden.

"So, you remember last week how Marshal Paulson followed me around?"

They nodded.

"Is she coming back?" Paige asked. "I thought things were okay now."

"I did too. But Finn—he learned some things today that make him think I might still be in danger. Marshal Paulson isn't coming back. The things he learned aren't concrete enough for her boss to put a detail on me again. But Finn's concerned enough that he's going to stay with us for a while."

The kids shared a look, making Kennedy's brows bunch. She knew that look. They were "talking." Neither said a word, but whenever they gave each other that look, she knew they were thinking the same thing. They didn't always enlighten her about what that was, either.

"How concerned should we be?" Pax asked. "I'd ask if we need to stay home, but we don't go anywhere except school."

"We need to be vigilant. Don't leave the yard, especially not alone. If you see someone you think is suspicious, tell Finn. Also, he'll probably be picking you two up from school for the foreseeable future."

That made them both frown harder.

"Why?" Paige glanced at her brother, then back to Kennedy. "Marshal Paulson didn't pick us up. Betty Ruth still did it."

"I know, but like I said, he heard some things, so we're just playing it safe." She held up a hand when Paxton gave her a curious look and opened his mouth to speak. "I don't know details. The person all this came from is on my docket, so when Finn and I talked just a little bit ago, I asked him to keep it general."

"A criminal gave him this info?" Paxton rolled his eyes. "That sounds legit."

"You'd be surprised how much people like that know. And this guy has a lot to lose if he lies. We aren't the only ones in danger. His family is too." She was well-aware that Gonzales would have left her and all the other judges in the dark if Herrera hadn't targeted his family.

Paige folded her hands and stared at them. Kennedy tipped her head, trying to see her daughter's face. She put her hand over Paige's. "You okay?"

Worried green eyes met hers. "I'm not sure I like your new

job. What happens to us if something happens to you? I don't want to live with Dad. Or Grandma. He's a jerk, and she'll just micromanage us."

Kennedy's heart broke. She hated that this was happening to her family. But the twins' fear was precisely why she agreed to let Finn stay. They'd all rest easier with him around. "I think everything will work out fine. That's why Finn's here. To make sure we're all okay. Just please do as he says?" She lifted an eyebrow, making eye contact with them both, waiting for them to nod before she continued. "Things won't always be like this. The man threatening us—Gustavo Herrera—is completely off his rocker. Most criminals I deal with aren't nearly so nuts, even at the federal level."

That drew a soft smile from Paige and a quick snort from Pax. Kennedy smiled, hoping to lighten the mood. She didn't want them to worry. She knew they would some—they were old enough to recognize the danger—but she didn't want it to consume them. "Do you have any questions? For me or for Finn? He said you can ask whatever you want."

Both teens shook their heads. Kennedy studied them for a long moment before nodding, satisfied they weren't holding back. "If you think of anything, don't hesitate to ask." She stood up. "I'm going to make up the guest room. Either of you want to help?" A smile flirted with her mouth. She knew the answer to that.

Paxton swung around, going back to his chair. "Nope." He picked up his headphones.

Paige popped up beside her. "He's one guy. What all needs to be done? Aren't there already sheets on the bed?" She headed for the door.

"Yes." Kennedy followed, pulling the door closed as they stepped into the hall. "But I need to put towels in the bathroom and make sure the pillowcases don't still smell like cardboard." The scent had permeated most everything fabric they owned. She'd washed a lot of clothing when they unpacked. Other stuff, she just let air out. She was hoping the bedsheets had aired sufficiently.

Paige wrinkled her nose. "Have fun. If you have to change the sheets, let me know, and I'll help you."

Kennedy smiled. "Thanks, sweetie."

Smiling back, Paige entered her room.

Feeling slightly better now that the hard part of this whole situation was out of the way, Kennedy spun on her heel and headed for the guest room.

# SEVENTEEN

Darkness enveloped Kennedy's yard. The street lights cast shadows, creating dozens of places for someone to hide. Finn squinted, looking for anyone lurking, but knew it was a futile effort; it was too dark. He let the curtain fall back into place and continued his check of the windows. Logically, he knew they were all secure—he'd checked them shortly after he came back with his suitcase. But he couldn't sleep, so he was up wandering.

A soft clink and a muffled male curse from the kitchen drew his attention. Automatically, his hand went to the weapon at his waist, but it only took a moment for his brain to register the voice. Relaxing, Finn strolled down the short hall, past the stairs. Paxton stood in front of the microwave, wiping up hot chocolate.

"Everything okay?"

The boy looked up. "Yeah. Sorry. I couldn't sleep. Sometimes a warm drink helps. Plus, I was hungry."

Finn nodded. He remembered being fifteen. The hunger never stopped. Walking forward, he grabbed a handful of paper towels and helped him clean up the mess. "What happened here?"

"I didn't close the microwave door when I took the water out. Bumped my head, which made me jerk, and I spilled hot chocolate everywhere. At least I didn't drop the mug." He pointed to the white ceramic coffee mug that only held a fraction of the liquid it should.

"It would have been easily replaceable by the looks of it, if you had."

"Yeah, but I don't want to upset Mom. I mean, she wouldn't be pissed. Not really. But it would just be one more thing that went wrong."

Finn straightened, a slight furrow wrinkling his forehead as he stared at the boy. "What else has gone wrong lately? Besides the obvious." He gestured to himself, indicating the situation with Herrera.

"My dad. My grandma." Pax shook his head and walked to the trashcan, throwing his soiled paper towels inside. "Life the last couple of years hasn't been too rosy."

"I'm sorry, kiddo. Do you want to talk about it?"

Pax lifted a shoulder, then leaned his back against the counter, bracing his hands on either side of his hips. He stared at the floor, kicking the tile with the toe of his sock-covered foot.

Giving the kid a chance to decide what he wanted to say, Finn turned, bending to open the cabinet beneath the sink. He wanted to clean the counter so it wouldn't get sticky. Finding what he was looking for, he sprayed the white quartz surface.

"Are your parents divorced?"

Finn set the spray bottle down and reached for more toweling. "No. But I had friends growing up whose parents were."

"You're lucky. It sucks."

"I bet it does. But your parents love you, even if they don't love each other anymore."

Paxton snorted. "Mom does. Dad only loves himself. I want to be mad that they split up, but I know it was for the best. The thing is, though, he wasn't always like this. When we were young, he was fun. I don't know what changed."

"I can't help you there, except to say you should talk to your mom. Tell her how you feel. Maybe she can help you understand."

His shoulder lifted again. "Maybe."

Finn tipped his head. "She wouldn't want you to worry about her."

"I know. Doesn't change the fact that I do. If I don't and Paige doesn't, who will? Dad should, but he stuck his head up his butt and ruined everything. Grandma cares, but she's too nervous to do more than fret. And Grandpa, well, he thinks we should all handle our problems like adults and that it's no one else's business. Said it makes us strong to do it alone." Pax rolled his eyes. "Everyone needs someone."

"I agree. You and your mom and your sister are lucky to have each other. But don't forget, your mom has your Uncle Ben too. And me. We'll look out for her. For you and Paige too."

Paxton looked up, a maturity beyond his years in his green eyes. "I'm glad you're here. I doubt Mom will admit it out loud, but having you in the house makes her feel safer. When she told us about what was going on, I could see the relief in her eyes when she mentioned you were staying with us."

That made Finn glad he took the time off to be here. His goal was to keep them safe. Making Kennedy feel that way was a bonus.

"How bad is this dude, anyway? Mom didn't tell us many details. She said she didn't know many."

"She doesn't, but that's on purpose. A lot of the info came

from someone on her court docket, so she asked to be kept in the dark. And I won't tell you much more, except Herrera is a bad dude. The man who gave us the info will go into witness protection after he serves his prison term—if he makes it through his sentence. His family will go into WitSec in the next couple of days. As soon as he signs the plea deal."

"Wow." Paxton blinked and looked away, thinking. "Now I'm really glad you're here." He met Finn's gaze again. "How long will this last?"

"I'm not sure. Gonzales has to testify against Herrera. That could be months."

"Months?" Paxton groaned. "There goes my summer."

Finn held out a hand in a stop gesture. "Not necessarily. We'll find stuff to do."

The boy's brows dipped. "Wait. If it's going to be months, how will you be able to stay that long? There's no way you have that much time off."

"True. But the next couple of weeks will tell us a lot about the threat level. If I have to, I'll pull in some backup. I have friends who would be willing to give some of their time to help out."

Paxton looked away again. "This is just weird."

Finn shrugged. He turned toward the pantry. "It is what it is." Walking inside, he found the hot chocolate mix and grabbed another packet before returning to the kitchen. "We all just need to make the best of it. Now," he held up the hot chocolate, "rinse out that mug and put more water in it."

Some of the tension left Pax's features. He picked up his mug and rinsed it, then filled it with fresh water. Finn filled a glass with cold water and drank it while Paxton's drink heated and the boy found himself a snack—a bag of trail mix.

"Thanks for helping me clean up my mess." Pax picked up his drink and the trail mix bag. "And for looking out for my mom—for us."

"Anytime, Pax. If you ever need to talk—about anything—I'll be around." And he meant that. He knew the importance of having a male role model to talk to. From what he'd seen, Kennedy was a great mom, but there were some things guys only talked about with guys.

With a nod, Pax left the room to head back upstairs with his midnight snack. Finn put his glass in the sink and glanced out into the backyard. Like the front, it was full of shadows too dark to see past.

"You're good with kids."

Finn jumped and spun around. Kennedy stood in the doorway in light gray pajama pants and a white sleep-shirt that read, "Just one more chapter before bed... Aaaaand it's 3am."

He shook his head and blew out a breath. "Where did you come from?"

A wide smile split her face as she walked closer. "Apparently, an inability to sleep is a common theme in this house tonight. I came down to get some tea. When I heard you two talking, I stood in the hallway bathroom and listened." She shrugged, unapologetic. "I'm glad I did. I knew he was worried, but it's nice to hear why, exactly. I didn't know he felt so isolated. I'll have to make a concerted effort to make sure we spend time with Ben and Gemma. Maybe I can get my other brother to come visit." She gave a short snort. "Though he's a lot like my dad. And my ex. So I doubt he'll make the time."

Finn opened his mouth, then shut it, unsure if he should ask the question rattling around in his head. Ultimately, though, curiosity got to him. "Pax mentioned his dad wasn't always the way he is now. What changed?"

Kennedy wrinkled her nose and reached for the tea canister tucked against the wall by the coffeepot. She opened the lid, removing a tea bag. "Greed got to him." She took down a mug and stuck it under the single-serve side of the dual brewer with the tea bag hanging over the edge. "He was always a go-getter. When we met, he had a life plan drawn out that took him to age forty." Her eyes met his. "Children weren't on that list. After we started dating, I mentioned I wanted kids, and he sort of hemmed and hawed about it, but eventually agreed kids would fit into the plan after law school. Then our birth control failed."

Looking away, she punched a couple buttons on the brewer, and it sputtered to life. "I was excited, even though I knew it would be a challenge to raise a child and finish school." She turned and met his gaze again. "But Pete wasn't the only one who had goals. I wanted it all, and I was going to have it. So what if part of the plan happened a little sooner? Pete didn't see it that way."

Finn leaned a hip against the counter and crossed his arms. "How come he didn't walk away then?"

"Image. And he was raised to deal with his responsibilities, not shove them away or pretend they didn't exist. I knew marrying him because I was pregnant probably wasn't the best idea, but like I said, I wanted it all, and I knew it would be a lot harder for me to obtain my goals alone. So, when he asked me to marry him, I said yes." She let out a long breath. "Things were fine when the twins were younger—for the most part. We were still in school, so the pressure to work all the time to advance in our jobs wasn't there yet. I went the prosecutor route, not wanting the pressure a defense attorney gets to climb the ladder. I was content with my government salary. What drove me was being the best I could be at my job. Pete— well, like I said, he had a plan, and that was to make partner in record time. He wanted to see his name on the letterhead and on the front of the building—no matter whose toes he had to step on to get it. Gradually, his ambition eroded family time until he was rarely home."

Something she said last weekend filtered through his mind. "He cheated on you, didn't he?" Finn's voice was a low growl. How any man could step out on a woman he vowed to love forever was beyond him. Especially one as classy and as kind as Kennedy.

She nodded. "With several women, actually. I found out because a friend of mine saw him leaving a hotel with one of his paralegals. When I confronted him, he didn't deny it. Told me things had been over for a while, but he stayed 'for the kids.'" She air-quoted and rolled her eyes. "I told him that was total crap. He wasn't around enough to use that excuse. He stayed because, one, a divorce—because he cheated—would make him look bad to his boss. Especially because he cheated on me with his subordinates. And two, he wanted the clout my position provided. I'd been steadily making a name for myself and had been elected to the state court of appeals. My success made him look good."

Finn let out a snort and dropped his arms. He was sure. Men like that only cared about what others could do for him. It didn't matter who that person was.

"Anyway, after that argument, he left and didn't come back. He even sent a moving service to pack up his things—which I had to supervise, so they didn't take anything that wasn't his or mutual property. Thankfully, one of my law school friends became a divorce attorney, and she helped me through the whole ordeal and made sure things were split fairly. Now, he just pretends we don't exist most of the time. It got to a point I couldn't watch the kids come home feeling rejected over and over again. When the position here opened up, I threw my hat in the ring."

He settled against the counter again. "Well, I'm glad you did. Even if current circumstances are less than ideal."

An ironic tilt lifted one side of her mouth. "Right? I know it won't always be like this, but it sure doesn't make for an easy transition." She lifted the tea bag from the hot water, swirling it for a moment before wrapping the string around it and squeezing out the excess water. Pulling open the drawer containing the trash can, she tossed it inside, then went to the fridge. "So how goes things, anyway? Is it all quiet on the western front?" She glanced at him as she removed the milk from the top shelf.

A smile erupted on Finn's face. "You're a history nerd, aren't you?"

She let out a soft laugh. "Somewhat." Returning to his side, she poured some milk into her tea. "It's always interested me, and it's a natural path to go into law from. I majored in it and political science in college." Retreating to the fridge, she put the milk away, then came back, grabbing a spoon along the way.

"I like old military history, but that's about it."

Kennedy opened the small sugar jar on the counter and added a spoonful to her tea. "That does not surprise me."

"Oh, how so?"

She shrugged and lifted her tea mug. "You're a fed. Don't most of them have some fascination with military history? Or were in the military?"

Finn tipped his head. "I guess."

"Besides, you have that air about you." She lifted her pinky and swirled it, then took a sip of the hot tea.

He quirked an eyebrow, an amused smile tugging at his lips. "An air? What kind of air?"

"You know, the whole alpha male thing. That bearing that says you'll take charge and be good at it. Ben has the same way about him."

A low chuckle escaped Finn's throat. She thought he was an alpha male? He supposed she wasn't too far off. He didn't venture into the caveman ways of "Me, Tarzan," and demand his friends and family fall in line, but he never shied away from being in charge. "Is that a good thing?"

She tipped her head back and forth. A touch of color

stained her cheeks, making Finn wonder what else was running through her head.

"It is. So long as you don't take it too far. I have no desire to be bossed around."

Wicked, naughty thoughts blasted through Finn's head. "Are you sure? It could be fun." The words left his mouth before he could stop them. But he didn't try to take them back. The fire that erupted in the depths of her pretty green eyes told him they weren't anything she wasn't already thinking. He edged closer.

She cleared her throat, but held his gaze. "You think so? I've never taken well to being told what to do. I like to have a say."

Finn shuffled another step toward her. "There's nothing wrong with that. But shouldn't someone be in charge? Drive, so to speak?"

She hummed, swaying toward him. Her tea cup stayed between them like a shield. "I guess it depends on where we're going and what the goal is."

He took another step, bringing her body within inches of his. "I think I know what my goal is."

"Yeah? What's that?"

Finn gave up any pretense about what it was they were talking about. "To find out how soft your lips are."

Her mouth parted on a soft gasp. Finn's entire body tightened. He reached for her mug and removed it from her fingers, setting it on the counter. With her shield gone, he closed the remaining distance. "Do you know what your goal is? Does it match mine?"

Eyes the color of green sea glass met his, searching. Desire blazed in their depths, but so did something else. An awareness that they were treading on the edge of some very deep water stepped up, front and center.

He lowered his head, maintaining eye contact and giving

her every chance to back away. A hairsbreadth from her lips, he paused. Raising a hand, he cupped the side of her neck and jaw. Smooth, warm skin met his fingers. The muscles in her neck worked as she swallowed. But still, she stayed put. Finn stroked the soft skin of her jawline and closed the gap.

# Eighteen

Explosions went off inside Kennedy's head, blinding her, even though her eyes were closed. But she didn't need to see to feel. Finn's mouth moved over hers, feeding the flames until they engulfed her body, warming her from head to toe. She clung to his shoulders, supporting knees weakened by the force of the desire flooding her system. Never in her life had a simple kiss sent her reeling quite so quickly and upended her world.

Finn pulled back, opening those beautiful gray eyes to stare down at her. Her breath came in short bursts as her body floated down from the high.

"That was rather—unexpected."

The low tenor of his voice washed over her, making her shiver and reigniting the desire. She forced herself to drop her hands before she clutched the sides of his face and kissed him again. That one kiss had already complicated everything, and she needed time to process it.

She cleared her throat. "It was, yes." Grasping the hem of her shirt, she twisted it around her fingers. She still wanted to pull him back down for another kiss.

*Escape.*

Her mind whispered the word. That sounded like a wonderful idea. She let go of her shirt and reached for her mug, intending to flee. "But I don't want to talk about it right now."

"Okay." His voice was still soft, but had lost the trace of desire, for which Kennedy was grateful. That low rumble it added made her want to do things that involved no clothes and the counter.

"It's late, and we're both stressed out and tired." Finn shifted, putting some distance between them. "But what just happened—we can't ignore it forever. Because it will happen again. That was—well..." His voice trailed off, and he raised an eyebrow.

Kennedy knew what he meant. And the word he was searching for. Incredible. Although, even that didn't do it justice.

She nodded, backing away. "I'll see you in the morning."

He raised a hand in farewell, and she fled. On swift feet, she hurried down the hall and upstairs to her bedroom. Inside, she closed the door, then spun around, leaning against it. Her heart thumped in her chest, and not from her mad dash upstairs.

What the hell? Why did she do that? Why did she let him do that? What happened to men only complicated things, and she didn't need the complication?

A soft groan escaped, and she pushed away from the door, marching to her bed. He'd looked at her with those sexy gray eyes, that's what. Those same eyes had sucked her in at the mountain cabin too. Here, though, she didn't have Marshal Getty and his flashlight to save her. She'd been at the mercy of their depths. What they said was true. Eyes really were the windows to the soul. And Finn had one of the kindest souls she'd ever seen.

Throwing back the covers, she set her tea on the night-stand and climbed into bed, arranging her pillows behind her so she could sit up. Grabbing the remote, she flipped on the television hanging on the opposite wall. She needed mindless entertainment to get her thoughts off what happened downstairs. Something funny she could get interested in.

But her mind wandered as she flipped through the channels. It lingered on the feel of Finn's mouth on hers. Soft and supple, but firm, he'd played her lips like a fiddle and made her body sing. She couldn't help but wonder what it would feel like if he moved on to other parts of her.

Hot now, she kicked the covers away, then huffed, eyebrows furrowed as she stared at the television, not seeing the show playing. She didn't understand why one man—who she'd only known a couple of weeks—could unsettle her so much. Sure, he was nice and funny. Intelligent and handsome. But so were a lot of other men she knew. What made Finn so special that she couldn't get him out of her head?

*You never let those other men kiss you.*

Kennedy ground her molars and told her inner voice to shut up. She didn't need the reminder. The impression of his lips on hers still lingered. Her mouth still tingled and felt puffy from the kiss. Her body ached for more.

Growling, she tossed the remote onto the bed and reached for the book on her nightstand. Maybe reading would be better, because the TV certainly wasn't distracting her like she'd hoped.

She flipped open the book and found where she left off. Her eyes widened as she realized she'd stopped just before the characters jumped into bed together. Slamming the book shut, she closed her eyes and drew in a long breath through her nose and forced her mind onto case law, hoping to banish images of what Finn might look like naked.

"Damn." She sat up and swung her legs over the side of

the bed, putting the book on the nightstand. Getting up, she walked over to the small bookshelf she kept in her room and found a different book, this one on the Galapagos, then retreated to her bed. Paper swished as she flipped to the first chapter. "Come on, tortoises. Enthrall me with your giantness." Kennedy rolled her eyes. Even if she did manage to lose herself in the book, she knew it would still be a long night. And that her dreams would be—eventful.

Nineteen

Still half-asleep, Kennedy took a mug from the cupboard and put it on the drip plate of the coffeepot. Inserting a pod, she pressed the button to make the machine brew, then stared at the counter while she waited. In moments, the rich scent of coffee reached her nose. She closed her eyes and took a deep breath. That alone cleared some of the fog from her brain. As predicted, sleep last night was elusive. Every time she tried to close the book and go to sleep, memories of Finn's mouth on hers, of the play of his muscled shoulders under her hands filled her mind and kept her from drifting off. She finally fell asleep reading somewhere around two or so. When she awoke to her alarm this morning at seven, the bedside light was still on and the book was in her lap.

Honestly, five hours wasn't bad for her. She'd run on less more times than she could count. But after the week she had, coupled with the stress of being the target of a crazy person, her body needed more than just a few hours rest.

She was going to do her damnedest to counteract it, though. After she drank this cup of coffee, she planned to hit up the treadmill. Running around her neighborhood would be better, but that wasn't an option at the moment. Endorphins were endorphins, though, no matter how she got them.

Light footsteps were her only warning a moment before Finn entered the kitchen.

"That coffee smells fantastic."

Kennedy's defenses went up, unable to deal with him yet. She pointed to the cabinet containing the mugs. "Help yourself." The pot sputtered out the last of her coffee, and she took the mug, stepping away. Not caring that she was likely to burn her tongue, she raised the cup, taking a sip. The hot liquid seared her mouth, but also cleared more of her brain fog.

"So, what are your plans today?" Finn put a mug on the drip plate and added a pod to the machine.

"Unpack. Catch up on case notes." She'd been putting off unpacking the last of the boxes, but since she was homebound, it seemed like a good idea to finish the chore. "I need to get groceries, too, at some point."

He leaned back against the counter, crossing his arms and ankles, and nodded. "Can you do the home delivery?"

"Probably. I don't have it set up here yet. I could always send Betty Ruth, though."

"Betty Ruth?"

"My housekeeper-slash-nanny. She moved here with us from Richmond."

Finn blinked. "You brought your housekeeper?"

Kennedy took another sip of her coffee and nodded. "She's been with us since the kids were little. When I told her I'd applied for the job here, she said she'd move with us if I got it. I didn't even have to ask."

"What about her family?"

"Her husband died fairly young. Heart attack at forty-four. She came to us shortly after that. They never had any children, and she didn't have any other family. We're her family."

"But she doesn't live here with you?"

"No. We found her a little house not too far away. She wanted her own space. I can't blame her for that. You've met my kids. They're great, but they can still be a handful."

"Do the Marshals know about her?"

Kennedy straightened, a frown tightening her features. "You don't think—"

"I think Herrera is evil enough to go after anyone any of you care about. When was the last time you talked to her?"

"Yesterday. She picked the kids up from school. She was here when I got home, then left after we ate dinner. We almost always eat supper together, then she heads home. She'll come clean while the kids are at school, pick them up, then make dinner for all of us. It's been that way for years."

"She's by herself on the weekends?"

"Usually, yes. Unless we make plans to do something together. The kids see her as a grandmother figure, so sometimes she comes with us when we go on an excursion. Should I call her?"

"It probably wouldn't hurt." His mouth twisted. "You should consider asking her to move in for a while too. I can move my things downstairs and sleep either on the couch in the living room or in your office."

Kennedy's frown deepened. She didn't have a big enough house for this. But she agreed with him. Betty Ruth could be a target.

Setting her mug down, she reached into the pocket of her leggings and took out her phone and called the older woman. With each ring, the pit in Kennedy's stomach grew deeper, turning into a chasm when it went to voicemail. She hung up without leaving a message.

"Could she still be asleep?" Finn asked when she pulled the phone away and ended the call.

"Maybe, but not likely. She's an early riser."

Finn turned back to the cupboards, opening the mug cabinet and removing two travel mugs. He thrust one at her. "Put your coffee in that, then go wake the kids."

"What?" She took the mug, but stared at him with a frown, confused. Awake more than she was a few minutes ago, she still wasn't fully tracking.

"We're going to check on her, but I'm not leaving any of you here alone."

Kennedy groaned, her shoulders slumping. He was right, but she still didn't want to wake the twins. "Do you have any idea how grumpy a teenager is when awakened early on a weekend?"

A grin slashed over his face. "Yep. They'll get over it."

"Yeah, next weekend." Grumbling, she put the travel mug and her full cup on the counter. "I'll be back." She walked away to his low chuckle.

Climbing the stairs, she went to Paxton's room first. He'd be the harder of the two to rouse. Kennedy opened his door and walked to the bed. He lay sprawled on his stomach, snoring just slightly, one leg poking out from beneath his navy blue comforter. She put a hand on his shoulder and shook him awake. "Pax. Sweetie, wake up."

He let out a soft snort, then a low rumbling breath. "Go away."

"You need to get up. We have to go check on Betty Ruth."

The boy stilled, then opened one eye, a wariness showing in its green depths. "Why?"

"Finn's worried about her. He wasn't aware of her or of how close she is to our family, so he had me call her to check on her. She didn't answer. We need to go over there, and you and Paige can't stay here alone."

He groaned and rolled over to sit up. "How long until this maniac gets convicted and is out of our lives?"

A quick scoff escaped Kennedy's throat. "Not soon

enough. Get dressed and come downstairs." She spun on her heel and left the room.

Waking Paige went much the same way, except instead of "Go away," she got, "What? It's too early." With both kids up, Kennedy went downstairs to finish her coffee.

In the kitchen, Finn was nowhere to be seen, which was fine with her. She could use a few moments to herself. Spying her coffee—which was now in the travel mug—she wandered to the pantry and grabbed a protein bar. It wasn't the breakfast she'd planned, but it would work. The wrapper crinkled as she tore it open and took a bite.

Her solitude only lasted through the time it took her to eat. As she swallowed the last bit of the bar, two sets of heavy footsteps thundered down the stairs. Finn reappeared in the doorway to the garage as the twins entered the kitchen.

Kennedy blinked at him. "Do you have some kind of radar?"

His brows dipped, then his expression cleared when she tipped her head toward the kids. He smiled. "Agent intuition. You guys ready?"

"Almost." Kennedy turned to the twins, who, despite their mad dash downstairs, still looked half-asleep. "Grab a breakfast bar of some kind and a drink. You can snack in the car."

They disappeared into the pantry. When they reemerged, Finn ushered them all into the garage.

"I'll drive." Finn rounded the rear of the car, heading for the driver's seat.

Kennedy paused, frowning. "But it's my car."

"Do you have a defensive driving certificate and hours of real-world practice at evading tails?"

Her frown deepened. "No." Spinning on her heel, she went to the passenger's seat and got in.

"Do you have the keys?"

She nodded. "They're in my purse." She pointed to the

leather bag sitting in her lap, which she'd snagged on her way out the door.

"Awesome, then let's go." He pressed the button overhead to open the garage door, then the button on the dash to start the car. It rumbled to life. "Everyone buckled?"

A chorus of grumbling assent came from the back seat.

Finn chuckled. "None of you are morning people, are you?"

"No." Kennedy leaned her head against the seat. "Especially not on the weekends."

"Not ever," Pax muttered.

"Hopefully, we can make this brief, and you can go back to sleep or just chill soon enough." He backed out of the garage, then turned to Kennedy, pausing at the end of the drive. "Which way?"

"Oh. Um, go left." She pointed out his window.

He backed onto the street, then set off down the road. Kennedy fed him directions to Betty Ruth's petite, but well-kept house that was about ten minutes away. When he turned into her driveway, there were no signs of life, but that didn't alarm Kennedy. The older woman parked in her garage.

Finn put the car in park. "Try calling her again."

Kennedy unlocked her phone and did as he asked. It still rolled to voicemail. She lowered the device, shaking her head. "Nothing."

His mouth flattened into a thin line. "Do you have a key to get inside?"

She nodded.

"Okay. Let's go knock first. If we don't get an answer at either door, I'll have you let us in."

"Do you think she's okay, Mom?" From the back seat, Paige's voice held a note of worry.

Kennedy glanced at her daughter. "I'm sure she's fine.

She's probably just sleeping still. Maybe she put her phone on silent."

The girl nodded, but Kennedy could tell she wasn't entirely convinced. She wasn't sure she believed her own words, but she had to hope.

Finn held out a hand to Kennedy. "Give me your keys."

She dug into her purse and produced them, dropping them into his palm with a clink. He curled his fingers around them and looked at the twins.

"You two stay here. No matter what happens, you don't get out of the car unless you'll die if you stay in it."

"Finn!" Kennedy's eyes widened with shock.

He spared her a glance. "I'm serious. Herrera doesn't play." He turned his attention to the twins. "If anything happens, you have your phones, right?"

They nodded, silent.

"Call for help." He took the key fob for the car off the ring and passed it to Paxton. "If you have to, drive away."

The boy swallowed hard, but took the fob. His eyes flicked to Kennedy. "Be careful."

"We will. And I think we'll be fine." She turned hard eyes on Finn, telegraphing that she thought he was being a little overzealous.

"Most likely, nothing will happen, but I believe in being prepared." He reached for his door handle. "Lock the doors behind us. Don't let anyone in except us."

Kennedy gave the kids another long look before climbing out. She shut the door and met Finn around front. "Did you have to scare them?"

"They need to recognize the danger. I meant what I said; Herrera doesn't play."

"I understand that, but geez." The harsh reality of their situation had never been clearer. She didn't like it. "Let's get this over with."

He gestured for her to proceed him. "By all means."

Kennedy walked up to the front door, glancing around as she went, nervous now. Nothing appeared out of the ordinary. The birds still chirped. A light wind still blew, ruffling the leaves and her hair. The rising sun warmed the world around them. It felt like a normal mid-May morning.

She ascended the steps and pressed the doorbell. It chimed in the house. Kennedy wished Betty Ruth's door had textured glass around it like hers, so she could see if the woman was coming. The heavy wood muffled any sound from the other side. She only heard the doorbell because it was loud.

After thirty seconds and no answer, apprehension skated up her spine. She glanced at Finn. A frown turned his mouth down.

"Try again."

Reaching out, she pressed the button once more. It pealed inside. Again, there was no answer. She banged on the door. "Betty Ruth?"

Finn walked into the chest-high bushes in front of the windows and cupped his hands on the glass. Leaning his face into the circle he created, he peered inside through the blinds.

"Do you see anything?" She came down from the stairs to stand closer.

He stepped back and shook his head as he turned. "No. Let's go around back."

Biting her lower lip, Kennedy glanced at the house, then the car. She could see the twins peering between the seats, watching. It was their attention that had her schooling her features and hurrying after Finn. She didn't want them to sense her worry.

Dew coated her shoes as she walked through the grass at the side of the house. They emerged into the backyard. Kennedy paused, eyebrows drawing together. The back door was open.

Finn held out his left hand, his right going to the gun at his waist. "Stay behind me."

That would not be a problem. She moved closer, hovering as close as she dared. He stepped into the house.

"Betty Ruth? My name's Finn. I'm here with Kennedy. Are you here?"

Silence met them. Finn glanced back. "Call out to her."

She didn't hesitate, knowing her friend would be more likely to respond to a familiar voice if she was scared. "Betty Ruth? If you're here, please respond." She peered around Finn's shoulder. The dining table loomed in front of them. He cleared the doorway from the mudroom. Kennedy turned her head to the right. The living room beyond was also empty.

Coming around the peninsula that separated the dining area from the kitchen, Finn sucked in a harsh breath. Kennedy turned to look at what caused his reaction. A scream built in her throat, getting stuck.

Betty Ruth lay, unmoving, on the kitchen floor in a pool of blood.

## TWENTY

Finn drew his gun, his gaze moving to the short hallway to his left. "Go to her. I'm going to check the other rooms quick. Call for help." With long strides, he moved to the hall.

This part of the house was like spokes on a wheel. Three doors fanned out from a short central hallway. In front of him, the bathroom door stood open. It was a small room with a glass-enclosed shower. No one could hide in there. He gave the door a push, and it hit the wall with no resistance.

Behind him, he could hear Kennedy on the phone, getting help. He tuned her out and glanced to his right. That room was a small office. Again, there was nowhere to hide except behind the door or in the closet. Finn pushed the door into the wall and moved inside to open the closet. It was full of cleaning supplies. Turning, he walked out and across the hall to the bedroom, quickly sweeping the room and finding no one.

He holstered his weapon and hurried back to the kitchen to help Kennedy.

"Is she alive?"

Kennedy had rolled the woman to her side and pressed a

towel to her back. She looked up, tears trailing silently down her cheeks. "Barely. She's been stabbed in the back."

Finn tamped down his rising anger. What was the point of harming Betty Ruth? Did Herrera hope Kennedy would pull herself off Gonzales' case? He'd just get reassigned to another judge. Was his plan to take out every member of the district court in Asheville?

He knelt beside her. "What can I do?"

"Find me some more towels. She's still losing blood. Somehow." Her gaze dropped to the floor and the puddle beneath Betty Ruth.

"I'll see what I can find." Finn got up and dashed to the bathroom. Behind the door was a linen cabinet. Inside, he found stacks of clean towels and grabbed several of the hand towels. They would be easier to wad up than the larger bath towels.

"Here." He returned to Kennedy's side and passed her a fresh towel.

She tossed the soiled one aside and pressed the clean one to Betty Ruth's back. "Where's the ambulance?"

"It should be here soon." The words were barely out of his mouth when the first wail of a siren in the distance reached them.

"Do you want to go direct them in and tell the kids what happened?"

"No. I don't want them to see me come out with blood all over me. You go."

Finn's gaze roved over her. He hadn't paid much attention to how she looked when he knelt next to her, but she had more than a little of Betty Ruth's blood on her shirt. She must have leaned into her to turn her over.

"Okay. I'll be right back. Yell, if you need help. I'll leave the front door open."

She nodded, and he got up and ran out of the house.

Clearing the porch steps, he jogged out to the car. Pax reached over the seat and unlocked the doors as he neared. Finn yanked on the handle and opened the door.

"What happened?" Paige demanded. "I hear sirens."

"Betty Ruth is hurt."

She gasped and reached for her door handle.

"No, stay put." Finn held up a hand.

"What? Why? I want to help."

"I realize that, honey, but it's a crime scene. You have to stay in the car."

"Crime scene?" Paxton pierced him with a look. "You said she was hurt. Someone did that? She didn't fall or something?"

"She's been stabbed." Kennedy would curse him for his bluntness, but he figured they'd find out the truth soon enough, anyway. "Your mom is keeping pressure on the wound." The sirens grew louder. It was a police car, not an ambulance. "I need to go greet the responding police officer and brief him on what happened." He took a step back. "Stay in the car." Slamming the door shut, he ran to the end of the driveway just as the police car pulled up to the curb and killed his siren. In the distance, Finn could hear another. He hoped that was the ambulance. Betty Ruth needed a hospital.

Finn took his badge from his belt and held it up as he approached. The officer opened his door and got out, his wary gaze locked on Finn.

"Finley Porter, ATF."

The man tipped his head. "Jeremiah Cassidy, Asheville PD. Why are you at a stabbing call?"

"The victim is related to a case I'm working. I've secured the scene. Whoever did it is long gone. My friend is inside, tending to the victim."

"Friend?" The officer closed his door and followed Finn toward the house.

"Long story short, I'm protecting a federal judge and her family. The victim is her housekeeper."

"Why would someone target the judge's housekeeper?"

"Because he's a sick son-of-a-bitch." They passed Kennedy's car and the twins and entered the house.

Kennedy looked up as they stopped in the entrance to the kitchen. The officer cursed.

"You're not the paramedics." She glared up at him.

"They're coming," Finn said.

Officer Cassidy glanced at him. "I'll go set up a perimeter and get a crime scene unit on the way. Flag down that ambulance." With one last look at the scene on the floor, he turned and hurried out of the house.

Finn crouched next to Kennedy. "How's she doing?" The woman was gray; her breathing shallow.

"Not good. Her pulse is weakening. She needs blood."

Sirens screamed closer. Finn peered around the wall, looking outside. The ambulance turned into the drive, stopping behind Kennedy's car. "They're here."

"Thank God." A fine tremor ran through her voice. "Are the kids okay?"

"Scared, but otherwise, they're fine."

She closed her eyes. "Maybe I should send them back to Richmond for a while. They can stay with their dad."

"I wouldn't. There's no guarantee the threat won't follow them. Then they'll be without protection. Or adult supervision from the way you three have talked." No, Finn wanted them all right here, where he could keep an eye on them.

A grunt of frustration escaped her. "Dammit."

Commotion at the front of the house drew their attention. Two paramedics, pushing a gurney laden down with bags of gear, mounted the steps and came inside.

The older of the two men crouched beside Kennedy. "What have we got?"

"Her name's Betty Ruth. She was stabbed in the back. I don't know how long she's been like this. We came to check on her when I couldn't get her on the phone." She moved to the side, relinquishing her duties to the professionals.

The man lifted the towel away to get a look at her wound. "How old is she?"

"Fifty-seven." She got to her feet and stepped back, so the other medic had room to work.

Finn laid a hand on her back while they watched, offering her some silent support. In minutes, the medical team had started fluids and lifted Betty Ruth onto the stretcher.

As they gathered their gear, the first medic handed Kennedy a wad of wipes. "For your hands." He offered her an understanding smile.

She sniffed and nodded, taking them. "Thank you."

"What hospital are you going to?" Finn asked.

He named the major medical center downtown.

"Okay. Tell the medical staff we'll be there as soon as we can. Kennedy?" He looked at her. "You're her next-of-kin, right?"

She nodded, wiping at her fingers. "We're all she has."

"I'll let them know." The medic gave a short nod, then looked at his partner and tipped his head toward the door. "Let's go." They whisked her out the door, taking the chaos with them.

Kennedy sagged against him, her face crumpling. Finn folded her into his arms, but she immediately pushed away.

"No. I can't break down. Not yet." Face turning to steel, she followed the ambulance crew outside. "Who do we need to talk to so we can leave?"

Both rear passenger doors on her car opened, and the twins got out.

"Mom!" Paige ran toward her, stopping as she saw the blood. "Oh my God!"

"Is Betty Ruth okay?" Paxton's voice was much more subdued, but no less worried.

"No." Kennedy's voice came out as a harsh whisper. Finn laid a hand over her shoulder and squeezed. She inhaled a deep breath. "But hopefully she will be." She glanced at Finn. "Where's the cop?"

He removed his hand, looking around. "I'll find him. Hang tight." He jogged toward the street and the cop car parked there with one goal in mind—get someone to take their statements, then get Kennedy and the kids to the hospital so they could be with Betty Ruth.

# Twenty-One

Keys jangling, Finn unlocked the interior garage door. Kennedy stood behind him, waiting silently, swaying under the weight of her exhaustion. She felt like she'd run a marathon, but she hadn't run a step. The ups and downs of multiple adrenaline rushes today left her utterly depleted. The medical team lost Betty Ruth shortly after she arrived, but managed to bring her back. It was still touch and go, but they said if she made it through the night, her chances were decent. She'd lost an enormous amount of blood from the puncture to the rear of her left lung. From what they could figure, she'd laid on the kitchen floor for a couple of hours before Finn and Kennedy arrived. Why she was there and not in her bedroom, they didn't know yet. The police were hoping she'd be able to shed more light on what happened when she woke up.

The door swung in, admitting them to the house. The kids immediately went upstairs, needing to decompress in their own ways.

"I need to call my boss and give him an update." Finn turned a gentle gaze on her. "Though I can do that later if you want me to stay with you for now."

She shook her head. Time alone sounded nice. She'd yet to truly process things. And she probably wouldn't until a little later when she went to bed. But some silence would be nice. "I'll be fine. Go do what you need to." He'd called his boss while they were at the hospital to let him know he'd been involved in an incident. She was sure the man wanted more information. She hoped he and Finn convinced the Marshals they needed to put the security details back on the judges and their families.

With a kind smile, Finn retreated to her office.

Kennedy wandered into the living room, not ready to go upstairs just yet. Exhausted, she flopped onto the couch with a groan. Her body went boneless as the soft cushions cradled her. She never should have sat down. Now she wouldn't want to get up and go to bed. Perhaps she'd just sleep here tonight.

Her phone rang, the sound muffled by the couch. Lifting her hip, she dug it from the pocket on the side of her thigh and looked at the screen. A different sort of groan spilled from her lips. It was her mom.

For half a second, she debated not answering, but experience told her Margaret Parsons Davidson Jewell would just keep calling. Kennedy slid her thumb over the screen and lifted the phone to her ear. "Hi, Mom."

"Hi, honey." A short pause came over the line. "You sound tired."

"I am. It's been a long day."

"What did you do? It's only eight o'clock."

"I know." Again, she debated not answering, but her mother was nothing if not resourceful. She'd find out what happened one way or another, then lambast Kennedy for not saying something. "Betty Ruth was attacked. We found her in her kitchen this morning, unconscious from blood loss."

Margaret gasped. "Oh my goodness!"

"She'll be okay." She hoped. "But it will take some time for her to recover." It would for Kennedy too. Seeing her friend lying there in a pool of her own blood had shaken her to her core.

"What happened?"

"Someone broke into her house and stabbed her." Tears pressed against her eyes. She blinked furiously. She would not cry. Not while talking to her mom on the phone.

"Oh my. I thought her neighborhood was safe? You told me she found a nice little house close to yours."

Pulling in a shaky breath, she answered. "It is safe. There were extenuating circumstances."

"Oh, don't use that lawyer speak with me, Kennedy Marie. What really happened?"

Kennedy's spine straightened. That voice still had the power to make her sit up and take notice. Margaret might fret about things, and seem like a bit of a basket case at times, but she was still a woman to be reckoned with. Margaret could be a pitbull. She'd get to the truth.

"There's been some trouble at my new job. A high-profile case is causing some issues for the judges and their families. We didn't think it would extend to Betty Ruth, so she wasn't under any sort of protection."

Loud silence met Kennedy's words.

"Does that mean you are?" Margaret's voice was hard.

Kennedy winced. Dammit. She'd wanted to avoid telling her mother about the situation. Not only would she worry, she'd turn mama bear and insert herself into things. "Everything is fine. The kids and I have security."

"Does your brother know about this?"

No, but he would soon enough. She couldn't hide Betty Ruth's attack from him. "Not yet. I'll talk to him soon."

"Good. Maybe you can do it tomorrow evening over a family dinner. I should be there in time for that."

Kennedy sat up, fatigue forgotten. "What? There's no need for you to come here, Mom. All is well, I promise."

Margaret snorted. "Sure it is. That's why your housekeeper is in the hospital. I'll be there tomorrow evening. Tim's been wanting to check out the Biltmore House, anyway."

Biting back a groan, Kennedy closed her eyes and pressed her fingers to the space between her eyebrows. She did not want her mother and her new boy-toy hanging around. "Mom, no. You need to stay away. If you come down here, it will just put you in danger. Finn can only protect so many people."

"Finn? Is that your security guard?"

"He's not a security guard. He's an ATF agent."

"Don't the Marshals protect the judges?"

Shit. Leave it to her mother to remember that detail. "Yes, but the circumstances are unusual."

Margaret hummed. "We could stay with Ben, I suppose. That would lessen the appearance that I'm there to see you."

Kennedy rolled her lips inward. Ben would kill her if Mom showed up out of the blue. "That's probably not the best idea, either. He's involved in this case as well, so he has his hands full too."

A sharp gasp came over the line. "Is this about that Herrera character? I knew he was bad news. Why can't the two of you have normal jobs, like Howie?"

Sighing, Kennedy's head dropped at the mention of her other brother. Howie was a marketing executive, like their dad. This wasn't the first time their mother had laid into her and Ben for their career choices.

"I just don't understand what it is about law enforcement that appeals to you two." She made a disgusted sound. "All those criminals."

"Mom, law is a very respectable career choice. And I like being a judge."

"Yes, so you've said."

Kennedy ground her teeth together, refusing to get into an argument. It was pointless. Motion drew her eye, and she glanced over to see Finn come into the living room.

*Bless him.*

"Mom, I need to go. Do not come down here. Not until it's safe."

"Fine. Oh! I never got to tell you why I called."

Closing her eyes again, she propped an elbow on her knee and spanned the width of her forehead with her hand, rubbing her temples. "Can it wait? I really need to go."

"I just wanted to tell you that I heard through the grapevine Pete's getting married again."

Kennedy froze, then forced her muscles to relax. What Pete did now was none of her concern. But it could affect her children. She wasn't even aware he was dating anyone seriously. "Oh?"

"Yes. Some young woman from what Sharlene said. Not much older than the twins." Margaret snorted. "He probably got her pregnant too."

This time, Kennedy didn't hold back the groan. She couldn't deal with this right now. "Mom, I'll talk to you later. Love you." She pulled the phone away and hung up, even as her mother continued to talk. Letting out a frustrated growl, she threw her phone onto the coffee table and sat back, covering her face with her hands.

"Everything okay?" The couch dipped as Finn sat down beside her.

"No." She dropped her hands and looked at him. "Apparently, my ex is getting married. To a younger woman. Mom thinks she's pregnant. The twins do not need this right now." They already didn't have the best relationship with him. What would this do to what was left?

Finn put an arm around her shoulders and tipped her into

his chest. Kennedy stiffened for a brief moment, then wrapped her arms around his middle and let him hug her. She didn't care that she was flirting with danger. It felt nice. He was like an anchor in a raging storm.

"No, but I think they'll be fine. They're pretty resilient, I've noticed."

"Yeah. I just hate piling stuff on them, you know? They need to be kids. To have normal teenage worries. Not crap like this." She raised a hand, letting it flutter, before dropping it back to his waist.

"Things will calm down, eventually."

"I sure hope you're right. It would be nice to have a semi-normal life again. But in the meantime, I get to figure out how to tell them."

"Don't."

She glanced up. "What?"

"Let their dad tell them. It's his news. He can explain why he's marrying a younger woman. You shouldn't always have to be the bearer of bad news. Just be there to support them afterward."

Kennedy's brow furrowed, and she looked away. Was he right? Should she stay out of it? Maybe she should. Especially since she didn't know all the details. She should probably call Pete, though, regardless of whether she told the kids or not. What happened in his life affected the twins, so she needed to be aware of the details. And if she decided not to break the news, she needed to tell him that so he could.

"I guess that's something to think about." A yawn stretched her jaw. "Oh. But I'm too tired to worry about it right now." She laid her head against his shoulder, breathing in his scent clinging to his shirt. It wrapped her in a warm cocoon, much like his arms. Kennedy closed her eyes.

"It's a little early to go to bed yet. Do you want to play cards or something?"

His voice rumbled through his chest, vibrating her ear. It traveled down her spine, sending a shiver through her and eliminating some of her fatigue. Her body now wanted to play, but not cards. She sat up, pushing out of his arms before she did something dumb. Like kiss him. Despite the hum running through her—and the memory of their previous kiss—she didn't want to go down that road. Not when she was exhausted and emotional. The way he made her feel scared her when she was well-rested and hadn't been on an emotional rollercoaster. Right now, she knew she couldn't handle it. One touch, and she'd probably cave. As nice as the physical connection would be, she didn't think it would be wise to start something with him when she wasn't herself.

Clearing her throat, she pushed to her feet. "Actually, I think I'm going to head upstairs. A long soak in the tub sounds nice. I need to unwind."

"Oh." He rose to stand in front of her. "All right. Well, if you change your mind, come find me. I'll probably be up for a while."

Kennedy nodded, backing away. She knew running from her feelings was cowardly, but she just couldn't handle him—handle the way he made her feel—right now. "Okay. Have a good night."

"You too."

Spinning on her heel, she left the room, fleeing temptation. Why did he have to be so damn nice?

# TWENTY-TWO

The phone on Kennedy's desk rang, making her jump. She'd been engrossed in case notes, trying to get up to speed on the cases currently on her docket for the week, and had blocked everything else out. It was a trait that served her well all through college, but sometimes left her unaware of her surroundings.

Taking a breath to calm her racing heart, she lifted the receiver. "Yes?"

"Your brother is here to see you." Suzie's voice came over the line.

"Ben's here?" She frowned at the door. Why would Ben come see her at work? "Send him in." She hung up and waited. A moment later, he came through the door, closing it behind him.

Her frown deepened as she caught the look on his face. Ben was typically serious, but there was an edge to his features that she didn't normally see. "Is everything okay?" Her heart thumped as a thought hit her. "The twins—"

"Are fine." He held up a hand briefly, then sat down. "We need to talk."

"About what?"

"Gonzales."

"I can't talk about him, you know that." She didn't even want to think about him. He needed to stay out of her mind so she could stay impartial.

"It's more the chaos his testimony has wrought. Someone tried to run Gemma off the road this morning."

Kennedy gasped. "What? Oh my gosh, is she okay?"

He nodded. "She did some fancy driving and got behind him, then turned and managed to lose the car. She called me from Meredith's babysitter's place."

Another gasp escaped her. "She had the baby in the car? Oh, man. This is getting ridiculous."

"I agree, which is why I'm here. I just got out of a meeting with Marshal Paulson and her boss. With Betty Ruth's attack and now the attempt on my family, they're putting security details back in place. Gemma got the car's license plate, which came back to a known associate of both Herrera and Gonzales. It gave them the proof they needed that the threat wasn't gone. I hand-delivered the info and made sure they acted on it. It's harder to say no to someone in person." A mirthless smile stretched over his face, then disappeared.

Kennedy's mouth flattened. She wasn't sure how she felt about the Marshals coming back. It meant Finn didn't need to watch over them anymore. As much as he unnerved her, she felt safer with him in the house.

"You should get a call soon, probably from Paulson, to let you know and to give you details. I also wanted to tell you that Gemma and I have decided to take a short vacation." His features tightened.

"You don't look too happy about that."

He shrugged. "Honestly, I'd rather stay and help the feds stop this nonsense, but this morning's events really freaked

Gemma out. She wants to leave, so we're going. Hopefully, the task force will make some headway while we're gone, because we can't stay away indefinitely."

Kennedy gave her brother a wide-eyed stare. It surprised her that Gemma would want to leave town. She remembered him telling her how she refused to leave when the serial killer threatened her. "Wow. I figured she'd accept protection before she'd leave town."

"If we didn't have Meri, I think she'd stay."

"What about the others involved in this? Piper and Cullen? And Carter? Tristan and Jake were involved too."

"My whole department was to some extent, but I'm a bigger target because I'm the boss. The guard never came off of Piper and Cullen. Carter has Maverick as an early warning system, and there's been no indication of anyone coming after Tristan or Jake and their families."

"Yeah, well, I never thought anyone would go after Betty Ruth, but—" she broke off, blinking hard.

"How's she doing?" His voice softened.

"Better. I called the hospital this morning for an update before I came in. They were still keeping her in the induced coma to give her left lung more time to heal, but she's stable. It'll be another couple of days before they wake her up, I think." The knife wound penetrated Betty Ruth's lung, nicking a smaller artery that fed the upper lobe. They'd repaired it surgically and replaced the blood she lost, but she needed time to heal. The coma and ventilator helped her body not have to work so hard. "And I meant what I said. I never thought they'd go after her. Tell the others—especially Tristan and Laurel—to be careful."

He gave a short nod. "I will. How are the kids handling things?"

Kennedy lifted one shoulder. "Better than I expected.

They were shaken up after Betty Ruth was attacked, but having Finn around helped. He makes them—makes us all—feel safer."

Ben tipped his head, studying her. "He sure jumped at the chance to help you."

Fighting the blush that wanted to erupt, she shook a finger at him. "Don't even start with me."

"Start what?" One corner of his mouth tipped up, and a teasing glint entered his eyes.

"Really?" She rolled her eyes. "I know where you were going with that statement. Nothing is going on with me and Finn."

He scoffed. "Liar."

Kennedy glared, making him chuckle.

"I saw the way you two looked at each other that weekend on the river. Take it from someone who fought that fight and lost—" He paused, tipping his head side to side. "Or maybe won is a better word. Anyway, it's not worth the mental effort to resist. The reward is so high it dwarfs any reasons you might have for keeping him at arm's length." His expression sobered. "He's not Pete, Ken. Not even close."

Kennedy blew out a breath, ruffling her bangs. "I know that. But I also know my life is in chaos right now—on more than one front. Adding a relationship to the mix would just be too much."

Ben hummed. "Maybe. Or he could be what you need to help you through the chaos. A bastion in the storm, so to speak."

The memory of feeling like Finn was an anchor in the storm hit her. She'd concede Ben could be right, but she wasn't ready to delve into those thoughts at the moment. Not at work.

The consternation brought on by her thoughts must have

been evident on her face. Ben held up a hand. "I get that there's more going on than I know, and I won't pretend to know how you feel, either. Just consider what I said. He could be what you—and the twins—need. Hell, you could be what he needs."

She frowned. "He needs something?"

Ben shrugged and stood. "Maybe. I know he's alone here. His family is in Florida, and I've never heard him talk about a woman. Why do you think I invited him to the cabin with us?"

Kennedy narrowed her eyes. "Are you seriously trying to set me up?"

"Well, I wasn't then. I just wanted to foster a friendship with him. He's a pretty nice guy. Maybe I'm just more insightful than I thought."

She rolled her eyes, but a smile played with her mouth. "Take your ego and get out of my office. I have work to do."

With a chuckle, he headed for the door. Hand on the knob, he paused, his expression sobering. "Be careful, Kennedy. Let Finn and Paulson and whoever else is assigned to you do their jobs."

Her amusement faded at the reminder. She nodded. "I will. Be safe. And stay in contact. I want to know you're still alive."

"That goes both ways." His smile returned. "You can keep me posted on how things go with you and Finn."

"Oh, shoo." She waved him out.

Laughing, he left.

Kennedy blew out another breath, ruffling her hair again. She shook her head and glanced down at the papers on her desk. Words swam in front of her. "Dammit." He'd obliterated her focus with his theories. Now all she could focus on was Finn's handsome face and the way he made her feel.

Her computer dinged, and she shook the mouse to wake it up. An appointment reminder popped up in the corner. It was time for her next court session. Rising from her seat, she closed the folder, then gathered her things. Catch-up work and thoughts of Finn would have to wait.

# TWENTY-THREE

Finn drummed his fingers on the steering wheel as he stared out the windshield at the twins' school. He didn't like this setup for pickup, but short of going inside and getting them before people started arriving to get their kids—or making them stay late—he couldn't do anything about it. They'd been adamant they didn't want to be treated differently. He couldn't blame them. It was hard enough being the new kid. There'd been no attempts at shooting anyone, which was the only reason he agreed to keeping things normal. Everything had been up close and personal. Herrera's goons liked to get their hands dirty.

The bell rang. Seconds later, the front doors opened and students poured out, peeling off in a multitude of directions as they headed for vehicles. Finn surveyed the crowd, keeping one eye out for the twins. They knew to look for his car, so hopefully, this would go smoothly.

He spotted Paige first. In white jeans with several stylish holes and a black, cropped, rock band t-shirt over a neon green tank top, she stood by herself as she studied the line of cars. He crept forward, waiting for her to notice him. Paxton walked up beside her and said something. The breeze ruffled his dark hair and billowed his plain blue t-shirt out behind him. Together, they scanned the car line.

Getting closer, Finn lowered the passenger side window and let out a sharp whistle. Several heads turned, including theirs. He waved, and they walked toward him.

"Hey." He offered them both a smile as they piled into the back. "How was your day?"

Pax raised a shoulder. "Normal."

"People suck." Paige glared.

Finn's eyebrows winged upward. "Uh-oh. What happened?" His brows dropped. "That kid who called you names wasn't at it again, was he?"

She pressed her lips together and shook her head. "No. The Marshals are back."

"And? You guys knew this. Your mom told you."

"Yeah, but no one else knew. Why is this happening?" Her wail filled the car, and she threw herself back against the seat.

The vehicle behind them honked. Finn ground his molars. "Hold up a second." He maneuvered the car forward, turning into the parking lot and pulling into a space. Once they were out of traffic, he turned around to face the twins.

"Okay, explain, please. Why are you so upset about having the Marshals around again? You didn't have a problem with it the last time."

She rolled her eyes and crossed her arms, letting out a huff. "Because no one knew. But now, people know and think we're like the mafia or something." She gestured to her brother, then herself.

"The mafia?" Finn held up a hand, thoroughly confused. "All right. Start at the beginning. How do people know about the Marshals, and what's been said?"

"I was in science class when Mr. Fulmer sent Alyssa Cavanaugh to the office to get a stack of papers he forgot. She came back a few minutes later, and when she sat down, she started whispering to her table partner, and they were looking at me with weird looks. I was like, well, that's weird, but I'm the new kid and she's a bitch, so I ignored her. Then I got to art—which she also has—and the whispers started all over with a different group. We've got more freedom in that class, and the next thing I know, she's pulling up a stool next to mine and asking me what Pax and I did to bring the U.S. Marshals to the school. Did we sell drugs for the mafia? Was my dad a hitman for them, and were we in witness protection, and that's why we moved here at the end of the school year? Had I ever seen a dead body?" She rolled her eyes. "Who asks that kind of crap?"

Finn let out a soft grunt, agreeing. That girl sounded like a piece of work. "What did you say to her?"

"I asked her what the hell she was talking about and why she'd think any of that. She said when she went to get the papers, there was a U.S. Marshal in the office, asking to speak to the principal regarding us." She gestured between herself and Paxton again. "I told her it had to do with my mom's work. She, of course, then thought it was Mom who was the hitman for the mafia." She paused and huffed again. "I didn't bother to correct her. She'll just believe whatever she wants, anyway."

Taking a deep breath, Finn glanced out the windshield, mind working. He didn't want there to be rumors floating around the school about the twins, but telling everyone the truth could do more harm than good. He looked at Paige. "You did the right thing, keeping the truth to yourself. It could put other kids in danger or even ostracize you more. There are only what, two weeks left in the school year?"

Paige nodded.

"Just do your best to ignore Alyssa and anyone like her. This will all blow over, and you two can start next school year on better footing." He glanced at Paxton. "Has anyone said anything to you?"

He shook his head. "No. I had a normal day. It'll probably be different tomorrow."

Oh, Finn had no doubt. Word would get around, and the story would get blown out of proportion. By the end of the day, Paige and Pax would be the children of some fictitious mafia don, who were on the run from their dastardly father. Or Kennedy would be turned into some sort of Mata Hari, now in hiding after killing the wrong lover. Kids had wild imaginations.

"Can we get ice cream? I need some chocolate goodness in my life," Paige muttered.

A smile tweaked Finn's mouth. "Sure. Just don't tell your mom I fed you ice cream before dinner."

"Mum's the word." Pax mimed locking his lips.

"Good. I don't want to get in trouble any more than either of you."

"Oh, whatever, man." Pax rolled his eyes. "She likes you."

Surprise widened Finn's eyes for a brief moment before he schooled his features. He hadn't thought the twins had paid much attention to his relationship with their mom. "You think?"

"Duh." Paige pinned him with a stare. "She gets all googly-eyed around you and watches you when she thinks no one is looking."

Finn cleared his throat. That was—interesting. "What do you two think of that? Would you be okay with your mom dating?" He fought to keep his breathing steady, when what he really wanted to do was hold it while he waited for their answer.

The twins looked at each other, something passing between them. It felt like they had an entire conversation, but didn't say a word.

They turned to him, nodding.

"If it's you, yeah," Paige said.

"Yeah. You're cool." Paxton's voice was quiet and thoughtful. "You listen to her. And to us. Dad doesn't. He acts like he does, but it goes in one ear and out the other."

Paige nodded. "I know she's kinda focused on us and her new job right now, but I wouldn't mind if you stuck around."

"Me, either." Paxton echoed his sister's idea, holding Finn's gaze.

A heaviness settled over Finn, but it wasn't a burden. It was more like a mantle of responsibility; one he wanted. This little family had burst into his life, and now he couldn't imagine what it would be like without them. He didn't want to go back to his solitary existence. He wanted to entwine his life further with theirs.

"Good to know. Let's go get ice cream." With a nod, he turned around. Now, he just had to convince their mom that merging their lives was a good idea.

# TWENTY-FOUR

Raucous laughter greeted Kennedy the moment she stepped in the door. A curious smile broke out on her face, and she followed the sound to the living room. Stopping in the doorway, her smile broadened. Twisted into a heap were Finn and the kids. They were playing Twister.

Paige spotted her first. "Mom! Spin the dial, would you? Finn can't reach it anymore." She giggled.

Kennedy's gaze flicked to Finn, who was twisted like a pretzel.

"Hurry, please? Before I get stuck like this." He looked at her, upside down from under his arm.

Laughing, she set her briefcase and suit jacket on the couch and walked over to the spinner, picking it up from its spot on the floor. "Whose turn is it?"

"Mine," Pax said.

Kennedy flicked the arrow and watched it spin. "Left leg, green." She glanced up.

Pax shifted his weight. His left leg was tucked beneath him on yellow. His right foot was under Finn on blue, and he had a hand each on yellow and green. Slowly, he wiggled his foot to the side, widening his stance. "Okay, I'm good."

She flicked the spinner again. "Right leg, blue."

"Really?" Paige groaned. Her right leg was currently on green. Blue was behind her. Balancing on her hands, she swept her leg back, touching a blue circle with her toes. "All right. Phew! That wasn't as hard as I thought."

With a smile, Kennedy spun the dial again. She glanced at Finn as it stopped, rolling her lips in to stop the laugh that wanted to break free. There was no way he could do this one.

"What?" He groaned. "I'm about to fall on my face, aren't I?"

She laughed. He currently had a foot on red, another on blue, his left hand between his legs on blue, and his right on green. "Probably. Left hand, red."

He stretched. "I am not this flexible." His fingers skimmed the circle. "Close enough. Spin it again."

Kennedy hurried through two more spins, twisting up Pax and unwinding Paige. She spun once more for Finn and gasped. "Left leg, green."

"Nope. No way." Grumbling, he wiggled his sock-covered foot over the board.

Paige laughed, watching him. Kennedy covered her mouth, holding back a serious case of the giggles. He made it halfway before his arms hit the junction of his pelvis and he toppled onto his butt.

Laughing, he rolled and bounced to his feet. "Man, that's a workout." Sweat beaded on his temples, and he lifted the hem of his t-shirt to wipe it away.

Kennedy's smile faded, and she nearly swallowed her tongue at the sight of his perfectly toned abs. The tanned skin and the dusting of dark hair set them off to perfection.

"Mom! Spin the dial!" Paxton's voice cut through the lust that had invaded her brain.

"Right." She looked down and flicked the arrow. "Right hand, blue."

"Oh, man." Pax studied the board. Paige was in his way. He lifted his right hand off the green circle and raised it over her back. When he rocked back to clear her body, he lost his balance and crashed to the floor.

Paige let out a whoop and stood. "I won! Yes!" She pumped her fist. "Gymnastics was good for something."

Kennedy laughed. "I'm glad I dumped all that money into the sport over the years so you could be good at Twister." She set the spinner on the end table next to the couch. "Come on. Let's go eat dinner."

"Oh, yeah. I'm starving." Pax hopped to his feet. "What are we having?"

Kennedy threw her hands into the air as she turned and headed for the kitchen. "No clue. Let's see what we can come up with." Betty Ruth usually took care of supper during the week. She hadn't said anything to Finn about it—not that she expected him to cook for them. "I think there's some bacon in the fridge. How about pancakes?"

"Breakfast for dinner sounds good." Paige headed for the refrigerator. Finn stepped up behind her and took the eggs, bacon, and milk from her as she spun around.

"You and Pax go clean up the Twister board, then set the table. Your mom and I will work on the food."

"Oh. Cool." She relinquished her hold and scampered away, Paxton on her heels.

Kennedy smiled at him as he came up beside her. "They're in a good mood." She opened the cabinet and took down a mixing bowl and her measuring cups.

"Now, yeah. Paige was ticked when I picked them up from school. Word got out they have the Marshals as shadows. Now speculation's running rampant. You're a mafia hitman, by the way."

Sputtering a laugh, she stared at him with wide eyes, then shook her head. "Kids sure have some imagination."

He chuckled. "That they do. Anyway, I sugared them up with ice cream, then helped them burn it off with games. We played cornhole outside for a bit, but it got too hot, so we came in, got a drink, then broke out the Twister board. The exercise helped her tremendously."

"That's great. I'm not even mad you gave them sweets before dinner." She reached for the flour canister, removing the lid.

He grinned. "Good. It won't be the last time it happens."

Warmth filled Kennedy's belly. She liked the impression he gave that he'd be around a while. It wouldn't help keep her life uncomplicated, but the woman in her sure did like it. "Keep it up and they won't want you to leave." She scooped a cup of flour into her mixing bowl.

He hummed. "What would it take for you to want me to stay?"

Kennedy's hands stilled on the bowl. She blinked twice, then looked up, a question in her eyes.

"I've been doing some thinking." His serious gray eyes met hers, and her heart skipped a beat. "We never talked about that kiss we shared, or what it meant. I know what I want it to mean, though."

"Oh?" She reached up and tucked a strand of hair behind her ear, then nudged her glasses back up her nose as she turned her gaze to the bowl in front of her. "What's that?" She looked at him again.

"That it's the start of something. Look, I know you have a lot on your plate. I don't want to add to that. But honestly, I'm not sure I would. I want to help. To be here to shoulder some of the burden. Especially with Betty Ruth out of the picture for a while."

She frowned, remembering how they'd had a similar conversation at the start of the weekend.

He held up his hands, reading the look on her face. "I'm not trying to keep away any guilt I'd have if something happened and I wasn't around. This is purely me—the man—wanting to be around a woman I find intriguing and kind and beautiful. And a great mom with a couple of amazing kids."

Heat bloomed on her cheeks, warming her face. "Oh. Thank you."

*Wow.* Did she really just say that? Mentally, she rolled her eyes at herself. He had her flummoxed. Trying to steady her thoughts—and her nerves—she reached for the eggs he'd set on the counter and opened the carton. She cracked one into the bowl and tossed the shell in the sink, then reached for the milk and her liquid measuring cup.

What did one say to that? It demanded a better response than *thank you.*

A laugh at the absurdity of her lack of dating skills at thirty-eight bubbled up. She poured the milk into the mixing bowl and set the glass measuring cup down with a clink on the quartz counter, stepping back.

"What?" A confused tilt lifted one side of his mouth.

Kennedy waved a hand and shook her head as she laughed, unable to answer.

"Are you all right?"

She nodded and sucked a breath in through her nose, attempting to control herself. "Sorry." Another laugh escaped, and she waved her hand again. "Oh my goodness." She swiped at the tears flowing down her cheeks, drawing in a hiccupping breath.

He crossed his arms and leaned a hip against the counter, raising one eyebrow. "Laughter is always a good response when you tell a woman you like her."

More laughter spilled free, but it was short-lived. She'd

calmed down. "I wasn't laughing at that—at you. It was me. You said such nice things, and my response was thank you. Thank you!" She rolled her eyes. "I couldn't help but think I'm thirty-eight and don't know how this"—she motioned between them—"works. I haven't dated anyone since I was in my early twenties. It's not the same when you're nearly forty and have kids."

Finn chuckled. He let his arms fall and pushed away from the counter, coming closer. Kennedy glanced up as he loomed large in front of her. Her stomach flip-flopped, and her skin pricked, urging her to lean toward him. She planted her feet. They needed to finish this discussion first.

"I'm a little better about the dating, but I've never dated a woman with children. I think it will be a learning experience for both of us." He reached out and took her hands. "We don't need to define what this is today. Or even tomorrow. All I'm asking is you let me in."

Deep in the recesses of her mind, a door cracked. Light spilled through, illuminating a part of her heart she thought she'd buried with her divorce. Part of her still wanted to run from the feelings he evoked. To hide, where it was safe. But he made her smile. More importantly, he made her kids smile.

Standing taller, she pushed that door open a little wider. "Okay."

The dimples in his cheeks popped out with his bright smile. "Yeah?"

She answered his smile with one of her own. "Yeah." The control she'd been holding on to slipped, and she leaned closer.

Slowly, his smile dimmed, desire taking its place on his features. He tugged on her hands, drawing her into his body.

Teenage voices, arguing, pushed them apart a moment before the twins walked through the doorway, bickering.

"Stop being so dramatic. All I asked was for you to put the

couch back." Paige rolled her eyes, heading for the plate cupboard.

"I'm not being dramatic. You boss me around all the time." Paxton went to the silverware drawer and yanked it open. Flatware clinked.

"I wasn't bossing. I asked." She shot him a look.

Finn let out a sharp whistle, making them all jump, Kennedy included. She put a hand over her heart, steadying herself not just from that, but from the emotions running rampant through her system.

"Are you really arguing about furniture?" Finn's brows dipped as his gaze flicked between the teens.

Both kids stayed tight-lipped. Finn let out a huff and shook his head.

Kennedy chuckled, and he looked at her.

"What?"

Her smile bloomed. "Welcome to the Davidson-Cobb residence. You've officially been initiated now that you've witnessed your first pointless teenage argument."

"Hey." Paige tried to frown, but her mouth refused. It kicked up on one side and her eyes sparkled with amusement.

Paxton walked past with a handful of utensils. He patted Finn on the shoulder. "Mom's right. Welcome to the family." He looked at Kennedy. "Don't forget to add him to the chore chart." Grinning, he walked out.

Finn watched him go, then looked at Kennedy. "I don't care what they say; I'm not cleaning bathrooms."

Laughing, and delighted at the new energy he'd brought to the house, she spun around and picked up a whisk. "Don't worry. I'll do that one. You can clean the drains."

He wrinkled his nose. "Yum."

# TWENTY-FIVE

Feeling like she had an entourage, the soft thud of rubber-soled shoes accompanied the sharp staccato of Kennedy's heels as she walked down the corridor to the nurses' station from the elevator. Betty Ruth was awake. Her lungs had healed enough for the doctors to bring her out of her induced coma this morning. When Kennedy called for an update on her lunch break, the nursing staff said she was already sitting up and talking. She couldn't wait to see her.

"Hello." A blonde nurse looked up with a smile as Kennedy paused at the desk, one twin on either side of her. Finn and Taylor hung back, keeping an eye out.

"Hi. We're here to see Betty Ruth Roberts."

The woman looked past her, smile fading. "All of you? Ma'am, this is the ICU. Patients can only have two visitors at a time."

"They're only along for support." Kennedy motioned to Finn and Taylor. "Do you think you could make an exception, though, and let my kids come with me?" She motioned to the twins.

"Oh. Hmm." The nurse pressed her lips together, considering the request. "I suppose that would be all right. Do you know which room she's in?"

"Ten-twelve."

The woman nodded, then pointed to her left. "It's right down there."

"Great, thank you." She stepped back and turned. "Come on, kids." Paxton and Paige followed her the short distance to Betty Ruth's room. Kennedy rapped her knuckles on the door, then pushed it open.

"Betty Ruth?" She stepped inside, smiling as she saw her friend sitting up. The TV played across from her, but the sleepy look on her face told Kennedy she hadn't been watching it.

"Hi." Voice raspy, a tired smile formed on Betty Ruth's face.

Kennedy walked closer, trailed by the kids. She stopped next to the bed and studied the older woman. Her short salt-and-pepper hair stuck out in a multitude of directions. Dark circles colored the skin beneath her eyes, and a paleness wreathed her features. She looked much older than her fifty-seven years. Kennedy reached down and took her hand. "Hi, lady." Tears swam in her eyes.

Weakly, Betty Ruth squeezed her hand. "None of that. I'm fine."

"Bullshit. You almost died."

"But I didn't. Thanks to you and that agent friend of yours. The nurses told me the two of you found me." A single tear trickled from her eye. "Thank you." Her voice, already nearly a whisper, was now barely audible.

Kennedy sniffed and looked out the window, trying to hold on to her emotions.

Paige reached out and touched Betty Ruth's leg. "When can you come home? We miss you." Her voice wobbled.

Kennedy let go of Betty Ruth's hand to take Paige's. The girl gripped it tight.

"As soon as they'll let me bust out of here." She attempted to shift, but quickly gave up with a short huff. "I miss my bed. This thing is terrible."

"Can we help?" Paxton walked around to the other side and bit one corner of his mouth, studying the older woman.

"How about we call the nurses?" Kennedy picked up the call-button remote. "So we don't pull on something we shouldn't or hurt her because we did it wrong."

Betty Ruth waved a hand. "It can wait. They'll be in soon, anyway, to take my vitals. They come every hour."

"Oh. Are you sure?"

Closing her eyes, Betty Ruth nodded.

Kennedy set the remote down and glanced around again. "Have they given you any indication of when they'll let you go home?" Her gaze stopped on the floral arrangements on the stand in the far corner. "And who sent you black roses?" Those weren't there when she stopped in yesterday.

Paxton walked toward the bouquet. "Maybe there's a card."

"I don't know," Betty Ruth said. "I haven't paid much attention. Been too sleepy."

"Do you see a card, Pax?" Kennedy turned to her son.

He peered into the bouquet. "Yeah." With two fingers, he plucked the small envelope from between the blooms.

"Let me see it." She held out her hand, and he brought it to her. Lifting the flap and removing the card, her eyes widened as she read. *Isn't black lovely? It's a pity you didn't die, so Ms. Davidson could wear it in mourning. Guess I'll have to try again.*

She looked at Pax. "Go get Finn."

His brows dipped for a fraction of a second before alarm widened his eyes. Turning on his heel, he dashed out the door.

"What does it say, Mom?"

Kennedy could hear the worry in Paige's voice. She clutched the card close, so the girl couldn't see it. "Don't worry about it." Neither of the twins needed to know the message's particulars. It was enough they knew Betty Ruth received something threatening.

"Mom—" Paige didn't get anything else out before the door opened. Finn walked in, looking like some sort of warrior out for blood.

Kennedy held out the card, and he took it. "It was in the black roses." She pointed to the corner.

He glanced over, then read the card. A muscle ticked in his jaw. "Okay. You all stay here. I need to talk to Taylor." With a quick turn and two long strides, he was gone.

"That must have been some note," Betty Ruth said.

Kennedy turned around. "Um, yeah. But don't worry. Finn and Taylor will handle it."

"I'm not worried." Her fingers rose and fluttered before dropping back to the blanket. "Between him and the young man the nurses said has been walking the halls, I feel perfectly safe."

Arching an eyebrow, Kennedy nodded. She was glad someone did. Betty Ruth might feel differently once she read the card. Those words would be etched into Kennedy's memory for a long, long time. Pursing her lips, she glanced at the television. "So, what are you watching?"

"No clue. I asked the nurses to turn it on to drown out the noise from the hallway. I couldn't sleep."

"Oh. Do you want us to go, Betty Ruth? So you can get some rest?"

Betty Ruth's head rolled from side to side on her pillow. "No. I like the company."

"Okay, then. We might as well get comfortable." She

motioned for the twins to have a seat on the couch under the window. Kennedy sat down in the chair at the head of the bed.

"You all talk," Betty Ruth said, her voice growing quieter. "And don't mind me if I doze off. It's nice to hear your voices."

Kennedy looked at the twins. "Tell her about your week at school."

Pax and Paige shared a look, then Paige started talking.

Worry kept Kennedy's back straight. With half an ear, she listened to the kids talk, her thoughts on the note now with Finn. He and the Marshals needed to stop what was happening before someone died. She didn't want to give Herrera the satisfaction of him being the reason she wore black.

# TWENTY-SIX

inn's footsteps echoed softly off the hallway walls as he strode through Kennedy's house to answer the door. After the events at the hospital yesterday, the Marshals went into evidence-gathering mode. Taylor had taken the card and vanished, leaving him out of the loop. He'd called late last night for an update, but she stonewalled him, saying they were still investigating. This morning, after he dropped the twins off at school, he went to her office, but she wasn't there and wouldn't take his calls. So, he left a voicemail and told her he would descend on her office and stage a sit-in until she arrived if she didn't come talk to him this evening. He couldn't effectively protect this family if he didn't know what to expect.

Flicking open the locks, he grasped the knob, swinging the door inward.

"Good evening." Taylor smiled.

He stepped back so she could enter. "Hello." Closing the door behind her, he locked it. "Let's go to Kennedy's office." He held an arm out, gesturing toward the hallway, then led her down the corridor. Once inside and the door was shut, he stopped in the middle of the room and crossed his arms, feet planted, pinning her with a hard look.

"Oh, don't look at me like that."

"Why not? You cut me out of the investigation."

"Technically, I don't have to tell you anything. You're only part of this because you've inserted yourself into the situation."

He dropped his arms with a scoff. "Don't give me that. I'm still a part of the Vargas-Ruiz task force. Herrera might be in custody, but that doesn't mean the investigation is over."

"No, but my job is protecting Judge Davidson and her family and all the other judges and their families. My concern is not the cartel itself."

"Noted, but we still need to work together on this. I want these attacks stopped as much as you do. Now, tell me what you know, please."

She let out a long breath, then walked over to the couch and sat down. Finn followed her and sat on the other end.

"I took the note to our lab and had them run a quick analysis on it. They found prints, but most of them matched Kennedy. The others we're still working on. But I'm betting they'll come back as either not in the system or to the florist. The roses came from Bailey's Florist here in town. I woke up the owner early this morning to ask for details on the sender. She said a man came into her shop yesterday around lunchtime and asked for a rush delivery of the flowers to Ms. Roberts. He paid extra and in cash."

Finn blinked. "Seriously? Did she provide you with a name and a description?"

Taylor nodded. "Just a first name. Steve. Though I doubt that was his real name. She said he was white and unremarkable. She went through mug shots, but didn't find him, so tomorrow, she's going to sit with a sketch artist."

Finn frowned. "White?" He hadn't expected that. Not

when dealing with the cartel.

Again, Taylor's head bobbed an affirmative. "Threw me for a loop too. Most of Herrera's cronies are Hispanic. We're on it, though."

"Did she have security cameras at her shop?"

"No. We're checking the shops around hers, but she said he came in with a hat and sunglasses on, as well as gloves, so even if we catch him on film, I doubt we'll be able to see his face. The card, he already had in his possession, and he paid cash for the flowers."

Finn frowned. "He already had the card?"

She nodded. "And before you ask, I'm checking the visitor's logs at the prison to see if Herrera passed on the note. We're also checking phone logs."

He glanced away, processing that. It's exactly what he would have done. "What about the other judges? Have there been any threats to them or their families? Surely, Kennedy can't be the only one. I would think there would be more heat on Judge Stechschulte."

Again, Taylor nodded. "Her family's dog was poisoned the same day Betty Ruth was stabbed. We also have reports from several of the magistrates that they received courier letters yesterday with a picture of Betty Ruth lying on her kitchen floor. The note with the image said, 'Don't let this be you or someone you love.' The elderly father of one of the other magistrates had someone run him off the road the day after Betty Ruth's attack. Luckily, the guy is a retired police officer and still remembered all his defensive driving training. He steered the car to a stop before he hit the other side of the ditch and flipped."

"Christ." Needing to move, Finn stood and paced to the window, looking out at the backyard.

"We're doing all we can, Finn, short of moving everyone to a safe house. That's not practical, and not just because it would effectively shut down the federal court here. We're talking over two dozen people. I'm just glad they mostly live together. My boss has already had to call in marshals from other offices."

He ran a hand through his hair. "So what happens now? It could be another year before Herrera's trial actually starts."

"If we can prove he's directing things from jail, we can limit his contact with the outside world to just his attorney."

"What if it's the attorney playing middleman?"

"We're looking into that too. If we find evidence of that, we'll arrest him for conspiracy."

Finn narrowed his eyes, studying her. Something in her gaze told him they'd put the attorney under surveillance. He nodded once. "Good."

She stood. "Now you know what I know, so stop harping on me, okay?" A smile softened her words.

He forced his shoulders to relax. One side of his mouth tilted higher. "I'll try. Just don't shut me out. Now I'm glad Kennedy doesn't have a pet."

A soft chuckle escaped Taylor's lips. "Trust me, so am I. Other marshals are now having to walk dogs. The one that was poisoned ate meat thrown over the fence. I guess he'll be all right, but it means no more pets in the yards. And their owners can't walk them because of the threat."

Finn shook his head. This truly was a nightmare for the Marshals. "If there's anything I can do to help, don't hesitate to ask."

She started toward the door. "I won't. You being here helps tremendously. I wish all my protectees had their own agent living with them. It's meant fewer marshals here and allowed us to redirect resources. Trust me. I appreciate you thrusting yourself into my investigation."

He grinned. "Happy to help."

She eyed him as she opened the door. "I'm sure you are."

Finn felt his cheeks heat at her implication. He wouldn't deny it, though. He was here for Kennedy and the twins—not to help the U.S. Marshals. "Let me know if anything changes."

"I will." They stopped at the front door. Hand on the knob, she glanced at him. "Watch yourself. I don't know where they'll strike next."

He nodded.

She let herself out. Finn shut the door and locked it, feeling both better and worse now that he knew where the investigation stood. He liked having information, but they weren't nearly as close to stopping the threat as he'd hoped.

Soft footsteps alerted him to Kennedy's arrival. He turned, offering her a small smile. "Hey."

She stopped in front of him, arms crossed. "Hey, yourself."

"I suppose you want to know what she had to say?" He hooked a thumb toward the door.

Kennedy nodded.

"Not a whole lot, actually. They've identified the florist where the flowers came from. The owner remembers the purchase, but can't give many details. She said the guy was white, said his name was Steve, and paid in cash."

Kennedy wrinkled her nose and let her arms drop. "That's not vague at all."

"Right?" Finn blew out a breath and ran a hand through his hair. "Taylor doesn't think they'll get any prints off the card, either. The florist said he brought it with him and wore gloves."

"In May?"

"They probably looked like driving gloves, which aren't unusual any time of the year."

She huffed and glanced away. Finn could almost see the thoughts running through her head.

"So what now?" Her gaze met his again.

"We wait. And stay vigilant. Not much else we can do." And it chafed. He wasn't used to sitting back, doing nothing. Even for slow cases, there was always something to be done. This situation gave him a new respect for victims' families and what they went through, waiting for detectives to solve cases.

Her soft growl matched the anger now burning in her eyes. "I hate this."

Finn reached out and skimmed his hands over her biceps. "Me too, honey. I wish I could do more. But I don't have anything to act on."

Her shoulders slumped, and she nodded. "I know. I'm just frustrated. At least it's the weekend. That'll make things a little easier on you. No running around, shuttling us from one place to another."

"It's not a hardship." He shrugged. "We might find it tougher to just sit around all weekend."

She smiled. "You and I might. The kids will find things to keep them entertained."

One side of his mouth lifted. "No doubt." They were modern teens with access to electronics. They'd find something to do.

"Maybe I'll do some baking."

"Baking?"

She nodded. "I haven't had a good baking day in a while. Can we hit up a local produce stand tomorrow morning? If I can find some zucchini, I'll make some different kinds of bread. And cookies. Though those won't have the zucchini. I need something that's just straight decadence."

Finn chuckled. "Sure. I definitely won't stand in the way of baked goods." He tipped his head toward the living room. "Come on. How about we watch a movie? Something funny. I could go for some laughs."

She smiled and turned toward the living room. "Same, Agent."

# TWENTY-SEVEN

Black robe flowing around her, Kennedy walked out of the anteroom she used as a courtside judge's chamber and stepped up to the courtroom door. George, the court officer on duty, smiled.

"Good morning, ma'am. Are you ready?"

She nodded. "As I'll ever be. Let's go see what sort of trouble people have gotten into over the weekend." Hers had been blissfully uneventful, but she knew that wasn't the case for many people on the other side of that door.

With a chuckle, George opened the door and stepped through. She heard him call for everyone's attention. She followed, quickly crossing to the bench. Sitting down, she looked out over the gallery. "You may be seated."

The first several cases flew by; they were for bail for various offenses. A longer evidentiary hearing came up, then she went back to bail. She staved off a frown as defense attorney Eduardo Baez came forward. He was the same attorney representing Javier Gonzales. She glanced down at her schedule, not seeing Gonzales' name. When he presented his client, Santiago Jimenez, who was accused of laundering cartel money, she realized Baez was one of the cartel's preferred attorneys.

"Your Honor, my client is the only source of support for his family, and requests the court set bail at twenty-thousand dollars."

The door to Kennedy's left cracked open. She sent a side-eyed glance at it, wondering who would interrupt her court in the middle of a hearing. Her bailiff backed up to speak to whoever interrupted, and she turned her attention to Baez. "Mr. Baez, your client laundered drug money to the tune of over a million dollars. He also owns his own business, which will continue to operate without him, yes?"

Baez nodded.

The bailiff closed the door and stepped back to his spot. Kennedy's mouth edged downward at the fierce frown on his face. She'd find out why soon enough. Just as soon as she finished this hearing. "Then that request is denied. Bail is set at one million dollars." She banged her gavel.

The sound still echoed through the courtroom when the bailiff approached the bench. "Your Honor. Kennedy."

Kennedy's eyes widened at the use of her first name. "What is it, George?"

"Ma'am." He swallowed.

"Just spit it out." Her stomach clenched. Whatever he had to say, she wasn't going to like.

"Your children's school called. Paxton's been taken to the hospital. He collapsed at lunch."

She gasped. "What?"

"Agent Porter is waiting in your chambers to take you to him."

Kennedy glanced at the door to the left. "Okay. Can you contact Judge Stechschulte as well as Judge Smith and Suzie MacKinnon? They'll need to reschedule the rest of my docket."

He nodded. Kennedy banged her gavel again, getting everyone's attention. "Due to a family emergency, today's remaining court sessions will be rescheduled. Someone from my office will contact you." She banged the gavel again and stood. Her bailiff called a hasty "All rise," as she scampered down the steps from her bench and walked swiftly to the door on the left.

On the other side, she turned right, then a quick left into the small office used as the judge's chambers. Finn whirled from his place at the window. The bailiff with him started slightly at her abrupt appearance. She spared him a quick look before zeroing in on Finn. "What do you know? What happened?"

"I don't know much yet. Just that he collapsed. The school called your office, and Suzie called me. I came down here, then, to get you."

Kennedy unzipped her robe and wiggled out of it, tossing it onto the coat rack in the corner. She picked up her suit jacket and swung her arms into it. "Let's go."

He picked up her purse from her desk and handed it to her, then the bailiff escorted them down the hall. In the main corridor, he took up position in front of the staff entrance and wished her son well. Kennedy thanked him and followed Finn down the hallway.

"They gave no indication of why he collapsed?" Kennedy grilled Finn as he led her to the elevator.

"No. Just that he was eating lunch when he suddenly got drowsy and passed out." His mouth flattened.

Kennedy's brow puckered. What could have brought an episode like that on? Paxton was a healthy teenager. "Where's Paige?"

"She's still at school, but the counselor pulled her from class. With Ben and Gemma out of town and Betty Ruth hospitalized still, I called Tristan to go pick her up. You need to call the school and authorize that, by the way. Taylor already left to meet the ambulance at the hospital."

Kennedy dug into her purse for her phone as they stepped onto the elevator. The signal died, and she growled, tapping her foot until the doors opened and they stepped out. As soon as the bars reappeared, she tapped the school name in her contacts and lifted the phone to her ear.

The receptionist barely uttered the school's name when Kennedy identified herself. "This is Kennedy Davidson. Paxton and Paige Cobb's mother. Let me speak to my daughter."

"One moment, please." The line clicked, rang once, then Mrs. Pickerington came on the line.

"Ms. Davidson. Paige is right here. She's fine."

"Let me speak to her." Kennedy's tone dared the woman to deny her.

"Of course." Crackles sounded as the woman handed the phone off.

"Mom?" Kennedy could hear the tears thickening Paige's voice. "Mom, he wasn't breathing."

Kennedy's heart stopped, then fluttered to life two times too fast. "What? Tell me exactly what happened."

"We were at lunch. Everything seemed fine, then he got quiet. I asked him if he was okay, and he looked at me and his eyes were all glassy, and he said, 'I'm really tired.' The next thing I knew, his eyes rolled up and he slumped into me. I couldn't wake him up, Mom. No matter what I did." Her voice dissolved into a sob.

"Hey. Paige, honey, it's okay. I know you did what you could. What happened after he passed out?"

The girl sniffed hard and drew in a breath. "I yelled for help. The other students at our table helped me lay him on the floor as the teachers ran over. The gym teacher, Mr. Ervin, checked his vitals and discovered he wasn't breathing, so he started CPR. He was still doing it when the ambulance crew arrived."

Kennedy's heart thumped harder. "Did they get him breathing?"

"Eventually. They gave him some stuff, and it brought him around. He seemed pretty coherent when they left with him. I wanted to go, too, but they wouldn't let me."

A dip formed between Kennedy's eyebrows, and she glanced at Finn. He gave her a questioning look, but said nothing as they continued into the parking garage to his car.

"Paige, Gemma's brother, Tristan, is coming to pick you up. He'll bring you to the hospital. I'm on my way there now with Finn. Can you put Mrs. Pickerington back on, please?"

"Okay."

Her heart clenched at the pain in that one word. "Good. I love you, sweetie." She wished she could reach through the phone and hug her.

"Love you too." More noise came over the line, then Mrs. Pickerington's voice.

"Hello?"

"Do you know what they gave him to bring him around?"

A long pause met her question. Dread filled Kennedy's stomach. "Mrs. Pickerington, please. Tell me."

"Narcan."

She sucked in a breath and muttered a curse under her breath. "I know you think my son is a troublemaker, but he would never do drugs."

Finn looked at her sharply. They'd reached his car, and he hit the button on his key fob to unlock the doors. He yanked on the handle, getting inside. Kennedy followed.

"I don't know what to tell you, Ms. Davidson. I just know he passed out, and the paramedics gave him Narcan to revive him. He denied taking anything."

"Of course he did, because he didn't. Is there security footage of the cafeteria?"

"Yes."

"Have you viewed it yet?"

"No. We've just gotten the kids who were at lunch back to their classes."

"Okay. The man who's coming to pick up Paige—his name is Tristan Mabley. He's a detective with Ferris County. Let him look at it, please?" Kennedy fastened her seatbelt as Finn pulled out of the parking spot.

Mrs. Pickerington sucked in a breath, and Kennedy could sense a protest brewing. "He might see something you all would miss," she said, heading it off.

"Oh. Well, I suppose that's true. I guess it wouldn't hurt."

"Thank you, Mrs. Pickerington. I appreciate it. He should be there soon."

"Sounds good."

Kennedy said goodbye and hung up. With a groan, she leaned her head back against the seat and closed her eyes.

"He overdosed?"

She opened her eyes and sat up. "That's what it sounds like. But he wouldn't take drugs. That's not him, Finn."

"I know. We'll get to the bottom of it. I'm glad you asked the school to let Tristan view the cafeteria footage. The sooner we get answers, the better."

"If there's nothing on the tapes, then what?"

"We'll look at other feeds from around the school. He got exposed somewhere."

Tears pricked her eyes. She nodded and glanced out the window, blinking back the moisture.

Finn's hand grasped hers, squeezing. "He'll be okay, Ken."

She squeezed back. "I hope so."

The remainder of the ride was quick; the hospital wasn't far. Finn parked in the E.R. lot and ushered her the short distance to the doors. Inside, Kennedy hurried toward the registration desk.

"My son, Paxton Cobb, was brought in by ambulance."

The young man at the desk typed the name into his computer. "Yes, I see him here. What's your name?"

"Kennedy Davidson." She dug her ID out of her bag and showed it to him.

He nodded and typed the information into the computer. "Have a seat, and someone will be out shortly to speak to you."

Kennedy bit back a growl, but didn't argue. She tugged on Finn's jacket sleeve and headed for a bank of chairs close to the doors leading to the treatment area. Perching on the edge, she folded her hands in her lap. They better hurry.

Finn wrapped a hand over hers, not saying a word. She appreciated both his silence and his support.

Minutes passed, and still no one came. Her foot bobbed, her heel gently clacking against the tile. They better come out soon, before she wore a divot in the floor.

The door swung open, and her tapping stopped. She willed the young blonde nurse to say her name.

"Mrs. Davidson?"

Kennedy shot to her feet. Finn held onto her hand, keeping her from running forward. She forced herself to take a breath and calm down. Letting her emotions rule was not how she normally operated.

"How is he?" she asked as she approached the woman. "The school said he was awake when the medics took him."

The woman turned, glancing back as she led them through the double doors. "He's still awake. We've had to administer another dose of Narcan, but he's doing well."

A small bit of worry lifted off Kennedy's shoulders. Finn squeezed her hand.

The nurse stopped in front of a treatment room and

pulled back the sliding door and the curtain, motioning them to precede her. Kennedy stepped inside and tried to keep her face a blank mask. She didn't want him to see just how worried she was.

"Hi, honey."

Tears swam in his eyes, and he looked away. "I didn't do anything. I swear."

Kennedy bit the corner of her lip, then let it go. She shook her hand free of Finn's and walked to Pax's bedside, stroking her fingers through his hair. "I know you didn't take anything."

"Do you remember what happened, Pax?" Finn stepped up beside her.

"It's a bit blurry. We were just eating lunch when I felt all woozy. The next thing I knew, I woke up, feeling like I'd run a marathon and there were paramedics hovering over me."

"What about before that? Did anything unusual happen? What about your food? Did it taste funny?"

Paxton's brows tipped down, then his forehead smoothed out. "I think everything tasted fine. I don't remember it being any different than usual. It was school food, so it sucked to begin with." He swallowed and licked his lips, wetting the dry skin. "There was something, though. We were sitting at the table and this kid walked up behind me and bumped into me." His eyes met Kennedy's. "It was the same boy who called Paige names."

Kennedy's face turned down in a fierce frown. "I thought the school switched your lunch periods so you wouldn't be together?"

"He was gone for like a day. I guess some class he's taking is only offered at a specific time and they couldn't find a way around it. At least, that's what Mrs. Pickerington told me when I asked."

Kennedy hummed. She and that woman were going to have words. "Okay. Why does that stick out?"

"Because he acted like it was an accident, but I could tell he was acting. And that he knew I knew he was acting. He dumped part of his tray on mine. I told him to watch it. He called me a skinny punk, picked up his drink and his apple, and walked away. After that, things get fuzzy."

She shared a look with Finn. Without a word, he took his phone from his pocket and walked out of the room.

"Am I going to be okay?"

Kennedy turned back to Pax and stroked his hair again. "You're going to be fine. You'll probably have to stay in the hospital for a day or two, just to monitor your condition, but once the drugs are out of your system, you should be fine."

He raised the hand not attached to the IV pole and rubbed his face. "If I ever had any urge to try drugs—not that I did— it's gone now. I never want to feel like that again."

"Good." Kennedy clenched her fist. She was just glad things didn't end differently.

# TWENTY-EIGHT

Finn left Kennedy at the hospital with the marshal assigned to Pax and headed to the school. After hearing Paxton's story, he called Tristan and told him he was on his way. That he wanted to see the video from lunch too. It bothered him to think that boy had slipped something into Paxton's food, but it made sense. He didn't know where else Pax would have ingested the drug. And it had been ingested. He quizzed the staff right before he left about whether they'd found a puncture mark anywhere on him. They hadn't.

Pulling into the school, he found a parking space, then headed inside, flashing his badge to gain entry.

"I'm Agent Porter with the ATF. I'm here about Paxton Cobb. My colleague Tristan Mabley should already be here."

The receptionist nodded and motioned him around the desk. "He's in the conference room with Mrs. Pickerington, Mr. Bagley, our principal, and Mrs. Gerschon, our assistant principal."

He rounded the desk. "Where's Paige?"

"She's with them."

"Thank you." Continuing down the short hall, he found the conference room. Five sets of eyes swung toward him.

"Finn!" Paige got up and ran to him, hugging him around the waist.

He wrapped his arms around her. "Hey, kiddo. You okay?"

"I guess so. How's Pax?"

"He's doing fine. Awake and talking. Your mom's with him." He let go, urging her to take a seat, then introduced himself. "Finley Porter, ATF. I'm assisting the Marshals with their protective detail."

The lone male school official held out a hand. "Dan Bagley. I'm the principal. This is Emma Gerschon and Lisa Pickerington."

Finn lifted a hand in greeting and sat next to Paige. "Have you viewed the cafeteria footage yet?"

"No," Tristan said. "We were waiting for you."

"Should she be in here?" Mrs. Pickerington pointed at Paige.

"I'm staying." Paige's voice rang with a firmness Finn hadn't heard before. She sounded like her mother.

"I think she'll be fine. She might be able to help us understand what happened." He gestured to the TV screen on the wall. "Let's watch."

Mr. Bagley picked up the remote and pushed some buttons. The video feed from Pax and Paige's lunch period began to play. They watched the students enter, forming a line against the wall as they snaked into the food buffet area, then out the other side, where they paid for their meals before finding seats.

Pax and Paige came into view, and Finn watched as they worked their way through the line and to a table. "Where's the boy who bumped into Pax?" He glanced at Paige.

She got up and went to the monitor, pointing to a kid five

people back. Finn kept his eyes on the boy as he came through the line, losing sight of him briefly as he went behind the wall that separated the kitchen from the dining area. When he reemerged, Paxton and Paige were sitting down.

The boy paid for his food, then took several steps, glancing around. He seemed to look like he was watching Paxton for a moment before he walked over to the condiment station and set his tray down. For several long moments, he stood there, his back to the camera, before he picked up his tray and walked deliberately toward Paxton's table. As he approached, he stared at Pax, then as he came up behind him, lurched to the side, dumping his drink and apple over Paxton's head. It landed on Pax's tray, knocking over his drink.

Pax looked up and said something. The boy smirked, replied, then picked up his apple—and the wrong drink.

Finn sat up. "Did you see that?"

"See what?" Mrs. Pickerington asked.

"Yep." Tristan sat forward and glanced at the principal. "Rewind it."

The man did so, then stared at the screen.

"Well, I'll be damned." Mr. Bagley shook his head. "He grabbed the wrong drink."

"Where's the trash from lunch? And we need to talk to that boy." Finn looked at the staff.

"You can't." Mrs. Pickerington said.

Finn frowned. "Why not?"

"His parents need to be present if he's questioned by law enforcement."

"That's true, Lisa," Mrs. Gerschon said. "But we can talk to him." She motioned to herself, the counselor, and the principal, then looked at Finn. "Tell us what you want us to ask."

"What was in the bottle? And make sure he knows we're going to test it for drugs and DNA." He looked at Mrs. Pickerington. "And I would call his parents. Also, wasn't that boy supposed to be in a different lunch period from Paxton and Paige after the first incident?"

She frowned. "We tried, but he's in advanced classes that conflict with the other lunch periods. Besides, there's only a couple weeks left in the year. We made sure they didn't sit together."

"Well, it didn't work!" Paige shoved her chair back, making it rock precariously, then spun on her heel and marched out.

Finn rose. "I'll go talk to her. Get that kid in here and call his parents. Tristan, call the locals and have them send someone over. We don't know if this is part of our federal case yet, so they need to be involved."

He nodded. Finn didn't wait for confirmation from the school staff before he went after Paige. Stepping out of the room, he looked left into a dead end. She had to have gone toward the main office.

The receptionist looked up as he appeared. "She ran into the bathroom." The woman pointed through the floor-to-ceiling window at the women's restroom just beyond.

He clenched his fists, knowing he couldn't follow her in there. "Could you go ask her to come out and talk to me, please?"

"Of course." Offering him a sympathetic smile, she got up and went through the door built into the wall of windows and entered the restroom. A few moments later, she and a teary-eyed Paige emerged.

"Is there an office we could sit in for a few minutes?" He laid a hand on Paige's shoulder.

The woman nodded and led them to Mrs. Gerschon's office, just past the front desk. Finn muttered a thank you, and she walked away.

"Hey, kiddo. Talk to me."

Paige sniffed and swiped at the moisture on her cheeks.

"I'm just so mad. Pax wouldn't be in the hospital—wouldn't have been drugged—if they did their jobs. I hate this school."

Finn had his own opinion, but kept it to himself. That was a discussion she needed to have with her mom.

"I'm sorry. I'm just angry."

"You have a right to be. But I'm going to get to the bottom of this. If that boy did drug Pax, he won't get away with it."

"I know. I trust you."

Something lit inside Finn's chest. From day one, he'd wanted Kennedy and her kids to trust him. Getting confirmation that at least one of them did hardened his resolve to protect this family and to be there for them. Through anything. He wouldn't—couldn't—let them down. "I'm glad, honey. I'll do my best, okay?"

She nodded.

"Come here." He lifted an arm and motioned her to come closer. "Give me a hug."

Paige wrapped her arms around him. Finn enveloped her and squeezed, then patted her shoulder as he let her go. "Come on. You can hang out with the receptionist lady while we wait on that kid and his parents."

Her brows formed a deep V over her eyes. "Why can't I sit in there like last time?"

"Because interviews are different than just watching security footage. And your emotions will not help us get answers out of him. He might just clam up and refuse to talk."

"Oh. I guess I see your point."

He offered her a soft smile. "Good. Come on." Ushering her back to the main office, he left her with the receptionist, then went back to the conference room. The principal was gone, but the two women remained with Tristan.

"I still can't believe Corey would do something like this," Mrs. Pickerington said. "He's one of our best students."

Finn bit his tongue. Someone needed to tell this woman

she shouldn't pick favorites. "We'll get to the bottom of it," he said instead.

Huffing out a harsh breath, she looked away. He shared a glance with Tristan, who shook his head, the look on his face telling Finn he'd come to the same conclusion.

Not long after Finn returned to the conference room, the principal poked his head in and asked Mrs. Gerschon to step out. Mrs. Pickerington frowned as she watched them leave, and Finn bit back a smile. At least the principal recognized that the counselor might be biased.

Ten minutes after the principals disappeared, raised voices filtered down the hall. One of them was Paige's. Finn spared a quick glance at Tristan before he got up and hurried down the corridor to see what the problem was.

A red-faced woman stood on the other side of the desk, pointing a finger at Paige, yelling at her that she was a liar.

"Whoa." Finn patted the air. "Let's calm down."

She turned her glare on him. "Who are you?"

Finn held up his badge. "Finley Porter, ATF. You are?"

Her spine straightened, some of the self-righteous anger fading from her eyes as a wariness crept in. "Melinda Edgerton. I'm Corey Edgerton's mother."

"Perfect. We've been waiting for you." He glanced at the receptionist. "Has the local police officer arrived?"

She pointed out the window to the parking lot beyond. "They just pulled up."

Finn glanced over to see a woman emerge from the cruiser parked at the curb. "Great. Send her back to the conference room when she comes in, please?"

"Yes, sir."

Turning to Paige, Finn pinned her with a look. She blew out a breath, then slumped in her seat, some of the fight leaving her. Satisfied she wouldn't cause any more problems, he glanced at Mrs. Edgerton. "If you'd like to follow me?"

Muscles in her face twitching and her eyes glittering like stainless-steel in the sunshine, she came around the desk and followed him.

"My husband is on his way. He was finishing a meeting."

"Great." Finn stopped in front of the conference room door and motioned her inside.

Back still ramrod straight, she waltzed past him. "Where's my son?"

"He's with Mr. Bagley and Mrs. Gerschon. They had some questions."

Her jaw worked, but she said nothing.

"Have a seat. Please." He nodded to the chair in front of her.

She set her purse on the table and pulled out the chair, perching on the edge. Once she was settled, an awkward silence fell. Finn hoped her husband arrived sooner rather than later.

Luck was on his side. Not long after the local police officer, Tracey Ingram, joined them, and he gave her a quick rundown on what happened, Mrs. Edgerton's husband, Justin, arrived. In his three-piece suit, the man walked into the conference room and honed in on Finn.

"You in charge?"

"No. She is." He pointed to Officer Ingram. "However, this might end up being my case. Depends on the answers your son gives us." He flashed the man his badge and introduced himself.

The man sucked his cheeks in slightly and nodded. "Where's Corey?"

"Right here." Mr. Bagley entered the room, Corey behind him. Mrs. Gerschon followed.

"Is this everyone?" Officer Ingram asked. She looked at Finn.

He nodded.

"Okay. Agent Porter brought me up to speed while we waited on everyone. Mr. Bagley, what did you learn from your conversation with young Mr. Edgerton?"

"Wait, you already questioned him?" Mr. Edgerton broke in. "I should have been present."

"It was a school matter, sir," Mr. Bagley said. "A student collapsed at lunch. Your son had direct contact with the boy and was a witness. We're just trying to figure out what happened."

Mr. Edgerton turned a sharp look on his son, then glanced at the principal. "What do you know so far?"

"A ninth-grader collapsed at lunch and stopped breathing. Your son bumped into him just minutes before it happened."

"So? That doesn't mean anything." Corey crossed his arms and glared.

"It might when we have it on video that you picked up the other boy's drink and left yours." Mr. Bagley put both hands on the table and leaned forward. "After you paused at the condiment station for nearly a minute, but didn't pick up any condiments."

Mrs. Edgerton gasped.

Mr. Bagley looked at Mr. Edgerton. "The boy who collapsed was revived by the paramedics with Narcan."

Corey snorted. "I knew that kid was a druggie."

"Corey." Mr. Edgerton's voice was sharp. "You will be silent unless asked a question. Understand?"

The boy pressed his lips together and stared at the wall. His dad turned back to Mr. Bagley.

"Is there any evidence Corey gave him a tainted drink?"

"Not yet," Finn interjected. "We have officers and agents searching the trash. We'll find the bottle and have it tested."

Corey sat straighter. "Wait. What? How will you know it's his?"

Finn looked the boy in the eye and took a guess. "It'll be the only one with fentanyl in it."

The young man went white.

Justin Edgerton stared hard at his son, but his words were for the others. "Would you all mind if my wife and I had a moment alone with our son?"

Officer Ingram looked at Finn, and he nodded, then stood.

"I think that would be fine." Officer Ingram rose and motioned for the others to follow Finn out the door.

In the hallway, Finn leaned against the wall.

"Do you think he'll tell his parents the truth?" Tristan came to a rest next to him.

Finn lifted one shoulder. "Maybe. His dad seems like he knew the kid was hiding something. Hopefully, he'll get him to open up."

Mr. Bagley sighed. "Even if he does, I'm not sure Mr. Edgerton will let him talk. He's a criminal defense lawyer."

Finn uttered a soft curse. Great. Just frickin' great.

Minutes passed. Through the door, they heard Corey raise his voice once, denying everything, then the softer rumble of his dad's and the barely perceptible murmur of his mom's. Finn crossed his arms and stared at the door, willing it to open and praying they'd get some answers and not a request for a lawyer.

Time stretched longer until Finn was ready to go back in and tell them their time was up. Arms still crossed, he drummed his fingers on his bicep, debating whether to do just that, when the door swung inward. A resigned and disappointed Justin Edgerton stood in the doorway.

"Normally, I would tell my son to say nothing. To wait for an attorney and not do anything to implicate himself. But something he told us warrants deeper investigation. He will talk to you, but I'd like the district attorney to consider lesser charges than the felonious assault he's likely facing." The man's eyes bounced from Finn to Tristan, to Officer Ingram, and back again.

"If he cooperates, I'm sure the D.A. will take that into consideration when filing charges." Officer Ingram stepped forward.

"Same goes for the U.S. attorney's office. If this turns out to be connected to my case, I'll put in a good word." Finn dropped his arms and pushed away from the wall.

Giving a short nod, Mr. Edgerton stepped back into the room, leaving the door open.

Curious what the boy could have said that caused his defense attorney father to waive his son's right to counsel, Finn didn't waste any time returning to his seat in the conference room.

As soon as everyone was settled, Mr. Edgerton turned to Corey. "Tell them what you told us. All of it."

Expression sullen, the boy glanced around at the myriad of adults, then took a deep breath. "Over the weekend, I went to the office with Dad before we went golfing. He said he had some papers he needed to look over quick. I sat out in the reception area, listening to music while he worked." Corey paused and looked at his dad, who nodded for him to continue.

"While I was out there, one of the other lawyers came in. He started to walk past me, then stopped and came over and sat down. He started asking me about school and how things were going. Said he heard I had some trouble with the new kid, Paxton Cobb. When I asked how he knew that, he said he knew Paxton's mom. That they were old friends from law school." He paused, flattening his lips.

"I should have known then something was up, because he asked me if I wanted to get back at the kid for getting me in trouble. He said Paxton's mom would get a kick out of her son getting what was coming to him for the way he acted."

Finn's posture shifted, his back going straight as he listened to Corey's story.

"And I wasn't going to do it." Corey's gaze flicked to his parents. "But then he offered me five hundred dollars. I get a good allowance, but it's not five hundred dollars good. So, I said sure, thinking he wanted me to just embarrass Pax in front of the school or something. Nope. The guy reached in his pocket and pulled out a small baggie of white powder. I tried to say no, but his whole demeanor changed then. He told me if I didn't do it, not only wouldn't I get the money, but he'd tell his friends about me. Friends who didn't 'take kindly' to people who backed out of deals." The boy air-quoted.

"I took the bag, afraid of what he'd do if I still refused. I figured I'd find a way out of it somehow."

"You should have come to us." Mr. Edgerton's voice was softer, some of his earlier anger gone.

"I know. But that dude's scary. And I didn't want him to hurt you or Mom."

"What happened after you took the bag?" Finn asked.

"He left and said he'd leave the money in the bushes out front of our house after I slipped Pax the drugs."

"Did he tell you what it was?" Tristan asked.

Corey shook his head. "He just told me to be careful with it when I opened the bag. That I didn't want to get it on myself. So, I opened it, tipped some into my drink, then wrapped the bag in a napkin and dumped it in the trash can at the condiment station." His face flushed and moisture gathered in his eyes. "I didn't know it would make him stop breathing. I thought it would just make him loopy or something."

Finn looked at Justin. "Who was the attorney who gave Corey the drugs?"

"Jack Cartwright."

Finn and Tristan both sucked in a breath and shared a look.

"One of Gustavo Herrera's attorneys gave your son drugs to give to another student?" Finn knew he sounded perplexed, but he couldn't help it. It seemed like such a laughable idea.

The man rolled his lips in and nodded. "I work for the firm representing him." He waved his hands. "I don't agree with it, and I've done everything I can to distance myself from the case. But my colleague has no such scruples. He's as scummy as Herrera. And unfortunately, one of our senior partners and the junior partner heading the case have similar attitudes, which is how he gets away with it." He grimaced. "I've been scuttling money away every month to open my own firm, which is the only reason I haven't quit yet."

"I think you need to do it anyway," Mrs. Gerschon said.

Finn agreed, but that wasn't the primary issue here. "Corey, did Mr. Cartwright say anything else about Paxton or his mom?" He highly doubted the man knew her from law school. This went back to the mole in the court's office.

"No."

With a nod, Finn looked at Mr. Edgerton again. "Did you mention to anyone at work that Corey was involved in an altercation at school?"

Justin nodded. "My secretary. She took the call from the school. I told one of our partners, too, over a round of drinks. We were just chatting, and it came up. Though if I had to guess who told Cartwright, it would be my secretary. I think the two of them have something going on."

"Good to know." Finn glanced at Tristan, then Officer Ingram. "Do either of you have any more questions?"

They both shook their heads.

He looked at Edgerton. "I think we have what we need for now. Your son's case will likely stay with Buncombe County.

But I'm sure Officer Ingram will put in a good word with the D.A., since he was cooperative." He glanced at her.

She nodded, looking at the parents. "I need to take him down to the station to process him for the assault, but I'll call the prosecutor's office right after, and we'll see what we can do."

Mrs. Edgerton, who'd been mostly silent, got up, teary eyes locked on her son. Her gaze flicked to her husband. "I need a moment." Without another word, she fled the room.

Finn felt for the woman. Corey Edgerton had an attitude, but until Pax showed up, he didn't think the kid had ever been in trouble. Not real trouble, anyway. Hopefully, the kid learned a lesson from all this and straightened up his act. Especially since he would spend the foreseeable future in jail and, once out on bail, in protective custody with his parents.

Holding back a sigh, Finn made a mental note to call Paulson when they were done here. He had another family to add to her protectee list.

# TWENTY-NINE

The soft snick of the front door opening, then closing, told Kennedy that Finn was home. Finally. She'd spent the rest of the afternoon at the hospital alone until Tristan arrived with Paige. He hadn't stayed more than a few minutes, just long enough to get an update on Pax and to make sure they didn't need anything. What she needed, though, he couldn't provide. Sure, he could give her answers, but she wanted to hear them from Finn. While he held her and told her everything would be okay. She hoped now that he was home she would get both.

Rising from her spot on the couch, she walked to the living room doorway and leaned against the doorjamb. "Hi."

He looked over as he twisted the deadbolt. "Hey." A soft smile lifted his mouth, showing a hint of his dimples. "I figured you'd be in bed already. I see you're dressed for it."

Kennedy glanced down at herself. "Yeah. It's the first thing I did after we got home. I needed out of that suit."

Finn strolled closer. He lifted a hand and pushed a lock of her hair back, untangling it from where it wound around the arm of her glasses. "You look exhausted. Why don't you go on up to bed?"

She reached up and took his hand, then turned, heading for the couch. "I will. After you tell me what you learned." She sank onto the cushions and pulled him down next to her.

He blew out a breath and raked his free hand through his hair. "Quite a bit, actually."

"Really?"

"Yeah. That student Pax mentioned, Corey Edgerton, he confessed. Told us everything. Someone from Herrera's legal team bribed him to drug Pax."

Kennedy's eyes went wide. "What? Who?"

"Jack Cartwright."

"I don't know him."

"Be glad you don't. He's a snake. Everyone on Herrera's defense team is."

"How did they get to Corey? Better yet, how did they know he and Pax went to the same school?"

"Corey's dad works for Herrera's law firm." He held up a hand. "He's not part of his legal team, though. Said he didn't want anything to do with the guy." His hand dropped, covering hers, where she still clutched his other hand. "Long story short, Corey was at his dad's office; Cartwright saw him and bribed him into cooperating. We think Cartwright got his information from the dad's secretary and whoever the mole is in the court's office."

Her whole face turned down in a fierce frown. "What's being done to find that person?"

"I know the Marshals are working on it, but I don't know much more than that. This will light a fire under them, though. Herrera's goon squad is getting bolder."

Kennedy didn't like that so little progress had been made. She hoped he was right, and they stepped up their efforts to find the mole.

Her dismay must have shown on her face. Finn tugged on her hand, shifting as he pulled her into his larger frame. "Hey, try not to worry. We're doing everything we can."

She'd started to relax into him, but sat up at his words, turning a glare on him. "Well, it's not good enough! Pax almost died! It shouldn't—" She broke off with a sob. Her face crumpled, and she dissolved into tears; the stress of the day finally took over.

Finn gathered her close. She sobbed into his shirt, not caring if she soaked it.

Making shushing noises, Finn stroked her hair and held her tight. He pressed light kisses to the top of her head. Kennedy latched onto the comfort he offered and let herself get rid of the bottled-up emotions, some of which had been simmering for weeks. Once the cork popped off, she couldn't stop it. They all spilled out until eventually, only drops remained, and her cries turned into hiccups and sniffs.

She lifted her head, looking at his chest and the wet stain on his gray shirt. Sniffing, she lifted her glasses, setting them atop her hair, and swiped at the tears on her face. "Thank you." Her eyes met his. "For letting me cry. I needed that."

Those sexy dimples popped out as one side of his mouth lifted. "No problem. Do you feel better?"

Her head bobbed. She swiped at her cheeks again. "Yeah. I'm still upset and worried, but I feel like I can cope with it all now." She blew out a long breath. "It's not just us, is it? We can't be the only ones targeted like this."

"No. There have been a few other instances, but yours has been the most serious. A lot of that has to do with your family dynamics. You're younger than most of the other judges, so your children are younger and more vulnerable. You also have extended family in the area in Betty Ruth. Only one of the other judges is from this area. The cards have aligned to make your family the easy target."

Kennedy's lips flattened to a thin line, and she bit back a growl. Pushing away from him, she stood up and walked to the window. "I just don't understand why Herrera would target judges not part of his case. Me. I get that we have Gonzales on our docket, but it would make more sense for Herrera to go after just the judicial staff trying his own case."

She heard the rustle of cloth as Finn got up, then the soft shuffle of his feet on the floor moments before she sensed his presence behind her. Warmth filled her body when he rested his hands on her shoulders.

"Regardless of what makes sense, the thing to remember is that Herrera is insane. Clinically a psychopath. He will do whatever makes his evil heart happy. Even if it doesn't make sense to us."

Kennedy leaned back, needing to be closer again. She dealt with evil every day in her job, but Gustavo Herrera was a different breed. No one else made her skin crawl or left a hollow pit of fear in her belly.

Finn's arms came around her shoulders, and he rested his chin atop her head. Kennedy raised her hands and wrapped them over his forearms.

"So, how's Pax? You're home, so I'm guessing he's all right."

"Yeah. They want to monitor him for a day or so. Make sure there aren't any ill effects from the drug and find an effective way to manage his pain. He's got some broken ribs from the CPR."

They stood that way for several minutes, not speaking. Beyond them, through the window, tree branches swayed in the breeze, playing peek-a-boo with the moon. The world outside was quiet, most creatures asleep.

Heaviness descended over Kennedy's limbs. Her crying jag had dispelled the tension in her body. Now she just felt drained. If Finn moved, she'd probably fall backward and land on her butt on the floor. He was the only thing holding her up.

A low chuckle rumbled through her back. "I think you definitely need to go to bed now. You just sagged into me."

She turned her head to look at him, a corner of her mouth ticking up. "That's probably a good idea." But she made no move to step away. Looking at him had been a terrible idea. Now she was ensnared in his steel-gray gaze.

His right hand came up to skim her jawline. He stroked a thumb over her lower lip. A zing of need shot through her, and her lips parted. Finn's pupils dilated. She heard his breath hitch. Slowly—agonizingly so—his head lowered until she felt his breath puff over her face. He slid his fingers higher, cupping the side of her head, and closed the distance.

Kennedy clutched his arm and locked her knees against the onslaught of desire that hit her the moment his lips touched hers. Her body remembered this feeling. The wonder of it was still there, but this time there was no shock to give her pause and allow her to think. No, this time, she turned in his arms and pressed closer, seeking more. She *needed* more.

With a soft grunt at her eagerness, Finn's hands drifted down her body to span her back. His large palms moved over the surface, leaving her wishing he would touch her bare skin. The friction still left behind a warmth that fanned the flames already burning inside her. Kennedy thrust her hands into his hair, raking her nails over his scalp. He let out a loud moan and deepened their kiss. She brought her hands around to brush the day's worth of stubble on his jaw. It rasped beneath her fingertips. It wasn't until he palmed the globes of her butt and tilted his hips into hers that some of her sanity returned. No matter how hot he made her, she wasn't ready to take this to the next level yet.

Pulling back, Kennedy framed his face in her hands. "We need to slow down."

Breathing hard, he nodded. "Yeah. Probably not a bad idea." He let her go and took a step back. "Damn." Swiping a hand over his face, he glanced away.

Mentally, she echoed that sentiment. But out loud, she said something different. "I'm going to say goodnight now."

Finn nodded again. "Great. Yeah. Perfect."

Kennedy stepped around him, hiding a smile. It was nice to know she wasn't the only one feeling the effects of their kiss. "See you in the morning."

He hummed. "Goodnight."

Keeping her eyes forward, Kennedy fled. If she looked back, she wasn't sure she wouldn't invite him to join her.

# THIRTY

A soft knock on Paxton's hospital door brought Kennedy's head up. She'd been buried in work, trying to stay on top of as much as she could and take some of the pressure off her fellow judges. She could review briefs and prep for court later in the week. Pax was making good progress—so was Betty Ruth—and the doctors were talking about releasing them both tomorrow. She'd already talked to the hospital about hiring a nurse for Betty Ruth. They'd referred her to a home health agency.

"Come in." Setting aside her laptop, she looked eagerly toward the door, hoping it was the nurse from the agency come to talk to her about Betty Ruth's needs.

But it wasn't. The door swung inward to reveal the marshal posted on Pax's room.

"Sorry to bother you, Ms. Davidson. There's a man here who says he's Paxton's dad. A Peter Cobb?"

Kennedy's eyes widened. She'd called Pete yesterday once things calmed down and Pax was settled in a room. Of course, she'd had to leave a message; Pete hadn't answered his phone.

When he didn't call her back, she'd assumed he just didn't care. She never thought he'd show up here.

With a quick glance at Pax, who was sleeping, she got up and followed the marshal into the hall. Sure enough, her ex-husband stood near the nurse's station, arms crossed, brows drawn down, fuming.

Biting back a growl, she walked toward him. He had every right to be here, even if she wished he wasn't. "Pete. It's nice of you to come. I wasn't sure you even got my message. You never called me back."

"I was going to, then decided I needed to see for myself that he was all right. But Mr. Muscles over there wouldn't let me pass." He uncrossed his arms to gesture to the young marshal who stood behind Kennedy, guarding Paxton's door.

"Yes, well, for good reason. Let's go someplace and talk." She'd been vague on the phone about what happened, not wanting to go into too much detail in a voice message. She was sure he had questions.

"Fine. Lead the way."

Kennedy led him down the hall to a small grouping of chairs set out of the way of foot traffic. She perched on the edge of one and waited for him to settle across from her.

"Your message was rather vague, Ken. What happened?"

"Paxton was drugged at school."

"You said that. Why? By whom?"

"There's a case going through the court system here. You've probably heard about it. Gustavo Herrera?"

Pete nodded. "What does that have to do with someone drugging our son?"

"Herrera's targeting the judiciary and their families in an attempt to disrupt his trial. Someone broke into Betty Ruth's house and stabbed her. She nearly died, but should make a full recovery. Extra precautions were put in place for me and the kids, and we thought they'd be safe at school."

"Obviously not." He looked down his nose at her.

She bristled at his tone, but kept the snarky response inside. It wouldn't help anything. "No. The boy who drugged him has a connection to Herrera. His father works for the law firm representing him." She held up a hand at the protest she saw brewing on his face. "The man is not involved in Herrera's case and actively tried to distance himself from it. One of the attorneys who is on the case, though, bribed the man's son into drugging Pax. From what the authorities have told me, the boy didn't know it would cause so much harm."

Pete snorted and rolled his eyes. "Yeah, right. Every kid that age knows how dangerous drugs are."

"When they're told what they are, yes. He wasn't aware he was given something so lethal. He said he thought it would just make Pax woozy, not put him into cardiac arrest."

Pete's mouth pursed, but he made no comment.

"He's doing fine now, though. And since it's the end of the school year, the school agreed to let him take his exams from home once he feels better. Same with Paige. Neither of them has to go back to school."

"Where is Paige?" He sat up and glanced around, a look of false interest on his face.

Kennedy curled her fingers, digging her nails into her palms. He hadn't even given his daughter a second thought until she brought the girl up. And he wasn't really interested now.

"She went to get some lunch. And before you ask, no, she's not alone." Kennedy hadn't been ready to eat when Paige declared she was starving, so Finn took her down to the cafeteria. They would be back soon. She hoped she could get Pete to leave before then. She doubted Paige wanted to see her dad. The girl never had anything good to say about him.

"Well, that's something, at least. Why haven't you called to tell me about the trouble you're in? The kids should have been in Richmond with me at the first hint of danger."

This time, she couldn't stop herself from rolling her eyes. "Like they'd be safer with you? You're never home. They would be on their own at your house, and they wouldn't have the team of U.S. Marshals and DEA and ATF agents looking out for them."

"So? The threat is here."

"You and I both know threats like this don't disappear just because someone leaves town. And Richmond is close enough Herrera could have people there. Someone here is feeding him information. It probably wouldn't be hard for him to find out where you live."

"Regardless, they're not safe here with you."

"They're not safe anywhere, Pete. But they're safer here with me and our team of federal agents than anywhere else." She tipped her head and frowned. "Where is this coming from? In the past, you've never been bothered when something happens to one of the kids. When Paige fell in gymnastics two years ago and broke her wrist, it took you several days to even call and ask about her. I had to leave you a message, then, too." She narrowed her eyes. "Does this have anything to do with that woman you knocked up? Did she put you up to this?" Kennedy took a chance that her mom's hunch was right and his new fiancée was indeed pregnant.

A slight widening of his eyes was the only indication he gave that she'd surprised him.

"How did you know about that?"

"Just because I left Richmond doesn't mean I cut all ties with the people I know there."

Red spots erupted on his cheeks, and his eyes turned flinty. "It was your mother, wasn't it? I should have known she'd find out. That bitch is the biggest busybody I've ever met."

Kennedy clenched her teeth and drew in a slow breath

through her nose. What had she ever seen in him? It didn't matter that he'd guessed her source correctly. Her mother might drive her batty on a good day, but she wasn't a bitch. "Well, when you knock up a woman not much older than your children, people talk."

"She's twenty-two. Plenty old enough."

Keeping her lips clamped tight, she just blinked.

"Rachelle thought it would be a good idea for me to come down and make sure Paxton was okay."

Kennedy's eyebrows went up. "When have you ever listened to the woman in your life? You never did what I thought you should."

"Yes, well, Rachelle is not you." He glanced away.

A pang of hurt sliced through Kennedy's chest, but it was quickly replaced by suspicion. He didn't want to look at her. "Who is she to you? Other than your fiancée and baby mama, I mean. Is she someone you work with?"

"It's none of your business." He leveled a hard look on her, but his hands fidgeted in his lap.

Like a lightning bolt, it struck her who she was. "It's Phillip Foster's daughter, isn't it?" She remembered meeting the man's family at a holiday party once. He had a daughter named Rachelle.

The red on Pete's cheeks emerged again, but this time it wasn't anger that prompted it. He stared down the hallway and didn't answer.

"Well, now I know why you're so eager to please her." She shook her head and stood. It disgusted her how much greed had changed him since they met. "Come on. Let's go say hi to your son, so you can report you saw with your own eyes that he's fine." Spinning on her heel, she marched down the hall, not caring if he followed.

Canvas shoes making a soft slap on the floor as she walked, she rounded the slight bend in the corridor and bit back a groan of frustration as she saw Finn coming toward her, a little wrinkle on his forehead.

"There you are." His gaze flicked past her to Pete. "Is everything all right?"

"It's fine." She stopped and turned so she could see both men. "Finn, this is my ex-husband, Pete. Pete, this is ATF agent Finley Porter."

Finn's shoulders straightened and his face hardened as he took in her ex. Kennedy knew what he saw. A handsome, dark-haired man, who, even in casual clothes, looked like a high-end lawyer. Pete had a lot going for him; it was a shame he could be a jerk. She hoped Rachelle Foster knew what she was getting into. Though, being the boss's daughter, she'd have more influence over Pete than Kennedy ever did. Pleasing Rachelle meant Pete kept his job, and maybe even moved up faster. She honestly wouldn't be surprised if he got the girl pregnant on purpose.

After a quick assessment of the man and Kennedy's posture, Finn stepped forward, holding out a hand. "Nice to meet you."

Pete took Finn's hand, his eyes doing some assessing of their own. Kennedy wasn't sure what he saw, but she didn't really care. If things continued down the current path between herself and Finn, he'd know soon enough that she was seeing someone. Either the kids or her mother would make sure he knew.

"You too." Pete let go of Finn's hand and let it drop to his side.

Kennedy didn't stick around to watch them continue to size each other up. She walked around Finn and headed for Pax's room. "Is he awake yet?" she asked Finn.

"Yeah. He woke up to the smell of food."

Despite the situation, Kennedy's mouth quirked. In true teenage boy fashion, food was a top priority for Pax. She was just happy she wouldn't have to wake him up so Pete could say hello. That would not go over well. Sleep was another of Pax's priorities. One he didn't like to have interrupted, even when he was feeling his best.

Pushing through the hospital room door, she paused at the foot of Pax's bed. He was sitting up, eating ice cream, smiling at something his sister said. Paige sat in the chair at the head of the bed, turned toward him as she ate a sub. Kennedy bit back another groan. They were getting along, the scare having helped negate some of the typical sibling bickering. Seeing Pete would bring down their moods.

They looked at her as she entered, their expressions quickly changing to ones of curiosity as they took in her fierce frown, then to frowns of their own when Pete walked in just ahead of Finn.

"What are you doing here?" Pax gave Pete a hard look.

"Your mother called and told me what happened. I came to check on you."

Pax rolled his eyes. "Yeah, right."

Pete bristled. Kennedy knew the twins' attitudes bothered him, but it was of his own making. She'd tried to get him to be more involved, but he'd repeatedly pushed them aside for his career. It shouldn't surprise him they were resentful.

Stepping closer, Pete opened his mouth to speak, but caught sight of Finn moving closer to Kennedy and paused. He aimed a disapproving look at Finn. "This is a family matter. You can go."

"Finn stays." Kennedy crossed her arms and looked her ex-husband dead in the eye. She knew she'd just given away their relationship, but she didn't care. She and the twins needed Finn here for support.

Pete's spine straightened. "I see." He raised an eyebrow as he looked at Kennedy. "Really, Ken? You're involved with your bodyguard?"

Thunderclouds gathered in Finn's eyes. Kennedy stepped in front of him, her voice low. "We are not talking about me. You're here to see your children." She tipped her head toward them.

He held her glare a moment longer before turning to the twins. Kennedy let out a breath and closed her eyes on a long blink. Finn walked up behind her. He didn't touch her, but she could feel the heat of his body. His proximity was enough to give her some comfort.

"Go home, Dad." Pax's voice was hard. "I'm fine. Mom and Finn have everything under control."

"So your mother has said. But I needed to see for myself that you're okay. You're still my son, and I care about you."

Paige rolled her eyes, but kept her mouth shut. Kennedy's heart broke at his choice of words. He'd said care instead of love. And she knew that distinction was deliberate. She'd listened to him rehearse legal arguments—and had him pick apart her words—enough to know that he knew exactly what he was and wasn't saying.

"That's nice. But it shouldn't take me nearly dying for you to come see us."

"You've only been in town a few weeks. I didn't want to create more stress for your mom while she tries to settle you all in."

"Oh, whatever." Paige glared at him. "What about the years we lived in Richmond after you and mom separated and you barely saw us? Even on your weekends with us?"

A muscle ticked in Pete's jaw. He glanced at Kennedy, but she stayed quiet. He could dig himself out of his own hole. The twins were old enough to decide for themselves what sort of relationship they wanted with their dad. She was done making excuses for his behavior in an effort to keep that relationship afloat. It would ring hollow, and the kids knew it.

"Yes, well, life's been busy." Pete's voice was tight.

Pax scoffed. "Guess you should get back to that busy life, then. Thanks for checking on me, Dad. I'm good. Bye."

As if on cue, Pete's phone rang. He took it from his pocket, glancing at the screen. "It's a client. I need to take this. Pax, I'm glad you're okay." With a nod at Paige, a quick look at Kennedy, and a glare for Finn, he headed for the door, answering his phone as he left.

"Why did you call him?" Pax glared at Kennedy.

"Hey." Finn stepped up beside her. "You might not like the man, but he's still your dad. And you're still a minor. He has every right to know what's going on with you. So watch your tone."

Pax had the good grace to look chagrined. "Sorry, Mom. He just makes me angry. Like, why did he even bother when he never has before?"

Kennedy offered him a soft smile and patted his leg through the blankets. She wasn't about to inform them of why he'd come, but she wouldn't lie about his motives, either, so she went with the vague option. "I'm not sure, sweetie. But try not to stress about it, okay?" She took in Paige as well. "Either of you. I doubt he'll be back now that he's seen for himself you're all right, Pax. Let's just focus on getting you well enough to get out of here. Okay?"

"Fine." Pax rolled his eyes.

"I guess." Paige picked at her sandwich.

Kennedy sighed and rubbed her temples.

"Man, you all are a bunch of sad sacks." Finn shook his head. "How about we don't let one person ruin our day, all right? Your mom is right. Let's focus on better days ahead. And you know what the first step toward that is?"

The twins shook their heads. Kennedy sent him a curious look.

He walked to the stand in the corner and picked up the card deck Kennedy brought to keep herself occupied. She'd played more hands of solitaire than she could count over the last day.

"Resetting our mindset with a rousing game of Go Fish."

The gloom left the kids' eyes, and they chuckled.

Kennedy smiled at him, a warmth settling in her heart. Yeah, there were definitely better days ahead.

# THIRTY-ONE

Yawning, Kennedy shut off the kitchen light, the last of the dishes put away, and ambled down the hall. She was ready to go to bed. Between the dozen briefs she read, the million emails she answered, and Pete's presence at lunch, she needed the oblivion of sleep. She just hoped she could fall asleep. Her brain wanted to go in every direction all at once. Fatigue didn't help.

Ascending the stairs, she paused in front of Paige's room, opening the door to peek in on her. The girl had gone to bed an hour ago, also exhausted from the stress of the last couple of days. Finn's light-heartedness had helped this afternoon, but she hadn't completely expelled the worry over her brother. Add Pete's unexpected visit to the mix, and she was on over-load, though she hid it well.

Curled up on her side, buried beneath the pale yellow comforter, she slept, though. Kennedy could hear her faint snore. Smiling softly, she closed the door and continued down the hall.

A thump from Finn's room made her pause, her hand

around her doorknob. Glancing back, she frowned. What was he doing?

Reversing course, she stopped outside his room and raised her fist, hesitating only a moment before she knocked. She heard movement on the other side, then the door swung open, and she forgot to breathe. Shirtless, the massive expanse of his chest glistened with sweat. Black athletic shorts hung low on his hips, revealing an enticing line of hair that disappeared beneath the waistband. His washboard abs heaved as he sucked in air.

"Hey. What's up?" He glanced into the hall. "Headed to bed?"

Kennedy licked her lips. "Um." What did he say? "Yeah. Bed." She hooked a thumb toward her room. "I heard a noise. I can see now you were just exercising." *Don't look down!* With every ounce of willpower she possessed, she kept her eyes locked on his. If she looked at his chest and abs again, she would not be able to keep her hands to herself.

"Oh, yeah. Sorry." His gaze heated.

A curse flew through Kennedy's head. She might have kept her hands to herself, but not her thoughts off her face.

"I dropped to the floor a little hard. I held my plank too long."

The image of him pressed up on those powerful arms—as he held himself over her—ran through her mind. She bit the corner of her mouth, holding back a whimper of need. Fatigue had also apparently removed the reins on her libido. That and the kindness and understanding he showed toward her kids this afternoon. He'd soothed their ruffled feathers and put things in perspective with just a few words, and they'd responded well. Pax had even apologized without prompting. She liked and appreciated the way he was with them. A sexy man who was good with kids was even sexier. And he was getting harder to resist. She wasn't sure she wanted to anymore.

"Kennedy?"

She blinked, his question drawing her from her thoughts. "What?"

He dipped his head and raised a hand to skim his thumb along her jaw, near her chin. "Are you okay?"

All the hair on her neck and scalp stood on end in response to his touch. The burn of desire shot down her spine to curl low in her belly. "I'm fine."

His steel-gray gaze held hers. He opened his hand and cupped her face. "I know you didn't come here for this."

Kennedy's core clenched at the low rumble of his voice. He could read the phone book to her and she'd listen with rapt attention. It was like fine whiskey. Smooth, but with some spice. Plus, there was the heat of desire coloring it. She could see that flare to life in his eyes. "No," she whispered.

"You can walk back to your room. Right now. And we'll go on like we have been. Slow and steady. I can wait. You're important to me, and I'm not going anywhere."

Rationale warred with Kennedy's desire to know every inch of this man. They were moving quickly, but she wasn't so sure that mattered. Her last relationship—Pete—had grown over several months before she entered his bed, and look how that turned out.

But Finn was different. She'd never been so drawn to a man. Not even in the beginning with Pete, when things were hot and heavy. Finn entered the room and she could feel his presence without even looking up. He set off a fine hum through her body with just a look. Everything about him spoke to her. He was more patient and softer around the edges than Pete ever was. Kinder and more thoughtful too. Did she really need more time to figure out if Finn was the right man for her? If he'd be there through all the ups and downs? Hadn't he already proved he would stay by her side?

She framed his face in her hands. "I'm not either."

His pupils widened and the gray of his eyes darkened. A stillness came over him as he stared down at her for a long moment before he wrapped an arm around her waist and tugged her into his room, sealing his mouth to hers.

Kennedy vaguely heard the door shut behind them and the lock click into place. She was more focused on the man holding her tight to his sweaty frame. Sliding her hands into his hair, she gripped the strands, kissing him back like a woman who'd walked through the driest desert and he was the giant, cold bottle of water waiting for her on the other side.

Together, they toppled onto the bed, wiggling up the mattress until Kennedy's head hit the pillows. He tucked her close, his lips leaving hers to trail down her neck and behind her ear. The same tingles that raised her hair a minute ago returned in force, racing down her body in waves. She clutched the back of his head with one hand and let the other skim over the tops of his muscled shoulders. Their legs tangled, and Kennedy couldn't stop the quick involuntary tip of her hips against his thigh. He needed to touch her soon. Before she went crazy from need.

Smart man that he was, he recognized her need for more and lifted his head long enough to draw her t-shirt over her head.

"I admired these at the lodge." He stared at her breasts. "Even then, I wanted to taste them."

A flush stole over Kennedy's body at his words. She wanted him to taste her breasts too. In an effort to encourage him to act, she drew her hands around to rest on his chest and tweaked his nipples. "What are you waiting for?"

He tilted his hips into hers and sucked in a quick breath at her touch. "Not a damn thing." He dipped his head, nipping at the skin above her bra cup.

Kennedy bit her lip, thrusting her hips up to meet him. She could feel the impressive ridge of his erection beneath his shorts, and her body ached to feel it deep within. Raking her nails across the hills and valleys of his abs, she let her fingers drift south to burrow beneath the silky nylon to the prize below. She filled her hand with him and listened to him moan.

Air drafted over her skin as he sat up. Rather than let go of him, she curled her hand; his shorts came down with his movement, exposing him to view. She licked her lips. He was as impressive as he felt. Her tongue darted out, wetting her lips. He wasn't the only one who wanted to taste.

Finn groaned again. "You're killing me."

She tore her gaze away to look at him. "Then do something about it."

Fire ignited in his eyes. It was Kennedy's only warning. In one swift movement, he rolled, putting her on top to straddle him. As she settled, he removed her bra and sent it sailing toward the door. His hands covered her breasts, pinching the peaks and making her moan.

He sat up, wrapping an arm around her and using the other to back up against the headboard. Settled, he leaned forward and latched onto her breast.

Kennedy bit back a shout, conscious they weren't alone in the house. The last thing she needed was to wake up Paige because she couldn't keep her pleasure quiet.

When Finn laved his tongue over the tip of her breast, she couldn't stop the squeak that escaped.

He looked up, a satisfied smile lifting one side of his mouth. "I understand why you stifled that. One day, though, I'm going to take you somewhere where you can shout my name and anything else you want without worrying about who hears you."

That sounded heavenly. She could imagine them naked on a private beach. Right now, though, she'd just settle for naked. Rising up, she moved to the side, unfastening the placket of her jeans. A pout turned her mouth down as the waistband of his shorts moved back into place, removing him from view. Soon enough, she'd uncover him again. But first, she wanted to get rid of her own clothing. Hooking her thumbs along the side of her hips, she shimmied, bringing the heavy denim down.

Finn groaned, eyes fixed on the skin she exposed. A wicked smile spread over her face, and she removed her hands. His gaze snapped to hers.

"Why did you stop?"

She shifted, getting off the bed. "It's kinda hard to take your pants off on your knees." Smile widening, she resumed her slow striptease.

"Vixen." He palmed himself through his shorts.

Kennedy whisked her pants down. It wouldn't do for him to set himself off before she had a taste.

Completely naked, she crawled back onto the bed. His eyes were a dark smolder now, the pupils crowding out much of the gray iris.

He crooked a finger at her, a rakish smile forming. "Come here, baby."

She moved toward him, but instead of straddling him, she reached for his shorts and tugged. He lifted his hips and helped her shove them and his boxer-briefs off. Free of all their clothes, Kennedy climbed up his long legs to settle over his hips. She rolled her own in a circle, teasing them both.

Finn gripped her waist, baring his teeth as he held onto his control. "Damn. We need protection." He pointed to his pants draped over the chair.

Kennedy made no move to get off. Instead, she rose up onto her knees and aligned their bodies. "I'm on the pill and clean. You?" She tipped her pelvis back and forth, wetting him.

His head jerked up and down as he groaned. "Clean."

That was all she needed to hear. Holding him steady, she sank down. Muscles that hadn't been used in years stretched to accommodate him with a burn. But it was a good burn. Finn pressed higher, holding her to him, and let out a low moan.

She rolled her hips in another circle, making him hit all the good spots.

"Oh, you're a tease," he growled, his voice sounding like gravel. He pierced her with a devilish look. "But two can play that game." His broad hands landed on her breasts. With his palms, he made small circles over the tips.

An airy moan escaped her. She raised her hips, then sank down again, making them both groan. Bracing her hands on the headboard's top rail, Kennedy rode him, drinking in the delicious friction created by their lower bodies. Her pleasure grew, wanting to break free, but she put reins on it, slowing her pace. She wanted to savor this as long as she could.

Finn had other ideas. With a growl, he rolled. The room swirled before Kennedy's eyes, and she found herself on her back, staring up into his hard face. Every line of his body screamed he was holding on by a thread. Good. So was she.

Getting to his knees, he slid free of her body, but didn't move away. Grasping her thighs, he pushed them wide. "I want to watch you come." He pressed a thumb to the top of her mound, swirling it. "I want to see you writhe, just for me."

An electric jolt shot through Kennedy, and her core pulsed. "Please, Finn."

One hand around his long shaft and the other still teasing her, he pushed deep. Kennedy grabbed a pillow and moaned into it. This position was even better than the last one. She felt every last, glorious inch of him.

Finn ripped the pillow away and sealed his mouth to hers, swallowing her moans. In moments, Kennedy flew apart at the seams. Light burst behind her closed eyes and flooded her brain. Fiery pleasure raced from her head to toes and back up in wave after wave, sucking the oxygen from her body. She felt Finn go rigid above her, then he locked her in a tight embrace as he rode his own climax.

With one last roll of his hips, his hold relaxed, and he sagged on his arms, his heavy weight pressing her into the mattress. Kennedy didn't care. Her limp body sank into the bed, boneless. If she could walk by morning, it would be a miracle.

Groaning, Finn rolled. Cool air whispered over Kennedy's heated skin, and she shivered. He wrapped one hand over her hip and pulled, tugging her into his large frame. She snuggled close, soaking up his warmth. A yawn stole over her face, reminding her she'd been on her way to bed when she got side-tracked.

A soft giggle escaped.

Finn lifted his head to look at her. "What?"

"Nothing. I was headed to bed. I'm just in the wrong one."

His low chuckle joined hers. He kissed the top of her head. "Do you want to go to your bed?"

Kennedy snuggled closer. "No. I'm good right where I am." She pressed a kiss to his naked chest. His smattering of chest hair tickled her lips. An ember sparked to life deep in her belly. She shifted her legs, trying to squelch it. They both needed to sleep.

He chuckled again. The hand on her hip drifted around her waist to run lightly over her back. Kennedy felt sleep pull at her mind, and her eyelids drifted closed. The bed shifted, and she cracked one eye open as Finn moved to pull the covers from beneath them. Warmth, in the form of the soft comforter and Finn's sleek body, enveloped her. Sleep tugged harder, and darkness edged her vision. The soft press of Finn's lips to her temple was the last thing she registered before she slipped into oblivion.

# Thirty-Two

Whistling, Finn turned the corner into the hallway that housed the ATF offices. Despite the fact his boss called and asked him to stop in, he was in a good mood. Great sex could do that to a person. That and the promise of a future he'd scarcely let himself dream about.

He grasped the long metal bar situated vertically on the wood and glass door bearing the ATF logo and pulled, letting himself in.

"Good morning, Agent Porter."

Finn smiled and waved at the receptionist, Jenni Drake. "Good morning, Miss Jenni." Continuing past her, he headed for the executive offices. Voices carried from the conference room across from his boss's office. He peeked through the glass and saw his boss, along with Nick Sharpe, and several other agents gathered together.

Rapping his knuckles on the window next to the door, he twisted the knob and stepped into the doorway.

"Finn. Perfect timing. Come in." His boss Gavin Trumbull motioned him inside. "We were just about to get started."

A slight frown marring the area between his eyes, Finn

walked to a seat, sitting along with everyone else. "What's going on?"

"We've been building a case against Jack Cartwright." Nick wasted no time diving in. "With Corey Edgerton's statement and the information we got from his dad, we started looking into the man."

"Oh? What did you find out?" Finn was willing to bet there were a whole host of skeletons in Cartwright's closet.

"He lives pretty high on the hog. Even for a lawyer. Especially a junior lawyer. His financial records don't reflect his lifestyle. The only deposits to his accounts come from his job, but he drives an Audi R8—with no car payment."

Finn let out a low whistle. That was an expensive car.

"We can't find evidence of mortgage payments, either, but he lives near the country club in a house worth more than his boss's."

"And he doesn't have family money?" Finn asked.

Sharpe shook his head. "Nope. He's a foster kid who came from nothing. Inner city Washington D.C."

"Okay. But all this is just conjecture. It can't get you a warrant. Though, with the Edgertons' testimony, you should have enough already."

"The kid is iffy. You know how judges feel about that sort of thing," Trumbull said. "So Sharpe went and talked to the office manager at Cartwright's firm, as well as Edgerton's secretary. They both told us some interesting things. Especially the secretary. She didn't want to get fired, so she told us everything she knew."

Finn hoped Edgerton still fired her. He knew if he were in Edgerton's shoes, he'd never be able to trust her again. "What did you learn?"

"The secretary witnessed him trade drugs for cash with a man who came to the house while she was there," Sharpe said. "Cartwright didn't notice her presence, and she never said anything to him about it. Which I don't blame her for. She's probably terrified of him. The office manager had even more to say than the secretary. She said she overheard a conversation between Cartwright and two other attorneys at the firm—all who are part of Herrera's legal team—discussing how they needed to find a way to get to Gonzales, because there was too much heat coming down from targeting the judges."

Finn sat up, gaze locked on Nick. "She's willing to testify to that?"

He nodded. "So is the secretary. The Marshals hate us now, but hopefully we'll soon be able to bring their number of protectees down to just a handful."

"So, what's the plan now? This isn't just an informational meeting, because I seem to be the only one who didn't know all this."

"Correct," Trumbull said. "We're putting together a plan to arrest Cartwright. Today. He hasn't been seen since Judge Davidson's son was drugged, but we have an arrest warrant, plus search warrants for his house and his office. We have search warrants for the two attorneys he was overheard speaking with as well."

A wave of victory swept through Finn, releasing a quick dose of adrenaline. Finally, they might get some answers and end this. "Sounds good. What have you all come up with?"

For the next thirty minutes, Sharpe and Trumbull went over the plan to split into teams and hit both Cartwright's house and the law offices at the same time. Finn was on the team breaching Cartwright's house.

With the plans hammered out, they geared up and piled into the vans to take them to their search locations. Finn drummed his fingers on the stock of the rifle slung over his chest and stared out the window as one of Sharpe's men drove. He hoped the raids netted them what they needed to stop the madness surrounding the judiciary. That they could identify and soon take down all the players. He had a feeling, though, that would be harder than they imagined. Finn doubted either team would find Cartwright today.

The van wove through the city streets until it turned into the exclusive neighborhood near the country club. Here, the stately homes rose several stories behind ornate metal gates and neatly trimmed hedges. They stopped half a block from Cartwright's house and got out.

Sharpe went over the breach plan, then they jogged up the street. Their tech whiz Garrett Somerhauler kneeled next to the code box for the gate and pried the back off, attaching a gizmo to it that cycled through passcodes. After a tense minute, the gate rolled back.

Knowing the opening gate could alert someone inside of their presence, they ran up the drive, half of the team heading around back. Once everyone was in position, Nick gave the order to breach.

Two of his agents swung a battering ram into the front door, splintering it after several tries. One by one, they filed inside, announcing themselves as federal agents. Finn peeled off to the right with Nick, clearing the living room and library before heading up the staircase. In minutes, they had cleared the residence. No one was home.

Finn let his rifle hang and propped his hands on his hips, mouth flat, as they all gathered in the foyer. He hadn't expected to find Cartwright home, but he was still disappointed. He'd wanted to nail the creep who bribed a kid to drug another kid more than he'd imagined.

"Spread out," Nick said. "Remember, we're looking for details on Herrera's drug operation and Cartwright's involvement in that. Find me something."

Turning away, Finn headed for the stairs. From what he knew about Cartwright, he seemed like a man who would keep his dirty secrets close. He wanted to search the man's bedroom.

"Finn, wait up."

Glancing back, Finn paused, waiting for Nick to catch up.

"You have the same idea I do, don't you? Bedroom?"

Finn nodded. "Let's see what we can find." He resumed his walk up the stairs, Sharpe on his heels.

Together, they headed for the left wing of the house, which was a massive master suite. Finn pushed the door open and stared at the gigantic room. At least it was sparsely furnished and neat.

"Where do you want to start?" Finn glanced at Nick.

"I'll take the closet." He motioned to the door on the wall to their left. "Why don't you look out here?"

"Sounds good." Finn moved toward the bed. Nick headed for the closet.

Pausing at the foot of the enormous four-poster bed, Finn surveyed the main room and decided he might as well start where he was. Rounding the mahogany post, he went to the nightstand and opened the drawer. A small baggie of white powder, a short straw, some tissues, and a few miscellaneous toiletry items sat in the drawer. He removed a small digital camera from his vest and snapped some pictures, then set an evidence marker on top of the nightstand before going around to the other side.

His nose wrinkled as he took inventory of the other nightstand drawer. Sex toys, lube, condoms, and a length of rope were jammed into the drawer. Cartwright had a kinky side. Finn had not wanted to know that.

Shoving the drawer closed, he knelt beside the bed and glanced under. It was dusty but empty. Rising, he ripped the comforter and sheets back, exposing the mattress. He hefted it, checking for hidden items beneath, but there was nothing sandwiched between it and the box springs below. Knowing there could be items hidden in the box springs, he moved the mattress, leaning it against the wall at the head of the bed, then probed the thin cover on the box springs. Near the top right-hand corner, the fabric gave. Taking a picture of the hole, he bent closer and shined his flashlight inside. A wad of cash and a bag filled with little bags of drugs sat nestled in the corner.

"Bingo." Snapping another picture, he left a marker near the hole. It was enough to put Cartwright behind bars for a long time. But it didn't tie him to Herrera.

Finn moved on from the mattress and searched the long dresser against the opposite wall. The top was clean, with only a dish full of change sitting amongst the décor. He searched the drawers, pulling them out and checking the wells, but found nothing. That just left the small couch tucked under the picture window.

He took the cushions off, unzipped them, and looked inside. Finding nothing, he stuffed his hands in the cracks, but got nothing more than crumbs and a penny. Next, he pulled the couch away from the wall. Seeing only dust bunnies, he flipped it up. A folder slid part way out of the pocket sewn onto the bottom lining. He snapped a quick picture.

"Nick." Finn called for his partner as he set the couch down and pulled it forward, then tipped it up.

"What did you find?"

"Not sure yet." He bent, holding the couch up with one hand, then took a second picture of the pocket before taking the folder from its pouch. He straightened, lowering the sofa to the floor. Nick stepped closer.

"Is this all you found?"

"No." Finn nodded toward the bed. "There were drugs in the nightstand and in the box springs. There's some cash hidden in there as well. How about you?"

"Lots of fancy clothes and accessories, but nothing incriminating. Open that." Sharpe pointed to the folder.

Finn flipped it open. A list of names and addresses stared back at them. One leaped out at him. "It's the judges' addresses." He touched Kennedy's, then turned the page.

"Whoa." Nick's voice was low.

Whoa was right. It was a list of family members. Right away, Finn saw Pax and Paige, as well as Betty Ruth. Ben and Gemma were on the list, too, along with their infant daughter. Tristan, Laurel, and their baby were on it also.

"Damn, this is thorough. How did they get all this information?" Finn skimmed the list, noting that each judge had at least one person listed.

"Probably been compiling it for a while. It looks like everyone involved with Herrera's arrest is on here, not just the judges." Nick pointed to the names of several deputies who'd been present at Cullen Tate's when Herrera was arrested. Their families were listed as well.

"This looks like a photocopy." Finn touched a line of text.

"It does. I wonder where the original is."

"And who drafted it."

"What else is in there?"

Finn flipped the page. The rest of the folder contained data on drug sales. "Looks like his dealing record." Cartwright was a bigger player than they thought.

"This should put him away for a long time. All right. Put a marker with that and let's go search another room."

Setting the folder on the couch, Finn dropped a marker with it and followed Nick into the bathroom. They pulled the lavish space apart, finding more drugs, but no more files. Finished with the master suite, they moved on to another bedroom.

It took several hours for the team to search the house. Cartwright had drugs squirreled away in nearly every room. In most places, it was just a bag or two. His office was the only other location where they found a significant amount of drugs. Like the bedroom, the bag was accompanied by a wad of cash. Finn's only disappointment was there wasn't anything more linking Cartwright to Herrera. Sharpe seized the office computer, though, and a tablet, so he hoped they'd find something stored either on the devices or in the cloud.

Arms laden with bags of drugs, Finn headed to the van to stow it all for transport. As he neared the vehicle, he caught Nick's eye. The man had his phone to his ear. He held up a finger.

"Take them to the office. I'll be back soon." He hung up.

Finn quirked a brow in question.

"The other team didn't find anything too damning at the law offices. More drugs in Cartwright's office. But the two attorneys who the office manager told us about arrived during the search. They've been detained and are heading to our offices for questioning."

"Awesome." He set the bags in a crate in the back of the van. "How much more do we have to load?"

"I'm not sure. Go check with Jones."

With a nod, Finn jogged back inside, finding Jones in the library. He helped gather the last of the bags, and they stowed them in the van. With the evidence gathered, they loaded up and headed back to the offices.

Sharpe tasked Jones and another agent with booking all the evidence into lockup, then told Finn to follow him to the DEA's interrogation area. They entered the viewing room, where Trumbull waited.

"Has anyone talked to either of them yet?" Nick asked.

Trumbull shook his head. "No. Your guys brought them in about half an hour ago. They've been stewing since then. The other guy is in the room next door."

"They probably haven't said anything, either, have they?" Finn moved closer to the window, studying the body language of the man on the other side. He sat slouched in the chair, giving off a relaxed air, but his twiddling thumbs and the hard set to his mouth said he was anything but relaxed.

"Just asked for a lawyer. One of the partners from their law firm is on his way."

Finn frowned. "He can't represent them."

"He can give advice, but in court, no. They'll have to hire someone outside their firm."

It only took minutes for the attorney to arrive. They gave him a few more with each client, then Finn and Nick went into the interview room with the senior lawyer. He had more to lose, but he also didn't need to kiss anyone's ass to move up in the firm. His name was already on the letterhead.

The metal chairs made a spectacular grating noise as Finn and Nick took their seats. Their suspect and his attorney scrunched their faces up, put off by the sound.

"Gentlemen, I'm Agent Nick Sharpe, DEA. This is Agent Finley Porter, ATF."

"Jeff Hester," the attorney replied.

Nick gave a quick nod in greeting. "We have some questions for your client concerning Jack Cartwright and Gustavo Herrera."

Finn sat back in his chair and let Nick do the talking. He would interject if he had a question or something to add, but he wanted to take the opportunity to watch Tom Kitchens. His body language could tell them a lot.

"You can ask anything you want," Hester said. "But my client won't be answering anything. And any information my client has on Mr. Herrera is privileged."

Nick tipped his head and shrugged a shoulder. "Only what pertains to Mr. Herrera's current charges. Anything that's happened since isn't covered."

Some of the light dimmed from Hester's eyes. Finn bit back a smile. The man had been hoping the agents he faced didn't know the law.

"Mr. Kitchens, are you aware Mr. Cartwright has been taking and dealing illegal drugs?" Nick asked.

Kitchens crossed his arms and stared at Nick.

"Or that he had a hit list of everyone involved in Mr. Herrera's case. And their families?"

Some of the color left Kitchens' face.

"Or that you were overheard discussing said list with Mr. Cartwright and Mr. Sandoval?"

"What?" Kitchens sat up, sweat beading on his forehead. "Who told you that?"

"So, it's true?" Nick countered.

"Tom." Hester shook his head. Kitchens sat back and crossed his arms again. His eyes darted to the side. Hester turned his attention back to Nick. "My client did not affirm your supposition, and he will not."

"I don't think he needs to." Finn tipped his head at Kitchens. "Sweaty forehead, pale skin, knee shaking under the table. I'm pretty sure we have our answer."

"Well, good luck getting body language to hold up in court." Hester's tone was droll.

"We won't need to. We have other evidence." Nick's voice was matter-of-fact, but the look in his eyes said he knew he had Kitchens by the throat. "If he wants any hope of beating a conspiracy charge, he needs to give us Cartwright. Where is he? What all has he done for Mr. Herrera?"

Muscles in Kitchens' jaw worked. He looked at Hester, who gave a soft shake of his head.

"Agents, without a deal on the table, my client will not say a word. This goes for Mr. Sandoval as well. I assume he's next?"

Finn's mouth flattened. He hated defense attorneys. Sharing a look with Nick, he pushed away from the table. "Don't go anywhere. Your charges are pending." Standing, he headed for the door. Nick's chair scraped the floor, and he followed Finn out.

In the anteroom, Finn let out a long breath and ran a hand through his hair. "He's guilty as hell."

"Agreed. But we need a deal before he'll give us anything. Let's talk to Sandoval. Maybe he'll crack, even with Hester urging him to stay quiet."

But their interview with the second man went much like the first. Hester kept his client silent, leaving Finn and Nick with no answers.

Frustrated, Finn went back to his office and sat down at his desk, running the facts of the case through his head. They had a lot of pieces to the story, but they still needed the rest of the puzzle to see the entire picture. He had a feeling they were missing some important players yet.

His phone buzzed on the desk, and he picked it up to see a text from Kennedy. Unlocking the device, he clicked on the message. An image of her taking a selfie with Betty Ruth, Pax, and Paige filled the screen. Beneath the picture, it said, *The gang's all together again. We're just missing you.*

Finn smiled, his frustration easing as a wave of something more tender filled his heart. Clicking in the text box, he replied.

*On my way.*

Gathering up all the gear he pulled from his car for the raid earlier, he left his office. His case was stagnant until the U.S. Attorney's office came through with deals for Kitchens and Sandoval. It was time for him to go home.

# Thirty-Three

The soft whir of the garage door alerted Kennedy to Finn's arrival. He'd taken to parking in the empty garage bay since he'd been staying with them. She didn't mind. It was nice to think he felt comfortable in her home. And after last night, she didn't want him to leave.

She smiled as the door opened and he stepped in. "Hi."

"Hey." His answering smile made her heart skip. "Were you waiting on me?"

Knowing he was referring to her presence in the kitchen, she shook her head. "I came out to make popcorn. The kids are watching a movie and requested it." She lifted a shoulder. "I'm indulging their laziness tonight."

Finn's smile widened. He walked closer. "Sometimes, that's all kids need." He bent his head to press a kiss to her lips.

Kennedy's heart skipped again. She kept her hands at her sides, knowing if she touched him, she'd deepen their kiss and just leave them both aching for more.

He pulled away, a tender but heated look in his eyes. "So, how did your day go? Did you get Pax and Betty Ruth home without any problems?"

The microwave dinged behind her, and she stepped back to take the popcorn out. "It went fine. I'm glad Paige came with me. She helped carry things."

"I'm sorry I couldn't come."

Kennedy waved a hand and put the second bag of popcorn in the microwave. "I know. Neither of us were expecting your boss to call you in. What happened, anyway? Something major, I'm guessing. You've been gone all day."

"Yeah." Quickly, he gave her an overview of his day. While he talked, she dumped popcorn into bowls and added seasonings.

"Wow. Do you think either attorney will give up Cartwright's location?"

Finn lifted a shoulder and stole a piece of the cheddar popcorn. "If the deal is sweet enough, and they know where he is, maybe."

"Well, in any case, it sounds like you guys have dealt a pretty good blow to the operation targeting us."

He took more popcorn, eyebrows drawn down. "Maybe. I think we just found the middlemen. What we need is to take the head off the snake."

Kennedy popped a piece of the cinnamon-sugar popcorn into her mouth. "How do you do that? Herrera's already in jail."

"We take away his access to the outside world. But we need one of the attorneys to confess that he put them up to turning over the list to his goon squad."

"How are you handling the corruption with his attorneys? He's entitled to representation."

"I know. I expect the U.S. Attorney's office to file a motion to have his counsel appointed by the court. This case is a mess. It might even end up moved out of the district."

Kennedy wouldn't be surprised if that happened. Every judge had their lives turned upside down because of Gustavo

Herrera's actions. It would have a direct impact on the court proceedings. She wouldn't wish her problems on anyone, but she wouldn't be sorry to see him go elsewhere.

"I don't want to talk about work, though. It'll still be there in the morning." He backed her against the counter, circling his arms around her waist. "I'd much rather get reacquainted with you."

Need erupted low in Kennedy's belly. She put her hands on his chest and fiddled with the row of buttons on his polo shirt. When his head descended, she met him eagerly, giving in to the desire. She was now resigned to living in a perpetual state of need. One look at those dimples and she was a pile of goo.

"Hey, Mom? Can we have—oops!"

Kennedy and Finn broke apart at Paige's interruption.

"Sorry. I can do without fudge drizzle." She grabbed both popcorn bowls from the other side of the island and drew them toward her. "I'll just take these. Carry on." With a bright smile, she spun and hurried away.

Groaning, Kennedy covered her face with her hands. Finn chuckled.

"At least we know she approves," he said. "She didn't seem upset to see us kissing."

Kennedy glanced up. "True. But that's not the way I wanted to break the news to them about our relationship."

"Well, let's go talk to them now." He took her hand and tugged her toward the door.

"What? Wait. No, I'm not ready." What would she say? She needed time to think about this.

"You said yourself that wasn't how you wanted them to find out. Instead of letting them wonder what's going on with us, we fill in the blanks now. Simple as that." He continued through the doorway and into the hall.

"No, it's not. Finn!" She yanked on his hand, pulling him

to a stop. "How can we tell them what's going on when we haven't even talked about it?"

A wrinkle formed between his eyes. "Good point." He changed direction.

Kennedy sighed. "Where are we going now?"

"To your office to talk about it." He pulled her through the door, then shut it.

Silence descended as they stared at each other. She knew what needed to be said, but didn't know how to say it.

"Tell me what you're thinking." Finn's quiet voice washed over her. "I can't tell."

She searched his gaze, looking for anything that would make her think he wouldn't respond the way she hoped he would. Taking a deep breath, she knew there was only one way to find out. She wasn't a coward, but the scars from her disastrous marriage ran deep. Putting her faith in another man was huge.

But Finn wasn't Pete. Not even close.

"I had resigned myself to being single. I'm thirty-eight, divorced with two teenagers, and I have a high-powered job. I knew the odds of finding a man who wanted to take on the craziness of my life were slim. But you came along and slipped in so seamlessly. I'm not sure if that means my life isn't as chaotic as I thought, or if you're just that amazing, but I'm not complaining. You've filled a void I didn't know needed filled. And as scary as it is to start a new relationship after all I've been through, I don't want you to leave."

There. It was out there. He meant something to her, and she wanted a relationship with him. Now he knew that.

Those dimples she loved so much appeared. "Good."

When he didn't continue, she arched an eyebrow and cocked her head. "Good? That's all you have to say?"

He chuckled. "I have plenty to say, Kennedy."

"Then say it." She needed to hear what was going on in his

head too. To know, one-hundred percent, that he felt the same way.

Finn framed her face in his hands. She fought the desire his touched provoked so she could listen.

"I have always been of the camp that if a family was in the cards for me, it would happen. Until I hit about thirty-five and had no prospects. Then I became more like you and thought that idea was well behind me. I never expected you. Or your kids. And I adore all three of you. I want to build a family with you, Ken. I don't want to leave, either."

Kennedy jumped on him with a joyful laugh, pleased beyond measure to hear him confirm this was more than just a fling for him too. Locking her ankles behind his waist, she held his smiling face in her hands. "I know it's too soon to put any labels on what we feel, but I'm falling in love with you, Finley Porter."

"Same, Judge Davidson." He brought a hand up from where it rested on her hip and cupped the side of her head, holding her steady to kiss her.

She sank into him with a sigh. If she ever got used to this —who was she kidding? She'd never get used to this. With a simple kiss, he sent her sailing toward the heavens. Every time.

Gentling the kiss, Finn lifted his head. "I would love to christen your couch, but we have another conversation yet."

Kennedy's thighs flexed involuntarily, bringing her center into contact with his, at the thought of stripping down and straddling him again. She pecked a hard kiss to his lips, then dropped her legs and stepped back, knowing he was right. "Yep. Let's go."

Finn adjusted himself with a grimace. "I'm glad I'm wearing jeans. And that you didn't do that again."

She let out a soft chuckle and glanced down. Only a faint bulge showed behind the zipper of his pants. "Think about your mom. That ought to kill it."

Laughing, Finn followed her out of the room. "Oh, yeah. It's dead now." He slapped her butt. "But I promise it will come back later."

Kennedy sent him a heated look as they reached the junction leading into the living room. "It better." Turning away, she pasted a smile on her face and walked toward the kids and Betty Ruth, who sat in the recliner, wrapped in a fluffy blanket. Kennedy spied the remote on the coffee table and picked it up, pausing their movie. They all glanced at her with curious looks. "Finn and I need to talk to you."

A wide smile spread over Paige's face. "I know what this is about."

Pax frowned and looked at his sister. "You do?"

She nodded. "I caught them K-I-S-S-I-N-G in the kitchen."

"Seriously?" Pax's eyebrows shot up and his head swung around to look at them. "Gross."

Finn's deep laugh made Kennedy smile. She fixed her gaze on the twins. "Paige is right. We want to talk to you about us." She glanced back at Finn for a brief moment. "We want there to be an us. And by that, I don't mean just him and me. I mean all of us." She drew a circle in the air, encompassing everyone in the room. "Because there is no us"—she waved a hand between herself and Finn—"if it doesn't include you. And we want to know what you think about that." She looked at Betty Ruth. "You, too, Betty Ruth."

The older woman waved a hand. "He's acceptable." A smile ghosted over her lips, and a twinkle appeared in her eyes. "But don't go by what I say. Listen to them." She pointed at the kids.

"I'm cool with it," Paige said. "He makes you smile."

"Yeah," Pax agreed. "And he's not a douche, like Dad."

"Paxton!" Kennedy stared open-mouthed at her son. She

shouldn't be surprised by his language, but sometimes she forgot he was nearly sixteen.

"What? It's true. We like Finn. He treats you like you matter. Us too. So if you want to date him or whatever, we're all for it."

"You don't mind that I might want to get married again someday? After what we went through with your dad?"

"No. Not when the guy you're with is cool." Pax's gaze turned hard, though. "Don't hurt her. I don't care that you're bigger than me. I will punch you in the face."

"And I'll jump on your back and claw at your eyes while he does." Paige narrowed her eyes, dead serious.

Kennedy just blinked. Good, lord. She cleared her throat. "Thank you, heathens. I appreciate the support."

Betty Ruth laughed, then moaned. "Oh, don't make me laugh. It makes my stitches pull."

Paige frowned. "Sorry. Maybe we should watch a different movie, then. This is sort of a comedy."

The older woman waved a hand. "You watch what you want. I'll probably just fall asleep."

Nodding, Paige looked at Pax. He lifted a shoulder, answering her silent question, then turned to Kennedy and Finn.

"We just want you to be happy, Mom."

"Yep," Paige said. "I wish we had been able to tell you that years ago. Maybe then you wouldn't have stayed with Dad so long. Neither of us has anything against you dating or being married. We just want it to be the right guy." She held a hand up, gesturing to Finn. "Finn seems like he might be that guy."

"I hope to be." Finn entered the conversation, conviction in his deep voice. "You and your mother are important to me." He glanced at Kennedy. "We're still feeling our way through this, but we both intend to see it through. To whatever that may be."

"Awesome." Pax grabbed a handful of popcorn. "Now that we have that settled, can we watch our movie again?"

Huffing a laugh, Kennedy nodded. "Sure. But you have to scoot over." She walked toward him, motioning for them to move down, then sank onto the couch beside him. Finn sat on the floor between her feet.

"What are we watching, anyway?" Finn reached for a handful of popcorn.

"*Jumanji*. The new one," Paige said.

"Hit 'Play,' Mom." Pax nudged her.

Kennedy pushed the button on the remote. Finn grabbed her legs and drew them over his shoulders, letting her use him like a footrest. Settling deeper into the couch, a contented warmth filled her. This was how evenings at home should be. She was thankful for this one and prayed they had many more.

# Thirty-Four

Kennedy shuffled through the papers on her desk, looking for the case report to go with the next name on her docket for this afternoon. She bit into the apple in her left hand, holding it with her teeth to free her fingers for the search. Being off so much last week put her behind. But the break had been nice, even if the circumstances weren't. She had a relaxing, quiet weekend at home with her kids and Finn.

A buzzing siren blared, making her jump and let out a soft shriek. She grabbed the apple and set it down, realizing the noise was the fire alarm. Her office door swung open.

"Ma'am, we need to go."

She nodded at the young U.S. Marshal assigned to her today, already rising from her seat. Pulling open her bottom desk drawer, she withdrew her purse, not wanting to be caught without it if they were locked out of the building for a while.

"Ma'am." The man motioned toward the door, his expression taut.

"I'm coming." She snatched her phone and office keys from the desk and followed him out.

The last of the interns walked into the hall as Kennedy stepped into the main office. She didn't waste any time following the young woman out. In the corridor, the siren blared louder, echoing off the marble floor and high ceilings. Voices intermingled with it, creating a cacophony that hurt her ears. She walked faster.

"Judge Davidson!"

Kennedy glanced back at the marshal's call as she reached the stairwell. He'd fallen behind.

"Slow down!"

Someone bumped into her, pushing her forward. She'd been swept into the tide of humanity exiting the building. Lifting a hand in a, "What can I do?" gesture, she kept up with the crowd, not wanting to get knocked down.

In the stairwell, the noise was even louder, the confined walls increasing the echo tenfold. Kennedy clenched her teeth and continued her descent, eager to be outside.

Finally, she made it through the small door on the ground floor and into the lobby. Pausing off to the side, she waited for her escort to emerge.

"Ma'am, please keep moving." One of the guards touched her arm, urging her to go outside.

"I'm waiting for someone."

"I'm sure they'll get out. You need to vacate the area, though." He stretched his arm out, hand behind her back, ushering her forward into the throng. His radio crackled to life.

*"Send fire to the second floor. We've got smoke up here."*

Kennedy glanced up at the gallery. A fine wisp of smoke hung in the air. Realizing this wasn't a false alarm, she cast one more look at the stairwell door, hoping her young escort would emerge. When several people stumbled out and there was still no sign of him, she let the guard usher her out.

Eyes darting around the lobby, she looked for familiar

faces. Where were Suzie and the interns? They were only a few steps ahead when she reached the stairs.

Sunshine hit her face as she stepped through the building's front doors. People streamed across the lawn and into the parking lot. Kennedy followed the crowd, still searching for someone she knew.

"Kennedy!"

She whirled, searching for the source of her name. Suzie waved near a row of parked cars. Relieved she wasn't out here alone, she jogged toward the woman.

"Well, this is exciting." Suzie rolled her eyes. "Hopefully, we won't be out long."

"I'm not sure if it'll be quick. I saw smoke."

Suzie's eyes widened. "Oh my." Her mouth flattened. "And you had the foresight to grab your purse. Damn. I left mine in my desk."

Kennedy wrinkled her nose, acknowledging Suzie's dismay, then looked around again. People still streamed from the building, but not in droves, like a moment ago. Firetrucks screamed onto the scene, divulging their firefighters, who quickly set up hose lines. Smoke now drifted out the front doors of the building.

Her gaze tracked over the crowd once more, looking for her escort. That marshal had vanished into thin air. She didn't see any of the others, either. But there were hundreds of people now standing outside; she couldn't see all the way to the back of the crowd.

"Judge Davidson!"

Hearing her name, she turned. A hand waved above the crowd. She stood on her tiptoes, trying to see who it was. It looked like one of the interns, but she couldn't be sure. She glanced back to ask Suzie, only to realize she, too, had disappeared.

"What the hell is going on? Did everyone take invisibility

pills this morning, or something?" she muttered. Shaking her head, she rose up on her toes again, looking for the person who called her name.

"Judge!" Arms waved in the air again, then a head popped up over the crowd for a quick moment.

Kennedy recognized the woman. It was an intern from her office—Frannie. Giving the area one last look for Suzie, Kennedy headed Frannie's direction. The woman still hopped, waving her arms, even as she pushed through the crowd.

"Oh, I'm so glad I found you!" Frannie grabbed her hand briefly and squeezed when they made it through the throng to each other. "Everyone disappeared."

"Have you seen anyone else? I found Suzie, but then she vanished."

Frannie looked past Kennedy, her bubbly smile dying. A harder, more pensive look appeared. "I thought I saw Danielle. Over there." She pointed away from the building toward the edge of the parking lot. "But then I saw you, and you were closer. Do you mind if we look for her?"

"Sure. We should probably try to find everyone from the office. The firefighters might need a headcount."

Frannie nodded and started walking. Kennedy followed and kept her head on a swivel, on the lookout for anyone from their office, or one of the marshals she knew. As the crowd thinned out and they still hadn't found anyone, she paused. "You know, we should find some higher ground. See if we can spot anyone that way. This isn't working. You're sure you saw Danielle back this way?"

"Yep. That blue jacket she had on today is unmistakable."

Kennedy hadn't seen her, so she couldn't comment. But she knew the jacket Frannie meant. It was one of Danielle's favorites. She didn't see anyone in anything that color over this way, though. "Frannie, I don't think she's over here."

"She's not."

Kennedy whirled, startled by the male voice so close. A man in a charcoal suit and navy blue tie stood several feet away. Sunglasses covered his eyes, and his rigid posture and blank expression sent a chill up her spine.

She glanced around, noting how far she was now from the majority of the crowd. Something wasn't right.

"Frannie, let's go back. Danielle must have changed direction. Suzie will be wondering where I went too." She started to walk around the man, but he stepped in her path. A shiver of fear went through her and made goosebumps break out on her skin, despite the heat.

"That stupid woman is probably gossiping about what happened." Frannie walked past to stand next to the man. "She doesn't care where you went." She glanced up at the man. "Hey, baby."

Kennedy's eyes widened. *Baby?*

The man gave Frannie a quick smile, transforming his face to handsome. The austere mask dropped back into place a moment later.

Frannie turned a cold smile on Kennedy. "That's right, Judge. You walked into a trap."

Kennedy's gaze darted around as her mind screamed at her she'd been a fool. Now she needed a way out. But if she went to either side, one of them would stop her. The only clear path was behind her, except it led away from help.

"We're going to get into that car over there." Frannie pointed at a dark blue SUV with tinted windows. "You're not going to make a fuss, or I'll stick you like a pig and let you bleed out behind a car. With all this commotion, how long do you think it'll take before someone realizes you need help? I'm guessing you'll be dead long before that happens." The bubbly girl who always had something to say to cheer everyone up was nowhere to be seen. In her place was a ruthless, unfeeling woman.

For just a second, Kennedy considered making a break for it. But they'd wandered to the very outskirts of the crowd. No one was paying any attention to her. And she didn't want to put anyone else in danger. Frannie had a knife, but what other weapons did the two of them have? She was betting the big guy had a gun.

A moment later, the man unbuttoned his jacket, sweeping aside one edge and exposing the butt of a pistol, confirming her suspicions. "Move." He nodded toward the car.

Gulping hard, Kennedy wavered. If she went with them, the chances of escaping were slim. But would she make it out of the parking lot alive if she resisted?

Frannie rolled her eyes. Reaching behind her back, she withdrew a long, thin knife as she took two steps forward and grabbed Kennedy's arm. "Don't make me hurt you. You're not supposed to die yet."

"Yet?" Kennedy frowned, staring at her, even as Frannie pushed her forward.

"Yes. Yet. Someone has plans for you. And you'll find out what those are soon enough."

Another wave of goosebumps erupted, her body chilled by the fear induced by that thought. What was in store for her next?

# THIRTY-FIVE

Finn tapped his fingers against his thigh, waiting for the cell door to open and let him through to the interview area of the prison. They'd hit a dead end in their search for Jack Cartwright, so he was back at the federal prison in Butner, hoping to get something out of Gustavo Herrera. The deals hadn't been good enough for Tom Kitchens and Alberto Sandoval, so they'd opted to take their chances with jury trials. But that left Finn and the task force with few leads.

A buzzer sounded, and the door rolled back, letting him through. Finn followed the guard through, vaguely noting the door clang as it hit the backstop.

"Is Herrera here yet?" Finn nodded to the door they paused in front of.

"He's on his way. It's lunchtime."

Another buzzer sounded, and the door at the opposite end of the hall opened. Finn's body went on alert as he saw Herrera standing there, chains around his wrists attached to his waist. His black hair was slicked back. A dark smile spread over his face when he caught sight of Finn.

"Agent Porter. You have perfect timing."

Darkness descended as the lights went out.

A thud and a grunt sounded from Herrera's direction, then the unmistakable sound of someone hitting the floor. The guard with Finn cursed, scrabbling at his waist as the clink of chains got closer. Finn's eyes strained in the dark. Why weren't the emergency lights coming on?

The guard lifted something free of his belt, a moment later clicking on his flashlight. It was just in time to shine off the metal chain coming at his face. The links smacked the guard in the temple, bending him double. The flashlight hit the floor and rolled away, its light bouncing off the wall and casting strange shadows.

Finn side-stepped into the middle of the hallway, facing Herrera. In the low light, he could see the man's teeth, bared in an evil smile. Finn braced himself as Herrera lunged.

Though smaller, the man was solid and hit Finn hard, burying his shoulder in his gut. The breath left Finn in a whoosh, but he held onto Herrera's jumpsuit, keeping him from getting past. With a hard tug, he brought the man down to the floor and rolled, trying to trap him to the ground.

A gunshot rang out, the bullet winging past his ear so close Finn felt the breeze. *Shit! Who was shooting?*

Herrera took advantage of the distraction and bucked, sending Finn to the side. Finn lost his grip. Cursing, he scrambled to his feet, but was forced back to the ground as another shot slammed into the wall to his right. He rolled into a deep shadow and crept forward.

Silhouetted by the light coming from the flashlights of other guards who ran to help, Finn saw a man standing in the hall, arm raised. Herrera ran through the still open door, and the man fired several more rounds down the hall. Finn heard one hit the guard who'd shown him in. The man let out a moan of pain, then a curse.

Saying a few choice words of his own, Finn watched the

gunman turn and fire at the guards coming toward them. Several of them dropped, the other retreating, and in moments, he and Herrera disappeared from view.

On his knees, Finn scrambled toward the flashlight and picked it up, then retraced his steps to the guard. The man lay on his side, blood pooling beneath him.

"Hey, man. Where are you shot?"

"Don't worry about me." The guard grimaced, his face clammy in the stark light. "Go get that son-of-a-bitch."

"Someone else is going to have to stop him. There are too many of you down for me to leave. And I'm unarmed." Punctuating his point, several more shots rang out in the distance. Finn wouldn't stand a chance against that; his gun and his phone were locked in his car, since neither were allowed in the prison.

He pushed the guard onto his back, trying not to think about Herrera getting away. "Let me see."

Groaning, the man raised a hand and pointed at his right side.

Finn inspected the area, finding a hole just below his ribcage. Blood ran out. His fingers moved to the buttons on the guy's uniform shirt. "What's your name?"

"Rich."

"Well, Rich, I think the bullet might have hit your liver." He got the shirt open to get a better look and probed the area around the wound. He didn't feel a bullet. "I'm going to turn you and look for an exit wound." Not waiting for a reply, he rolled him up and looked at his back. There was blood, but no hole. Gently, he let him back down. "I don't see an exit. Is there a first-aid station close by?"

"Um, yeah. Where we checked you in. There's a cabinet with supplies."

"Okay, hang tight." Finn rose to his feet and hurried away, keeping close to the wall in case Herrera and his buddy came back. He made it through the door, stopping to check the guards who were down and finding them all dead. Pushing away the remorse, he ran into the office. Rich would be, too, if he didn't stop the bleeding.

It only took him moments to find what he needed. He also tried the desk phone, but it was dead. Whoever cut the power also cut the phone lines.

Turning away, medical supplies in hand, he took a step toward the door, but stopped when the light crossed something shiny. His heart dub-stepped as he realized it was a cellphone. Someone hadn't been following the rules. Finn stooped and grabbed it. He clicked the button on the side, praying it wasn't locked. A keypad appeared.

"Dammit!" Shoving the device in his pocket, he ran back down the hall.

"Took you... long enough." Rich's breathing had turned labored. He was grayer too. Finn wasn't sure his limited first-aid skills would be enough to staunch the blood flow.

"I tried to call for help. The landline's been cut. I found a cellphone, but it's locked." He opened the med kit and removed several large gauze pads.

"That's... Dunleavy's. He sneaks it in... to text his girlfriend."

"Do you know the PIN?" Finn tore open the packets and pressed them to Rich's side. The man hissed, and Finn grimaced in apology. "Sorry."

"'S'okay." Rich gulped in some breaths and moaned again. "Oh, God, that hurts." He swallowed and took another labored breath. "And yeah. The PIN... is his girl's birthday. Zero-nine-three-zero."

Finn took the phone from his pocket and typed in the code. The home screen came up. "Yes! I'm in." He touched the phone icon and called 911. The dispatcher picked up after a couple rings, and Finn quickly identified himself and the situation.

"Can you tell me how many are injured?"

"I've got one here. And three dead. Hang on." He got up, going to the end of the hall to check on the guard Herrera knocked out. The man was alive, but unconscious. Finn didn't see any blood, but the man had a large goose egg on the side of his head. "There's another unconscious. Looks like a head wound. I haven't been past this hallway to tell you about others."

"Okay. I'll relay your information to responding officers. Can we call you back on this number if need be?"

"Yes."

"Great, thank you. I've sent help."

"Thanks." Finn hung up and went back to Rich. Dropping to his knees, he cursed when he saw the gauze. Blood had soaked through all of it.

The medical box clattered as Finn dug through it. He found the rolled gauze and ripped open the package, unspooling it. "This is gonna hurt, man." Finn put the gauze to the wound and leaned.

Rich moaned long and loud.

"Sorry, but I need to stop the bleeding." Finn glanced down the hallway. Help needed to hurry.

Minutes passed, and Finn went through the rest of the roll. Rich's breathing grew shallower, and the color seeped from his face. Fearing the man would die in the next couple minutes, Finn called 911 back.

The man's greeting barely cleared the line before Finn started talking.

"I just called from inside the prison. Agent Porter. The man who's injured is bleeding to death. Rapidly. Are medics close?"

"I'm not sure. Let me contact the incident commander." The line clicked as the dispatcher placed Finn on hold.

Letting out a growl, Finn hung up and put the phone away. He didn't have time to wait on that. "Okay, man. We're getting out of here." And hopefully, the coast was clear.

He sat Rich up, then bent, putting the man's arm over his shoulders, and hiking him across the top of his back. With his other hand through Rich's legs, he straightened, holding the guard in a fireman's carry. Saying a prayer, he made his way down the darkened hall.

At the hallway junction, he paused, peering around the corner. Not seeing anyone, he kept going. As he neared the front of the building, more guards laid motionless on the floor. He wanted to stop to check on them, but knew he needed to get Rich out of the building. He couldn't do anything for the downed men without jeopardizing the critical patient he already carried.

Rounding another corner, light filtered in from outside, quickening Finn's pace. He burst through the door to the wide walkway leading to the offices outside the fence. Movement inside made him slow. He didn't know if it was a guard or if it was Herrera and his one-man hit squad. Though he was betting Herrera went through the intake gate. They could have run through the yard, bypassing most of the doors in the facility.

The door opened.

"Freeze!"

Finn stopped.

"Identify yourself."

"Finley Porter, ATF. I have an injured guard who needs urgent medical attention." The man on his shoulders moaned.

The guard's gun dipped, then he motioned Finn forward. Wasting no time, Finn brought the man inside and laid him on the floor. Blood had soaked through to Finn's clothes. Rich was deathly gray.

"Shit." The guard who let him in took in Rich's appearance. "Jacoby! Go get the med kit." He turned to Finn. "Are you hit?"

"No."

"What happened? The alarms went off, and we got a report of shots fired, then nothing."

"Gustavo Herrera escaped. He had help. A guard, or someone dressed like one. There's several more men shot back there." Finn pointed toward the door. "I was here to meet with him. The guard who escorted Herrera to the interview room is down, but alive. Rich was my escort. The ones who came running after the first shots are all dead. I passed several others on my way out, but didn't check them because I had Rich."

The guard cursed again. "Okay. I'll send some people in to get them out." He lifted the radio mic on his shoulder and requested backup to the front of the prison. Jacoby appeared with a beefy med kit while he did.

Finn dug into it, finding the things he needed to try to stop Rich's bleeding. Another guard, who was trained as an EMT started an IV line.

"I called 911 from inside." Finn reached into his pocket and handed the guard the phone he found. "One of the dead guards apparently didn't like to leave his phone behind."

The man took it. "We called too. They should be here soon."

Within minutes, first responders filled the parking lot beyond the doors. Thanks to the fluids the guards started, Rich was still alive when an ambulance crew whisked him off to the hospital. Finn stood back and watched the chaos. So far, six guards were dead and seven others were injured.

"Agent Porter."

Glancing over, he saw Jacoby coming toward him.

"Sir, there's a phone call for you."

Finn frowned. "For me?"

"Yes, sir. Nick Sharpe?"

Figuring Nick had heard about the escape, Finn followed Jacoby into the security office and picked up the phone the man indicated.

"Porter."

"You need to come home. Now."

Finn's frown deepened at the urgency to Nick's voice. "What? Why? Herrera—"

"Forget Herrera. Kennedy's been taken."

The blood drained from Finn's head. He grabbed the back of the chair and locked his knees to stay upright. "Say again?"

"There was a fire at the courthouse. In the chaos of the evacuation, she's disappeared. The office manager, Mrs. MacKinnon, tried calling her. So did the Marshals. Everyone else is accounted for except for Judge Stechschulte and an intern. Francesca Romero. A check of the local hospitals doesn't turn up a match for any of them. They're just gone."

A string of curses flew through Finn's head. "Have you checked security feeds yet?"

"Of course I have." Nick's tone was sharp. He blew out a breath. "Sorry. I'm just pissed. With all the security we had in place, somehow, we've had three people vanish at once. And before you ask, the cameras caught Kennedy talking to Mrs. MacKinnon, then Ms. Romero. She walked out of sight with the intern. Judge Stechschulte went across the street in the evacuation. We lost her in the crowd."

Finn raised a hand to rub his face, then paused. He was still covered in blood. "Okay. I need to get cleaned up, then I'll be headed home. Has anyone told the families yet?"

"Not that I know of."

"Okay. Don't tell Kennedy's. Let me talk to them. I'll go there first."

"Sounds good. What's the word on Herrera? Paulson messaged me there'd been an incident at the prison."

"He escaped."

"Well, shit."

"Yeah. He planned this. Probably from the moment he was arrested."

"Have you checked on Gonzales?"

Finn's eyes widened. "No." In the chaos and confusion, he hadn't even thought about their witness. "I'll do that, too, before I head back."

"Good. Keep me posted."

"Yep." Finn hung up and looked at Jacoby. "I need eyes on Javier Gonzales."

"We're doing an inmate count now."

"That's good, but I need you to send a man to his cell and make sure he's alive. He's the main witness against Herrera."

Jacoby's eyes widened. He lifted the phone receiver and put in the request.

"There some place I can wash up?" He motioned to his bloody hands.

"Down the hall." Jacoby pointed, eyes on the security feeds.

"Thanks. I'll be right back."

Finn hurried to the restroom and ran his hands under hot water, soaping, rinsing, then soaping again. His jacket was ruined, so he stuffed it in the trash. Not even the best dry cleaners in the world could fix that. His shirt was stained, but not soaked like the coat. He had a spare in his car and would switch it out when he left. Urgency propelled him out of the restroom and back to the security center.

"Excuse me. Who are you?" A man in a suit straightened

from where he leaned over Jacoby's chair, watching the monitors.

Finn flashed his ID. "Finn Porter, ATF. I'm the one who brought your injured guard out."

"You mean you're the one who let an inmate escape." The man pinned Finn with a glare.

Expression hardening, Finn squared his shoulders and faced the man he assumed was the warden. "Maybe you should look at your internal hiring practices before accusing me of anything. I tried to help your men. It was a guard who helped him escape." He glanced at Jacoby. "Did you find Gonzales?"

The downturn to the man's face told him all he needed to know. "Fuck. He's dead, isn't he?"

Jacoby nodded. "Shiv to the heart."

Finn grimaced. Ouch. "Keep us in the loop. I need to go back to Asheville. There have been some developments there."

"What kind of developments?" The warden stepped away from Jacoby, turning to face Finn. "If this involves my prisoner—"

"It does, but it'll be up to other agencies to track him down. You worry about the population you have left. And your dead and wounded guards." He backed toward the door. "I'll email you my statement on the incident. And no, I didn't get a good look at the guard who helped him. It was too dark." Now in the hall, he turned to leave. "Someone from the task force will be in touch." Not waiting for more questions—or protests—he jogged away. He needed to be in Asheville. Not just for Kennedy and the kids, but because he had a feeling there were more answers to this there.

# THIRTY-SIX

The skin on Kennedy's wrists burned, raw from the rope tied around them. After Frannie and her well-muscled boyfriend ushered her off to their waiting vehicle, they tied her up and stuffed her in the backseat. She'd flexed her wrists when they did so, hoping to create a little space so she could get free, but all she'd succeeded in doing so far was to make herself bleed.

She glanced to her right. Judge Jill Stechschulte sat next to her, barely conscious. Dried blood matted her hair over a lump on her forehead. They'd stopped behind the buildings across the street long enough for some guy to shove the battered judge in the vehicle. Kennedy had done her best to stop the bleeding and clean her up, but all she had—all she could reach, was the pack of tissues she kept in her suit jacket. They'd taken her purse from her when they stuffed her in the car.

Kennedy resisted the urge to touch her waist. Having a feeling they would leave her bag behind, she'd slipped her fingers into the outside coin pocket as they walked and removed the AirTag she'd kept in there ever since they became a thing. When Frannie tried to take her purse, she fought, knowing they'd get physical. She'd played up the altercation and dropped to the ground when Frannie punched her. With a quick roll of "pain" she stuffed the tag in her underwear, where they'd be the least likely to check. It was worth the hit to the jaw to get that device on her person. She just hoped someone thought to look for it. Her phone was with her purse now inside a dumpster across the street from the courthouse.

The car turned off the highway to a bumpy side road. Kennedy had no idea where they were. Somewhere in Virginia, that much she knew. They'd passed a sign hours ago when they crossed the state line. Now they were in the middle of nowhere. It was nothing but trees outside her window.

Several miles down the road, the car slowed and turned onto a dirt track, taking them deeper into the woods. She braced her bound hands against the driver's seat, holding on as they bumped over the uneven ground. Jill tipped, her reactions slow from her head wound, and banged her head into the window. Kennedy let go of the seat and grabbed the woman, pulling her toward the middle. She spread her feet, using her knees in place of her hands to keep them steady.

Eventually, the road ran out, and they stopped.

"Where are we?" Kennedy looked out, hoping to see something she recognized, but there was nothing but trees.

Frannie tossed her a hard look over the seat, but stayed silent. She and her boyfriend got out, opening the rear doors. Large hands gripped Kennedy's arms, pulling her from the vehicle.

"I can move on my own, you know," she growled. "No need for manhandling."

In answer, his grip around her bicep tightened, and he shoved her forward.

Gritting her teeth, she quit arguing and concentrated on her footing. Heels—even low ones like she had on—weren't suitable for hiking. Thankfully, they weren't too pointy, so she didn't sink into the dirt.

Leaves slapped her face as the man hauled her through the woods. Every step tightened the ball of nerves that had formed in her belly. They were well and truly in the middle of nowhere. She glanced at Jill, who stumbled alongside Frannie. The younger woman was working hard to keep the judge from collapsing, her head wound taking its toll.

"Ian, trade me." Frannie stopped with a huff. "This one's having trouble walking."

Stopping, Ian rolled his eyes. "Weren't you just telling me the other day you didn't need help with heavy things?"

"That was a box, asshole. Not a hundred-and-fifty-pound woman who's four inches taller than me."

He snorted. "Not my fault you're short, pumpkin."

Frannie propped one fist on her hip and glared.

"Fine," Ian growled. "Come take her." He shook Kennedy's arm.

Frannie pulled Jill with her, thrusting her toward Ian as she reached for Kennedy's other arm.

"You behave for Frannie, now." Ian tapped Kennedy's nose.

Her anger surged. What a prick. "When I get out of this, I'll make sure you two spend the maximum amount of time possible behind bars."

"I admire your confidence. But we've never been caught, and it's not happening this time, either." Ian put his shoulder into Jill's abdomen and lifted her over his shoulder.

Ian's words sent a jolt of worry through her. Who were these people? Some sort of murderous, modern-day Bonnie and Clyde?

"Let's go. They're waiting." Ian glanced back at Frannie and Kennedy as he walked forward.

For a split second, Kennedy debated asking who "they" were, but she was sure she didn't want to know.

Their trek continued for another ten long minutes before she caught a glimpse of a four-wheeler through the trees. Another few feet and a large tent came into view.

Frannie let out a short snort. "You know, when he said to bring them to his camp in the woods, I pictured an RV. I hope he doesn't expect us to stay here too."

"We'll do whatever he wants. He's paying us well."

She rolled her eyes, but didn't protest. "You owe me a tropical vacation after this."

"Baby, I'll buy you a whole house wherever you want with what we'll get from this job."

Kennedy was determined they wouldn't see a penny. She just had to figure out how to get away with Jill in tow. Leaving the woman behind wasn't an option.

The quick zip of someone opening the tent flap filled the immediate area, and a man emerged.

"I told you to get here quickly."

"We did." Ian pushed Jill, and she stumbled forward, landing in the dirt with a weak cry.

Kennedy tried to pull away from Frannie, but the woman dug her fingers in.

"Speeding when you have two kidnapped women in the car isn't a good idea. I drove as fast as I dared. That one needs medical attention." Ian pointed to Jill.

The other man shrugged. "She won't be alive long enough for it to matter."

Tamping down the fear, Kennedy forced herself not to react to that statement. When the time was right, she'd fight tooth and nail. But right now, she needed to play this smart. Wait for the right opportunity. Or for help to arrive.

"Bring them inside. He's waiting." The man motioned for them to follow and ducked back into the tent.

Frannie pushed her forward, stepping around Jill, who Ian scooped off the ground and dragged inside. Kennedy's blood ran cold as she ducked through the tent flap and got her first look at who "he" was.

"Good afternoon, Judge Davidson. Judge Stechschulte. It's so nice of you to join me here in my temporary abode." Gustavo Herrera held his hands out, gesturing to the gray tent walls.

Bile rose in her throat at the slimy smile he sent her way. "How did you get out of prison?" Alarm slammed into her gut, making her nauseous. Finn was supposed to interview him today.

"Violently."

Blood rushed through Kennedy's ears. Finn had to be okay. He needed to be there to hold her when she got out of this mess.

"I'm glad my brother met your expectations," Ian said.

"And then some. He was quite effective." Herrera glanced at the man who greeted them. "You did well in your hiring choices, Jack."

"Thank you, Mr. Herrera."

The pleased look on Herrera's face vanished. "Don't look so happy. You still failed in one aspect. Where's Piper Riordan? Or that damn K-9?"

Jack swallowed hard, his eyes wide with a hint of fear. Kennedy felt a perverse sense of satisfaction that her captor was also scared shitless.

"She's out of town. It seems she and her fiancé took a trip when the trouble started. I haven't been able to locate them."

Herrera stared at him, hard, for another moment. "And the K-9 and his handler?"

"They're nearly impossible to get to. Deputy Townsend wired his house with cameras and motion detectors and never leaves the dog unattended. Not even outside."

"Then blow the place up! A few well-placed gas cans and whoosh! No more annoying K-9." Herrera raised his arms, making a large circle as he let them fall back to his sides.

The younger man nodded once. "I'll speak to the men."

Herrera waved a hand, then looked at Ian and Frannie. "You two do it. Since you've proven yourselves so effective."

"That wasn't part of our contract, sir," Ian said.

"I'm making it part of it. With compensation, of course."

A mirthless smile slashed over Ian's face. "We'll get right on that. Do you need us to stay to help with these two?" He motioned to Kennedy and Jill.

"No. Jack and I can manage them just fine, I think. Plus, your brother is wandering around"—he twirled a finger in the air—"somewhere."

Again, Herrera aimed a slimy smile at Kennedy. She stifled a shudder. If he tried to touch her, that was when she would fight to the death.

"Good. We'll take our leave then. My love?" Ian held a hand out to Frannie.

Giving him a genuine smile, Frannie shoved Kennedy toward Herrera. "Let's go, babe."

Kennedy didn't see them leave. She was too busy fighting to get out of Herrera's arms. He'd caught her as she catapulted toward him. In her heels on the uneven ground and with her hands tied, she hadn't been able to stop. But she didn't want to be anywhere near him. Going limp in his arms, she sank out of his hold and rolled to the far corner of the tent. "Stay away from me!"

Herrera laughed. "Relax, Ms. Davidson. You're safe for now."

Kennedy reached up with her bound hands and readjusted her glasses. She kept her gaze on him, even as he turned away.

"You, Judge Stechschulte, are not." He reached down and grabbed Jill's arm, lifting her to her feet.

With glazed eyes wrought with fear, Jill looked at him. "Please. Let me go."

"Not a chance. You've not approved a single one of my motions yet. You really should have suppressed Ms. Riordan's testimony." He gave her a push toward the tent door. "Jack? Keep an eye on Judge Davidson. Don't let her run off. She's my entertainment for later."

"Yes, sir."

"No!" Kennedy lunged for the door, trying to stop him from leaving with Jill.

Jack ran between her and Herrera, pushing her back. "You don't want to go out there, trust me. He'll just do to you what he plans to do to her."

"Let me go, you bastard!" She pushed against him. "How can you let him do this?"

"Because, like you, I have no choice."

That made Kennedy pause. She looked at him, studying his face. His blank expression gave away nothing. "We always have a choice."

"With Gustavo, the choice is to live or die. I choose to live. You should too." He pushed her down, more gently this time. "Sit."

Kennedy settled onto her butt, continuing to stare at the door. A faint rustle of leaves reached her ears, but nothing else. For long minutes, she sat there and prayed, tears trickling down her face as helplessness overwhelmed her. She prayed that whatever Herrera did to Jill, it would be quick. She didn't want the woman to suffer.

The wind shifted, and soft cries and pleas for mercy floated into the tent. Kennedy clutched her fists, digging her nails into her palms, and tried not to listen. When a short blood-curdling scream sounded, Kennedy shifted, drawing her knees up and burying her face in them, holding in a sob. As the echo died away, peace returned to the forest, and she heard nothing more than the breeze rustling the tent.

She didn't even look up when Herrera came back a minute later. From his footsteps, she could tell he was alone. She dug her nails deeper into her palms, desperately holding onto the sobs that wanted to break free. It would only draw his attention. She would mourn Jill's loss later. Right now, she needed to stay alive.

"What? No tears?" Herrera crouched in front of her.

Kennedy lifted her head to glare at him.

He gave a soft laugh, genuine amusement glittering in his eyes. "You are one tough *mujer, Juez* Davidson." He reached out and skimmed her cheek with one finger. Kennedy turned her face away. "I like strong women. They're the most fun to break."

Bile rose in her throat. Closing her eyes, she drew a deep breath in through her nose and faced him again. "Why are you doing this? Why me? Or my friend? I've been in town less than a month."

Herrera reached for a milk crate and dragged it over, sitting on it. "That may be, but I've known about you much longer. Your brother is a thorn in my side. Him and that *maldito* department he runs. I couldn't get to him or his deputies. Even his wife is overly cautious. But you? You were too easy. Until that ATF agent showed up." His mouth turned down. "But hurting you—hurting your family hurt all of them."

Kennedy swallowed. "How did you do all this? You've been in jail." Her gaze flicked to Cartwright, who sat on a stool in the corner. He had a bottle of water between his hands, slowly rolling it back and forth as he listened.

"I don't leave things to chance," Herrera said. "I will admit, going after Ms. Riordan like I did was not my finest moment, but when you surround yourself with good people, even the worst situations can have good outcomes." He looked at Cartwright. "I paid for his education, making sure he was set up to help me if I ever needed it. Jack's been a great asset since he was a teenager. Right, Jack?"

The other man's head bobbed. "I do my best."

Kennedy narrowed her eyes. "It's people like you who give attorneys a bad name."

He shrugged. "I lead a good life, and that's all I care about. It's all I ever wanted."

She looked at Herrera. "You used a *child* and turned him into a criminal."

"I saved him." Herrera's accent thickened, and he pointed at his chest. "He'd be dead if not for me. He was nothing more than a street urchin. Now look at him."

Oh, Kennedy saw him, all right. She saw the man beneath. The one that was still that scared child. Only now he was scared of just one thing—Gustavo.

"So, what do you intend to do now? Why are we in a tent in the middle of the forest?"

"This is temporary. Jack's associates have been busy clearing a path for me to leave the country. We'll stay here for a few days until some of the heat dies down, then he and I will be on a plane to Colombia. You, *cariño*, will have served your purpose at that point and will not be joining us."

Her heart stopped, then raced, only to skip beats again as fear rushed through her. From the look in his eyes, she could tell what her "purpose" was, and what he intended to do to her when it was time for him to leave. Bile rose in her throat again.

But she couldn't let him see her fear. She wouldn't give him the satisfaction. Instead, she stared at him, defiant.

He chuckled and skimmed her cheek again. "Yes, I will quite enjoy you." He dropped his hand and stood. "But for now, I think it's time to eat. Jack? Tell me you brought the food I asked for."

Kennedy closed her eyes, letting out a slow breath as she reined in her terror. She had to find a way out of here before he made good on that promise.

# Thirty-Seven

Finn turned into Kennedy's driveway, bumping over the curb after an interminably long drive back. Even being on the phone with Nick and various other agents most of the way hadn't made the time go faster. It just made him more anxious to be home.

He brought the car to a halt and shut off the engine, hopping out. Jogging up the walk to the front door, he let himself inside.

"Pax? Paige?"

Taylor emerged from the living room. Finn's gaze turned flinty. He was still angry the Marshals failed to protect Kennedy. But he'd express that sentiment later. Right now, he had a more pressing concern. "Where are the kids?"

"In their rooms."

"Do they know?" They better not. He'd made it clear he wanted to be the one to tell them.

"No."

With a nod, he turned and ran up the staircase. Reaching Paige's room, he knocked. At her soft, "Come in," he opened the door.

"Hey, can you come with me? I need to talk to you and your brother."

"Sure." She put down her phone and took off her headphones, getting off the bed.

Finn turned and walked to Pax's room and knocked, then opened the door.

"Hey, Finn." Pax frowned. "What happened to you?"

Frowning, Finn glanced down, looking for blood. He'd changed his shirt, but he thought his pants had escaped ruin. "What do you mean?" His trousers were clean.

"You're wearing a t-shirt with dress pants. You left in a suit."

"Oh." Mouth flattening, he walked into the room and motioned for Paige to sit. "We need to talk."

"What's going on?" Paige asked, perching on the bed.

Finn braced his hands on his hips. "There's no way to ease either of you into this, so I'm sorry." He paused and ran a hand through his hair, then over his face. "Your mom is missing."

"What do you mean, missing?" Pax asked.

"There was an incident at the courthouse—a fire. And when the firefighters gave the all-clear and everyone went back inside, she was nowhere to be found."

The twins shared a look, but stayed silent.

"The Marshals are looking for her. I'm going to head to the federal building in just a few minutes and join the search."

Pax logged off his computer. "We're coming with you."

"No." Finn held up a hand. "It's safer if you stay here with Taylor."

He scoffed. "I don't care. I want to look for Mom."

"Me too." Paige stood.

Finn sighed. "Guys. I really need you to stay here. I get that you want to help. That you want to be part of the search, but—" He broke off, gathering his thoughts. "Your mom would want you to stay home where you're safe. And I need you to stay here, so I don't have to worry about something happening to you. I need to be able to put all my focus into finding her. Do you understand?"

Again, they shared a look. Words Finn couldn't hear passed between them before they looked at him.

Paige nodded. "Fine. We'll stay home. But you have to keep us in the loop. She's our mother."

He could do that. "I will. Any clues we find, I'll let you know."

"Good," Pax said. "You can start now. What do you know so far?"

As quickly as he could, Finn gave them a brief summary of what he knew, which was disgustingly little.

"Did they look for her phone?" Pax asked when he finished.

"I'm not sure, but probably. It's likely one of the first things they did to try to locate her. If she was kidnapped, though, I doubt her captors would let her keep it. They know those things can be tracked."

Paige's face lit up. "Call whoever it is you need to call and ask if she had her purse."

Finn frowned. "What? Why? She wouldn't get to keep that, either."

"No, but if she had it with her when they took her, she might have been able to slip the AirTag she keeps in it into her pocket."

Eyes going wide, Finn blinked. "Your mom keeps an AirTag in her purse?"

Both teens nodded.

"She was mugged several years ago," Paige said. "The thieves got everything and were never caught. When Apple came out with the AirTags, she bought a bunch and put them everywhere. We have them in our backpacks, and I carry one in my purse. She always sticks them in our luggage when we travel too."

Finn stepped to the door and leaned into the hallway. "Taylor!" Ducking back into the room, he looked at the kids. "You're sure she had an AirTag in her purse?"

Again, they both nodded.

A ray of hope made his heart beat faster. "Are either of you able to access it?"

"Yeah." Pax picked up his phone from his desk. "She shares all the tags on the 'Find My' app." He unlocked his phone, then handed the device to Finn.

"Christ, Finley. Are you trying to shout the house down? What's wrong?" Taylor entered the room.

"Kennedy had an AirTag in her purse."

Taylor frowned. "We found her purse when we pinged her phone. They were both in a dumpster across the street from the courthouse."

Finn zoomed out the map on Pax's phone. Several devices showed up, but a lone AirTag popped up in Virginia. "Yes!" He turned the device to show it to Taylor. "She's in Virginia."

Astonishment rounded Taylor's eyes. She took the phone. "I'll call the team." Spinning on her heel, she hurried out of the room.

"She's going to be okay, right?"

The wobble in Paige's voice put a lump in Finn's throat. He cleared it and nodded. "You have my word I will do everything I can to bring your mom back to you."

A tear trickling from Paige's eye was Finn's only warning, before she launched herself at him, hugging him around the waist. He wrapped his arms around her and held on tight, needing the comfort as much as she did. Finn wasn't sure what they would do if he couldn't bring Kennedy home alive.

# Thirty-Eight

Determination lengthened Finn's stride as he walked into the U.S. Marshals' office at the federal complex. After Taylor called the team with the info about Kennedy's AirTag, they'd called a meeting. One to which he hadn't been invited. He only knew about the meeting because he was in the room when Taylor's boss called and told her to switch out with another marshal and come to the office. Over her protests, he'd followed. They would have to put him in a cell to keep him out of the room while they discussed this operation.

"Agent Porter—"

Finn held up a hand, silencing the front office manager as he walked past her desk. "I'm here for the meeting."

He heard her sputter and lift her desk phone from its cradle, but he didn't stop. Striding down the hallway, he found the meeting room and opened the door.

Conversation ceased as a dozen heads swiveled toward him.

"Agent Porter, I'm sorry, but this is a closed meeting." Taylor's boss, Marshal Ty Kearns, stood at the front of the room, looking at the map projected on the whiteboard.

Finn stepped inside and closed the door. "I'm staying."

Kearns held his gaze for a moment, then glanced at Taylor.

"Finn." She took a step toward him.

"You will have to arrest me and throw me in lockup to get me to leave. I need to be part of this. Even if I just sit in the background. Don't shut me out." The look in his eyes implored her to understand.

With a sigh, she looked at her boss. "He knows this case well and could have insights we overlook."

Kearns' mouth flattened. "You get in the way, and I will do exactly what you said."

Finn gave a short nod. "Noted."

Giving Finn another long look, Kearns turned back to the map. "To catch you up, Agent Porter, we've tracked Judge Davidson's AirTag to a remote part of Shenandoah National Park outside of Charlottesville, Virginia. We're looking at mounting a reconnaissance mission at dawn, with, hopefully, a rescue shortly after."

Finn glanced at the clock. "It's only six-thirty. There's still several hours of daylight left."

"Right, but by the time we get resources together, it will be dark. In that area, we need to know what we're up against before we move in."

Seething, Finn stared at the board. "And in the meantime? Are we just supposed to pray Herrera doesn't kill them?"

"There's no evidence he has any of the women," Kearns replied. "We don't know where he went after he escaped."

Finn scoffed. "He broke out of federal prison at the same time Kennedy, Judge Stechschulte, and the intern went missing. He has them. Every minute we wait, the higher the chance we don't bring them home alive, let alone unharmed."

"And I've taken that into consideration, Agent Porter. But I also have to consider the people going in and their safety. I understand you're eager to recover Judge Davidson, but you can't let your emotions overrule your rationality. If you can't do that, then there's the door." Kearns gestured to the door behind Finn.

Muscles in Finn's jaw worked. He needed to be part of this rescue, but he couldn't stand here, listening while they planned something that was twelve hours away. With a long, hard look at Taylor, he turned on his heel and walked out.

The door opened and closed behind him. "Finn." Taylor's voice carried down the hallway, but he didn't stop. He heard her jogging to catch up, but still kept going.

"Finley." She grabbed his arm and yanked.

He spun and looked down at her, knowing the anguish he felt was all over his face.

She studied him for a moment. "What are you going to do? If you interfere, Kearns will make sure you end up in federal lockup. At the very least, you'll lose your job."

"I don't care, Taylor. You know Herrera. Know what he's capable of. If Kennedy dies or Herrera—" He broke off and swallowed hard, glancing away. He couldn't even think about the things Herrera could be doing to her. Shaking his head, he looked at Taylor. "Kearns is guaranteeing at least one of them ends up with some sort of physical harm by delaying the mission. I know where she is. I'm not waiting."

Again, Taylor studied him. "We can't help you if you get in trouble. No one will be there yet."

"I know. Let me worry about that."

She rolled her lips in and paced away, then looked back. "Nothing I say will stop you, will it?"

"No."

"Please be careful."

He nodded. "Are you going to tell Kearns?"

She shook her head. "You didn't really tell me your plan, so—" She shrugged, raising her hands, palms up. "As far as I'm concerned, you were upset and decided to go home."

A wave of relief washed over him. "Thank you, Taylor."

"Don't. I still think this is a terrible idea. But I also think Kearns is playing it too safe. Bring them home."

"That's the plan." He backed away, then turned, taking long strides as he left the Marshals' offices.

In the corridor, he broke into a jog, plans spinning through his head as he made his way through the building to his car. If he took off now, he could be in the vicinity of the AirTag in about five hours. It was still much longer than he wanted, but it was the only option.

Finn's phone rang as he drove out of the parking lot. Glancing at the car display, he saw Ben's number. He touched the button on his steering wheel to connect the call.

"Hey, Ben."

"Paxton called. Tell me what you know." A hard edge colored Ben's voice—one Finn had never heard before. He understood it, though. Ben loved Kennedy too.

"Everything went to shit. Herrera escaped, and someone abducted Kennedy, Jill Stechschulte, and an intern. Kearns wants to wait until dawn, so he can make a plan with all the contingencies. I'm not waiting. I'm in the car and heading north now."

"By yourself?"

"Yes. There's no time for backup. She's five hours away."

"You hope. What if they found the AirTag and left it there to confuse us?"

"Then I'll find the AirTag. But I can't stay here and wait."

A softer voice in the background came over the line.

"Hang on, Finn. What?" Ben's voice grew quieter as he turned away from the phone. "Okay."

Finn tapped his fingers on the steering wheel.

"Sorry. Gemma was listening. She's calling Brooke."

"Brooke? Why?"

"Because the woman has access to a helicopter."

Finn let off the gas. "What?" He turned into the parking lot of a small shopping center, too distracted now to continue safely. "Ben, as much as I'd love to fly up there, I can't put a civilian pilot in danger. Plus, it'll be dark in a few hours. Can they fly in the dark?"

"Not sure. Hang on."

Again, Finn heard Gemma's voice in the background.

"Brooke's going to call you, so I'm hanging up. Call me back."

"Yep." Finn hit disconnect, then stared at the screen, willing the phone to ring again.

The soft burr of an incoming call filled the car and an unfamiliar, but a local number appeared on the infotainment screen. He tapped the green icon. "Brooke?"

"Hey, Finn. I figured it would be easier to talk to you instead of relayed information through Gemma. It's just awful what's happened, but I want to help."

"I appreciate that, but I can't put your pilot in danger. And this will be dangerous. I don't know what kind of weaponry Herrera has or how many men are with him."

"Ezra is a former SEAL pilot. It wouldn't be the first time he's flown into an unknown, dangerous situation."

Finn blinked. "Oh."

"Let me call him and explain what's happened. As much as I want to help, it's still his decision. But I have a feeling he'll say yes."

"Is he certified for night flying?"

"Yes. Our chopper has instrument flight capabilities, so flying at all times of day in all legal conditions is one of the job requirements. Give me just a few minutes." The line clicked, going dead in his ear.

Heaving a sigh, Finn let his head drop back against the seat. Hope wanted to crowd out the fear, but he tamped it down. It was too soon to hope he could get there faster. That he could spare the women the pain Herrera would surely inflict if given enough time.

Several interminable minutes later, his phone rang. Sitting up, he touched the screen to answer yet a different number. "Porter."

"Agent Porter, this is Ezra Chastain, Appalachia Resorts' chief aviation officer." The deep voice with its heavy Cajun accent that filled the car held a note of authority Finn appreciated.

"Thank you for calling so quickly. What did Brooke tell you?"

"That your woman and two of her colleagues have been abducted by a psychopathic drug lord. Her words, not mine."

Despite the situation, Finn chuckled. "She got it in one."

"She also said you need someone to fly you into a potentially dangerous situation. I told her I'd call and get the particulars, but I'm not agreeing to anything yet."

"I understand. I'm just glad you're willing to hear me out." He gave Ezra a quick rundown of what he knew and what the potential for danger could be.

"We would need to land several miles away and hike in. If I fly too close, they'll hear. If Herrera is as unstable as he sounds, he could decide to kill the women, then run."

That's what Finn was afraid of. "How far away do you want to be?"

"Depends on the weather. It's been hot here. And humid. If it's the same wherever up there, we can probably feel safe at about three miles. This is assuming I can find a clearing that close. You said Shenandoah National Park, right?"

"Correct."

Ezra hummed, then clicked his tongue. "Okay. My weather app shows similar weather there as to what we've had here. Do you have more exact coordinates?"

"They're on my phone. I can send them to you."

"Do that. I'll check a satellite map and try to zero in on a landing site."

"Does this mean you'll help?" Finn tightened the reins on his heart; it wanted to gallop away with hope.

"Yes. The danger is limited. Even if it weren't, I'd probably still say yes. I hate the cartels. Send me the coordinates and meet me at the resort. Go inside and tell the front desk staff you're meeting me. If I'm not there yet, they'll make you comfortable."

"Will do. Thank you, Mr. Chastain."

"It's Ezra." He hung up.

Finn picked up his phone and texted the coordinates for Kennedy's AirTag to Ezra, then put the car in gear and swung the vehicle around. He needed to run home to change clothes and get the gear he should have before he blindly headed north. He'd call Ben back on his way to the resort.

Taking a deep breath, he did his best to shove his emotions into a box. He needed a clear head to get them all out of this alive.

A sliver of the hope he'd been holding back broke free. He clenched the steering wheel and said a prayer. *Hang on, baby. I'm coming.*

# THIRTY-NINE

Finn left the car running under the portico at the resort main lodge and ducked inside. He wasn't keen on lugging his gear—which included a high-powered rifle—through the lobby. Hopefully, there was a place he could unload out of sight.

"Good evening." A woman behind the large wooden reception desk smiled as he walked toward her.

"Hi. I'm here to meet Ezra Chastain."

"Oh, yes. He called earlier. Your name?"

"Finn Porter."

"That's the one he gave us. Let me call him and see if he's arrived yet." She picked up the phone, punching in some numbers.

Finn tapped his fingers against his leg, feeling the press of time. It had been nearly thirty minutes since he spoke to Chastain. The flight would take a couple of hours. He was anxious to get in the air.

"He said he just pulled in a few minutes ago. Do you know where the helipad is?"

"No." He'd never been to the resort before.

"It's around back of the lodge." She glanced past him through the fourteen-foot front doors. "That's your car?"

He nodded.

"Drive into the guest lot. At the rear of it is a gated parking lot for staff." She picked up a sticky note and wrote a code on it, handing it to him. "That will get you inside. You can leave your car there. The helipad is behind the lot. You can't miss the chopper sitting there."

"Great. Thank you."

She smiled again. "You're welcome."

Turning on his heel, he exited the lodge with long strides and rounded the front of his car, getting in. It was a quick trip through the parking lot to the staff lot. As he entered and rounded the back of the building, he could see the helicopter on a concrete pad atop a small hill. He parked as close as he could and got out, getting all his gear from the back of his SUV.

Nearing the chopper, a tall, dark-haired man came around the side of the aircraft. He stopped when he saw Finn.

"You Agent Porter?"

"Yes." Shifting his gear, he got his right hand free and extended it. "Thank you for agreeing to this."

Ezra shook his hand. "Not a problem. Just don't tell my wife. She's out of town." He flashed a quick smile. "Not that she'd stop me. But I'd get that eye roll and the lip pout." He shook his head. "Plus, I'd rather not worry her, so your timing is great." His mouth flattened as his smile died. "Not that any of this is good."

Finn waved a hand. "I understand what you mean. Are we ready to go?"

"Almost. I just need to finish my flight checks. Why don't you store your gear and get in? You can sit in the co-pilot's seat." He gestured to the left side of the chopper. "It shouldn't be more than about five minutes." Finn nodded and walked around him to put his things in the rear of the aircraft.

True to his word, Ezra climbed into the pilot's seat four and a half minutes later. He handed Finn a set of headphones, then donned his own and started flipping switches. The rotors spun up, but it was quieter than Finn expected. He imagined it had something to do with the nature of the helicopter. It was meant for rich executives, after all.

"Okay. Based on the coordinates you gave me, we're looking at about two hours' flying time. I scouted landing sites on the satellite map, but obviously, terrain changes. I'll get you as close as I can." Ezra's tinny voice came through Finn's headset.

"I appreciate that. Thank you again for doing this."

"No problem. All right. Here we go."

The chopper left the ground; the enormous lodge suddenly looked like a child's toy as they rose above the tree-tops. Finn kept his gaze on the scenery outside and tried to let it calm his mind. Running tactics wouldn't help. He didn't know what the area looked like. Forested; he knew that much. He just hoped Herrera didn't have too many men with him. The fewer around to hear Finn coming, the better.

But even the beauty of the Smokies couldn't hold his thoughts at bay, so he turned to his pilot. "Brooke said you were a pilot for the SEAL teams?"

A corner of Ezra's mouth kicked up. "One day, I'll get her to say it right. I was a Night Stalker. Army. Not Navy. But I did fly SEAL teams—and Delta Force teams."

Finn's mouth twitched. "Noted." He wouldn't want to be misnomered, either. "Why did you get out, if you don't mind me asking?"

"I got married. It just didn't hold the same appeal after I met Amy. Especially since she lived in the D.C. area and I was stationed in Kentucky."

"How did you end up down here, then?"

"I haven't been here long, actually. About a year. Amy left her job in D.C. to be closer to me at my base, but it didn't take me long to realize my job scared her. And she was more important to me than my job, so I started looking around for something in the civilian sector. An old friend of mine was the McGintys' pilot. He heard I was looking for a change and he recommended me for the job. When the McGintys offered Amy a job, too, I couldn't turn it down."

"So, she works for them too? Doing what?"

"She's their historian. They just opened a small museum inside the resort dedicated to the business and the local area. Amy spearheaded the project and now runs the place."

"Wow. That's great."

"Yeah. She's pretty proud of it. And I'm grateful to the McGintys for giving her a job."

Finn turned, hearing something in the man's voice. He gave Ezra a curious look.

The man chuckled. "Brooke created the position—and the museum—to lure me here."

"Seriously?"

Ezra nodded. "When I applied for the pilot's spot, I told her grandpa and dad that I could only accept if my wife found a job. Brooke made sure she had one." He lifted one shoulder. "I've come to learn that's just Brooke. She's a great lady."

Finn agreed. It seemed the woman was on a mission to better the lives of those around her. He was grateful.

The two men made small talk through the rest of the flight. Halfway through, Finn called the twins to have them check the AirTag's location and make sure it hadn't moved. According to the map, it was still in the same place. That both worried him and made him happy. They wouldn't need to divert course, but it could mean he was going to stumble over a grisly sight.

Those thoughts threatened to undo him, so he focused on his conversation with Ezra, learning more about the pilot. The man, who hailed originally from a small town just outside of New Orleans, was entertaining and highly intelligent.

Coming up on the tag's coordinates, they fell silent. Finn's nerves increased, but Ezra's calm, collected piloting helped keep them in check.

"I'm going to switch on my floodlight." As they'd flown, the sun had set. It wasn't completely dark, but the light was low enough, all the shapes on the ground blended together. "The tree canopy is dense enough no one should see it. Keep an eye out for a clearing. I need at least a hundred feet all the way around." Ezra reached for a switch and light flooded the ground below.

Finn peered out the window at the ground. Treetops whizzed by, much closer than he'd like. They weren't skimming the canopy, but they weren't far off. Swallowing his fear, he concentrated on the task. The helicopter dipped, and Finn glanced at Ezra, whose attention was on the ground.

"Did you find a spot?"

"I think so. Hang on."

The chopper dipped lower, hovering just above the trees. Finn peered down at the small hole in the canopy. It looked much smaller than a hundred feet across. "You can't be serious. That's not a hundred feet."

"Actually, it's about a hundred and twenty." Ezra descended.

Finn held his breath. Leaves whipped around the chopper as they passed below the treetops. Branches swayed in the rotor wash. The skids hit the ground with barely a bump.

"Damn." Finn let out his breath. "That was smooth."

In the darkened cabin, Ezra sent him a bright smile. "Gotta keep the skills sharp." His smile faded. "Go get your stuff and bring those women back. I'll be here." He reached for the instrument panel and started flipping switches again. The engines throttled back, and the rotors slowed.

Finn twisted the handle on his door and got out, going to the back door and letting himself into the cabin. Donning his vest, he grabbed his backpack and rifle, dragging them to the door.

"Does your phone work up here?" Ezra asked, now standing outside the chopper.

"Let me check." Finn took his phone from his pocket, tapping the screen. A single signal bar shone in the corner. He grimaced. "Not well."

Ezra hopped into the cockpit and opened a compartment behind the seats. When he emerged, he held two radios. "Use this." After fiddling with the dials, he handed one to Finn. "It's set to the resort's private frequency. No one else should be on it. If you need me, call. When you find them, call. We can be out of here quickly if you give me a head's up."

Finn took the radio and stowed it in the zippered pocket on his pants.

"One more thing." Ezra ducked inside the chopper again, this time digging into a metal box behind his seat. "You might need these." He tossed something at Finn.

Catching it, Finn glanced at it, eyes going wide. "Night vision?"

Ezra nodded. "I grabbed them on my way out of the house. Thought they might come in handy."

"You have no idea." Finn put the band over his head, adjusting it.

"Oh, but I do. You need more than luck in this situation."

He couldn't argue with that. "Thanks." Slinging the backpack over his shoulders and buckling it around his waist, he picked up his rifle. "Watch yourself."

"Don't worry about me. I can handle myself. Bring me some passengers."

With a sharp nod, Finn ran into the trees.

Away from the landing site, he brought out his compass and checked his heading. The terrain rolled, but there were no steep cliffs or high ridges in his path to the AirTag coordinates that he'd been able to tell from the air or from the topographical map he'd looked at earlier. Stowing the compass, he settled the goggles over his face and switched them on. The forest lit up around him in shades of green.

That pesky emotion he'd been battling all evening reared its head again. Finn tamped it down. He couldn't hope. Not yet. Not until he found her.

# FORTY

The run through the forest took Finn just over thirty minutes. He was grateful for Ezra's forethought. Without the goggles, it would have taken him much longer. He'd have been forced to walk instead of run. They also let him see the camp well before he would have otherwise. The lantern lit inside the tent shone like a beacon.

Finn slowed as he neared, staying out of sight. He stood at the edge of the camp for several minutes, watching for movement, but the site was silent.

Why would Herrera choose to camp in the wilderness with three prisoners? It just didn't seem like something he would do. The man liked his creature comforts. But Finn had to admit, in terms of hideouts, it was a good one. Well off the beaten track, the tent was the perfect place to lie low for a while.

A shadow passed in front of the light burning inside. A moment later, a man emerged. Finn zoomed in. It wasn't Herrera, but he knew that face. That was Jack Cartwright. The lawyer glanced around, then walked behind a tree. Finn heard the sound of him peeing in the dirt.

Now was a good time to move. Pushing away from the tree concealing him, he circled the area, checking for others who might be out on patrol. Halfway around, he made a gruesome discovery.

Bile rose in his throat when he whipped off the goggles to check on Judge Stechschulte. On her back, she was naked from the waist down, her shirt torn. Sightless eyes stared up at the trees and blood coated her neck and abdomen from stab wounds. Fear threatened to overwhelm him that he would find Kennedy in a similar state nearby.

Closing his eyes, he said a prayer for the judge, then drew in a steadying breath through his nose and stood. He couldn't let himself think like Kennedy was dead. He couldn't fall apart. Not unless he found her that way.

With one last look at Jill, he put the goggles back over his eyes and continued his circuit of the camp. No other bodies— alive or dead—appeared in his path. Except Cartwright. Done relieving himself, the man had lit a cigarette and leaned against a tree.

Finn crept through the forest, doing his damnedest not to alert the man of his presence. He had surprise on his side, though, which enabled him to get within feet of Cartwright before a twig snapped under his boot.

Heart skipping beats as his adrenaline spiked, Finn lunged. He wrapped one hand around Cartwright's middle and the other over his mouth, masking his surprised shout. A searing pain went through the back of Finn's left hand as Cartwright stabbed his lit cigarette into it, but he didn't let go of the man's waist. Clenching his teeth, he dragged the lawyer deeper into the woods.

"You're going to stay silent, or I'm going to break your neck, understand?" Finn growled in his ear.

Cartwright struggled. Realizing the man wouldn't go silently, Finn grabbed a fistful of his shirt and spun him around, landing a solid right hook to his face. The lawyer crumpled, then rolled. Finn dove on top of him and hit him again. Dazed, Cartwright groaned.

Finn took off his pack and dug into it, looking for the tape and rope he packed. As quietly as he could—though after that scuffle, he wasn't sure it would make a difference—he tore off a piece of tape and slapped it over Cartwright's mouth. With the man silenced, Finn used a length of nylon cording to tie him up.

Satisfied the lawyer wasn't going anywhere, Finn left him on the forest floor and picked up his pack. Readjusting the goggles on his face, he hurried back to the edge of camp. Herrera stood outside now, holding Kennedy to his chest.

"Oh, baby," Finn whispered. She looked okay. A little disheveled and scared, but okay.

Determination hardened his features. He aimed to keep her that way. Lowering himself to the ground, he found a rock in the dirt and set the barrel of his rifle on it. He lifted the goggles up and looked through the scope.

"Whoever's out there, come out!" Herrera yelled into the darkness. "I will gut her like a feral hog."

Finn saw the knife at Kennedy's throat. But it wasn't a gun. He wouldn't have to worry about a reflex making Herrera squeeze the trigger when he put a hole through the man's skull.

The unmistakable sound of a pistol hammer cocking came from behind him. Finn froze. He'd missed someone? Or had Cartwright gotten free?

"Stand up."

The voice was most definitely not Cartwright's. *Fuck!* Finn's mind spun as he worked through things. If he got up and faced the guy, it gave the man an advantage; he'd be able to see Finn's intent.

He took his hands off the rifle, but stayed put. He needed him to come closer. Finn just prayed he wouldn't shoot first.

A foot hit his ankle. "I said stand up."

*Bingo.*

Finn rolled, thrusting a foot between the man's legs as he twisted, bringing him down. A shot went wild as the man fell. Bouncing to his feet, Finn drew his sidearm. "Federal agent. Put the—" He didn't get to finish his sentence. The man brought his gun up. Finn fired two shots, both striking the man in the chest. Blood bloomed on his shirt as he slumped to the ground.

Hurrying forward, he kicked the man's gun away and checked his pulse. It was still there, but weak. Finn doubted he'd last long; his shots had been dead center. Turning, he peered through the trees at the camp. Herrera and Kennedy were nowhere in sight.

"Dammit." Retrieving his rifle, he moved closer. A soft feminine squeal from his right sent him past the camp and into the trees. "Kennedy!" There was no point in hiding his presence anymore.

"Finn!"

He ran faster, thankful more than ever for Ezra's goggles. Ahead, he could see Kennedy struggling with Herrera. He had one arm around her waist, the knife in the other. She had both hands wrapped around his forearm as he tried to bring it down.

Finn stopped. Lifting his goggles, he raised his rifle and looked through the scope. This wasn't the shot he wanted to take, but if he didn't try, Kennedy would die. "Herrera! Let her go!"

The drug lord paused, his head turning toward the sound of Finn's voice. "I'm glad you showed up, Agent Porter. You can watch your lady die." He whipped his head around to look at Kennedy once more.

Finn fired. The crack of the rifle echoed off the hillside. Kennedy screamed, letting go of Herrera's arm to drop to a crouch and cover her head. Herrera hit the ground beside her, part of his skull now missing from the high-powered round.

"Kennedy!" Finn dashed toward her, landing on his knees at her side. She threw herself into his arms with a sob. "Baby, are you all right?" His hands skimmed her head and down her shoulders and back, checking for lumps. She clung to him tighter, making it impossible to assess her. He gave up and hugged her tight. "Honey, it's over. You're safe." He kissed her temple, letting her cry. Eventually, her sobs quieted, and she lifted her head.

"Jill. He—" She broke off and rolled her lips in, tears coursing down her cheeks.

"I know, baby. I found her. She's gone." The sight of the judge's body was not one he'd forget anytime soon. "Where is the intern who went missing with you?"

"She was part of it. She lured me away from the crowd, and she and her boyfriend—some big brute—brought me and Jill here. They left not long after." Another sob broke from Kennedy's chest, but she reined in her tears. "Can we go home now? I need to see my kids. Are they okay?"

Finn bit back a curse. He needed to call that in. Soon. His arms tightened around Kennedy. "They're fine. Pax was ready to come with me."

She barked a laugh-snort. "Of course he was."

Finn got to his feet, bringing Kennedy with him. "Come on. I'll call our ride and the local authorities to clean up here so we can go home."

Kennedy seemed to realize, then, that he was alone. "Where is everyone?"

"I'm alone. Well, except for the chopper pilot who brought me here. That AirTag idea of yours was genius. I'm going to sew one into the lining of every pair of boxers I own."

Finn expected her to laugh, but she stared at him through wide eyes. "You came by yourself? Why didn't you have a whole team?"

"Because the team was still planning your rescue. They don't even plan to be on the ground here for another eight hours. I couldn't leave you in his clutches that long." He swallowed hard, thinking of what could have been. "I know what he's capable of."

She grabbed his face and kissed him. "Thank you."

"You don't need to thank me, baby. I love you. I will always come for you."

The tears came back, but Finn could tell these were happy ones by the bright smile that lit her face. "I love you too."

He gave her another hard, fierce kiss. "Let's go home."

# FORTY-ONE

Exhausted beyond belief, Kennedy stumbled through her front door. All she wanted was to take a shower and go to sleep. After she hugged her kids.

"Mom!"

Two sets of footsteps thundered downstairs to accompany Paige's shout. In moments, she was enveloped by both teens in a hard hug. Tears threatened again, and she blinked furiously to keep them at bay. She was safe. Herrera was dead. It was over.

Pulling back, she touched their faces. "I'm okay. A few scrapes, but no major trauma. Finn tells me it was the two of you who thought to mention my AirTag. Thank you." Her voice trailed off into a whisper. She swallowed around the lump in her throat. "You saved my life."

They hugged her again, and she squeezed tight, happy to have them in her arms.

"I knew I heard your voice." Betty Ruth came down the stairs, leaning on the railing.

Kennedy disentangled herself from the twins to give the older woman a hug. In the distance, she heard a phone ring.

"I'm glad you're safe, dear." Betty Ruth pulled back and glanced at Finn. "You better hang on to that one. He moved mountains for you."

A soft smile on her face, Kennedy looked at him. "I know." She didn't plan to ever let him go.

"I'm sorry to interrupt, but Agent Porter, that was Marshal Paulson." The young man who'd been assigned to her family stepped into the foyer and waved his cellphone. "Marshal Kearns is on his way over. She said he's not happy. He's got Agent Trumbull with him."

Kennedy could imagine not. Finn had upstaged the man.

"Of course they're coming now." Finn sighed. "He could have had the grace to wait until morning."

Headlights washed over the front of the house. Kennedy glanced through the frosted window, but could only make out a dark shape.

"Kids, let's go make your mom and Finn some tea. I bet they could use it." Betty Ruth held out an arm, motioning for the kids to follow her to the kitchen.

The teens looked at Kennedy, and she nodded. "Go on. We'll be fine. Maybe convince Betty Ruth to add a splash of whiskey to that tea?"

Pax flashed her a quick smile, but his eyes reflected his worry when he looked at Finn. She gave his shoulder a gentle shove. "Go. Everything will be okay. You'll see."

He nodded, but she could tell he didn't one-hundred percent believe her.

"I hope you didn't just lie to him." Finn kept his voice quiet as he watched the twins trail Betty Ruth down the hall. "Kearns threatened to make sure I lost my badge if I interfered."

"Let him."

He turned a sharp look on her. "What?"

"Let him. I'm sure you could easily find a position in a

private security firm. You did just single-handedly take down one of the most notorious drug lords in the Appalachians. Though I will miss seeing you at work."

Finn smirked. She had a point. It might be a less stressful line of work too. "We'll have to make up for it at home." Reaching for the wall, he flipped on the porch light. "Wouldn't want Kearns to trip as he comes to watch Trumbull fire me."

Kennedy chuckled. "Open the door."

Turning the knob, he pulled the door inward. Kearns and Trumbull ascended the steps. They glanced up in surprise.

"Gentlemen. Come in." Finn made a sweeping motion and stood to the side.

Kearns glared and stepped in. Trumbull shot him an amused look. Finn bit back a smile. Maybe he wasn't getting fired after all.

Shutting the door, he turned and faced the men.

"What were you thinking?" Kearns asked. "I told you not to interfere. Not only did you disregard my orders, you put a civilian pilot and aircraft in danger." The man's face turned red as he spoke. "It was reckless and insubordinate."

"I'll thank you to lower your voice in my house." Kennedy held up a hand. "Shall we go into the living room?" She gestured to the room to their right.

With a huff, Kearns spun on his heel and marched into the room. He stopped near the couch and put his hands on his hips. "Well?"

"I did what I had to do." Finn stopped ten feet away, giving the man a hard look. "And I don't regret it. I just wish I'd gotten there sooner so I could have saved Judge Stech-schulte." Though, from what Kennedy said, Herrera killed her almost immediately. He would have had to have been right on their tail to get there in time.

The mention of the judge's death took some of the wind

from Kearns' sails. "That still doesn't excuse your reckless behavior."

Finn stayed silent.

"Tell us what happened," Trumbull said. "We got the gist of it from the local feds who cleaned up after you, but we want to hear your account. And start at the beginning. How did you end up with the McGintys' personal pilot?"

Kennedy sank onto the couch and pulled Finn down with her. If they were going to make her relive her night, she wanted to be comfortable.

Trumbull sat down in the wingback chair by the fireplace. Kearns leaned against the mantle. He still looked pissed, but the curiosity in his eyes told her he also wanted to hear their side of things.

"I was on my way home when Ben Davidson called to find out what was going on." He hadn't been on his way home, but he figured telling Kearns that would make the man more amenable to listening to the rest of the story. "His wife is good friends with Brooke McGinty. Gemma was right there when I filled Ben in, and she called Brooke and asked if there was any way her pilot would fly me to the AirTag's coordinates. He then called me and asked for details and decided it was an acceptable risk. We landed several miles from the coordinates. There was very little danger to Mr. Chastain or his helicopter."

"So, other than flying you there, he had no role in tonight's events?" Trumbull asked.

"Correct."

"What happened when you got there?" Kearns asked. "Why didn't you call for backup when you found the camp?"

"There wasn't time. While I was circling the perimeter, assessing the site, I found Judge Stechschulte." His mouth turned down at the memory. "Then, as I came around the other side of the camp, I came up on Jack Cartwright. I still hadn't seen Kennedy or Herrera—or anyone else, for that matter. I wanted to get information from Cartwright, maybe use him to get to Kennedy, so I snuck up behind him and took him down. But he proved less than cooperative, so I bound and gagged him. Our scuffle drew Herrera's attention, and he came out of the tent with a knife to Kennedy's throat."

Unconsciously, Kennedy reached up and touched her neck. She could still feel the cold bite of steel against her skin.

"Herrera called out, but couldn't see me through the darkness and the trees. I laid down to steady my rifle and that man I killed came up behind me out of nowhere. We fought, and I managed to squeeze off two shots with my sidearm before he could bring his arm around and shoot me."

"It was after that Herrera dragged me away from camp," Kennedy added. She could only assume he wasn't sure who was still in play and thought he might yet need her as a hostage. "He caught sight of Finn, and at that point, tried to stab me. I don't know how, but I got hold of his arm and held him off. It gave Finn the time he needed to save me." She doubted she would have lasted longer than a few more seconds if he hadn't shot when he did. Her arms had been on fire, burning from the effort to keep Herrera from bringing the knife down.

"The man who ambushed you is precisely why you needed to wait for backup. You never should have gone into that situation alone. None of my marshals would have dared—"

Kennedy rolled her eyes. "I'd be dead if he'd waited. Even before Finn showed up, Herrera was getting restless. He'd been on the phone off and on the entire evening, setting up transport to get him out of the country. He didn't plan to take me with him." They'd told all of this to the agents who descended on them in the forest.

"I hope you've tasked agents with finding the people on the other end of those phone calls," Finn said. "And in finding the two people who kidnapped Kennedy and Judge Stech-schulte."

Trumbull nodded. "Actually, Deputy Townsend and his K-9 just took them down. I don't have all the details, but they were outside his house."

Kennedy's eyes widened. They certainly hadn't wasted any time in doing Herrera's bidding. She was glad, though. They were the last of the threat still lurking.

She patted her knees. "Well, good." Satisfied they'd covered most everything, she stood up. She was done playing the gracious host. "Look, I'm exhausted. Finn is too. We gave our statements to the agents on-scene. You can read all about it by making a simple email request, I'm sure. If you plan to fire Finn, get it over with so we can go to bed, please."

She heard Finn swallow a chuckle. Trumbull gave her a surprised look, while Kearns continued to glare.

"There's no need for that, ma'am." Trumbull rose. "I think a two-week suspension without pay and a formal repri-mand is plenty." His eyes sparkled, and he held out a hand to Finn. "Good work, Agent Porter."

Finn stood and took his boss's hand. "Thank you, sir."

Kearns sputtered. "Gavin—"

Trumbull released Finn's hand and looked at Kearns. "Stuff it, Ty. You know it's just your hurt pride that's made you so upset. Finn's been reprimanded. The situation threatening the judges' safety has been rectified. It's time we all got some rest. I know I'm going to sleep like a baby now that Gustavo Herrera is dead." He stepped toward the door. "Let's go."

With a glare at Finn and Kennedy, Kearns followed Trumbull from the room. They let themselves out, the door shutting with a thud as Kearns slammed it.

Kennedy laughed and turned to Finn. "Two weeks without pay, huh? What are we going to do? You might need to stay here so you can keep your utility bills low. Save some money." She looped her arms around his neck.

Grinning, he wrapped his arms around her waist. "Works for me. I was actually hoping we could make that a more permanent arrangement."

She lifted an eyebrow. "Yeah?"

He nodded. "Yeah. What do you say? Will you move in with me?" His brows dipped. "Er, make that, can I move in with you?" He chuckled.

Kennedy's head fell back as she laughed. "Yes. To both."

Palming the back of her head, he held her steady and smiled softly, studying her face. "I love you, woman."

She framed his face, holding that beautiful gray stare. "I love you too. Now kiss me."

"Yes, Your Honor."

His lips swallowed her joyful laugh.

Thank you for reading Smoky Mountain Judge! I hope you enjoyed it. Want to read Ezra's story? Sign up for my mailing list. Newsletter subscribers get his story for **FREE**. You can find the sign-up form on my website, ashleyaquinn.com. My list also receives sneak peeks of my latest work and access to exclusive giveaways. Also, please consider leaving a rating or review on Amazon and/or Goodreads. It would be greatly appreciated!

Thanks again for reading!
    - Ashley

# About the Author

Ashley started writing in her teens and never stopped. Her first novel, Smoky Mountain Murder, came out in 2016, and she has since published two more series and has plans for more. When not writing, you can find her with her nose stuck in a book or watching some terrible disaster movie on SyFy. An avid baseball fan, she also enjoys crafting and cooking. She lives in Ohio with her husband, two kids, three cats, and one very wild shepherd mix.

Website: https://ashleyaquinn.com

goodreads.com/ashleyaquinn

amazon.com/Ashley-A-Quinn/e/B07HCT4QST

# Also by Ashley A Quinn

**Foggy Mountain Intrigue**

Smoky Mountain Murder

Smoky Mountain Baby

Smoky Mountain Stalker

Smoky Mountain Doctor

Smoky Mountain K-9

Smoky Mountain Judge

**The Broken Bow**

A Beautiful End

Wildfire

In Plain Sight

Close Quarters

Scorched

Light of Dawn

**Pine Ridge**

Sweetness

Loner

Shark

Katydid

Homespun

www.ingramcontent.com/pod-product-compliance
Lightning Source LLC
Chambersburg PA
CBHW061318190726
48288CB00002B/561